T0198848

A DILEMMA
FOUND ON THE
COLOMBIAN
OIL FIELDS

DONALD MCGEE

authorHOUSE®

AuthorHouse™
1663 Liberty Drive
Bloomington, IN 47403
www.authorhouse.com
Phone: 1 (800) 839-8640

Published by AuthorHouse   02/17/2017

ISBN: 978-1-5246-5786-4 (sc)
ISBN: 978-1-5246-5784-0 (hc)
ISBN: 978-1-5246-5785-7 (e)

Library of Congress Control Number: 2016921620

Print information available on the last page.

Prologue

My name is Rolly (Rolland) Farrington. Before I was born my father and grandfather were among the richest men in America. They each owned large estates on the East and West Coasts. Their fortunes came from investing in land, companies, everything. But when the Great Depression of the 1930s hit, they lost everything, and that's when I was born. To keep from going to prison, my father unloaded everything he owned, leaving him dead broke. I never met my grandfather. He committed suicide a year after I was born. To survive we ate pork-less canned pork and beans, and meat-less hamburger. To this day, I can't stand looking at macaroni and cheese, beans, or peanut butter. I grew up wearing discarded clothes and shoes with holes. I thought everybody lived like us until my first day in school. I expected to see other kids dressed in hand-me-down rags like me, but as I looked around class, I saw most kids wearing new clothes and shiny new shoes. How come they weren't poor like me? I learned later that they weren't rich; it was that their fathers had good jobs and earned a decent living. I was a sorry sight to those boys. They treated me like dirt. They shunned me. However, two of the prettiest girls in class, Becky and Lucy, felt sorry for me and asked me to share lunch with them. They liked that I was tall and not bad looking. They gave me things like mittens for winter or food to eat. I tried to repay them by helping them solve math problems. I later learned they didn't need my help but just wanted to make me feel good. I hated being pitied.

I swore I would escape this life of poverty. I was going to get rich. Richer than what my parents used to be. To start I swore never to marry and have kids. They just drag a man down and ruin his chances of becoming wealthy. How was I going to accomplish this goal? . . . I had no idea.

Later I found my answer—Colombia. However, I was unaware of the dangers awaiting me in the Andes that were destined to change my life forever.

Chapter 1

TEEN AGE

When I was fifteen Grandma Fenton died, which might have been my first step in defining how I will reach my goal. I didn't know her well because she lost her big home due to my father's mishandling of her affairs, so she went to live with my Uncle Hank. He had sent money for our family to take a bus from San Jose, California, to Bakersfield to attend her funeral. Dad refused to go. He hated Hank. Jealousy topped his list of reasons, followed by Hank's whoring, boozing, and his unforgivable good luck finding oil on his worthless, barren land.

Hank met us as we climbed down from the bus. This was my first meeting of my much maligned uncle. He was about five feet five with thick shoulders and slim waist. A crop of light brown hair sprinkled with gray topped his tanned, worn and wrinkled face. His piercing blue eyes seemed to burn right through me—was he mad at me? No I think that's just the way he looks. He had a reputation, according to my mother, living a rough-and-tumble life and taking orders from no man. I admired that lifestyle.

I was a scrawny kid about five feet six. Hank told Mom: "Your little runt needs some fattening up. Tell you what—when he turns sixteen let him come and stay here with me all summer. I'll put him to work so he can earn money for himself while I stack plenty of beef on his puny body. I'll build him up to be a man. Looks to me like he's got a good enough frame, just needs a lot of meat on them bones."

"We'll see about that later." She didn't sound convinced about that being a good idea. "Well, tell me, when's Ma's funeral?"

"Tomorrow, eleven o'clock, at some kind of funeral home; they said they'll dig up some preacher for a short service. I told them we ain't church-going people. He just said it don't matter."

1

"Good, I haven't been in a church in forty years," Mom added.

We drove several miles over dirt roads as a crimson sun was setting. Uncle Hank's spread stretched for acres over dry, spindly weed-choked dusty brown earth. Paint on his huge creaky old mansion was mostly scoured off by wind and winter rains. Five bedrooms, six baths, a large kitchen, sumptuous living room, and a gaming room with a great stone fireplace impressed me. I planned on owning a place like that someday. His barn looked weather beaten like his house. It had a shiny, sturdy lock on its doors to keep his Cadillac safe from thieves.

From Uncle Hank's cook/housekeeper, Noana, I learned how good solid food tasted. Uncle's freezer was full of thick steaks, hamburger, lamb chops, chickens for frying and ice cream. It was unbelievable. The next morning, before the funeral, I smelled an unfamiliar aroma I hadn't known before—bacon. I fell in love with those crisp, greasy strips.

Uncle Hank drove the three of us into town to attend Granma's funeral at eleven o'clock. Hank went to meet the preacher. That took one minute. The funeral itself didn't seem to take much longer. That made my uncle very happy because that gave us enough time to catch a bus back to San Jose.

The summer I turned seventeen Uncle Hank met me at the Bakersfield bus station. Right away he put me to work with two high school boys from town. It was hard work: digging irrigation trenches that connected to Hank's new water well. The loose, sandy soil was easy digging, but after working long hours we were dog tired. Other jobs included chopping weeds, feeding livestock, and mending fences. Sometimes when the wind flew from the west I could hear big oil drilling rigs in the distance. My uncle told me to stay away from them—too dangerous, he said.

It wasn't all work in summer's burning sun, though. Around sundown Hank dug out a baseball and two gloves. In his youth he had been a semi-pro baseball player in Bakersfield, and after a few days throwing the ball around, he said, "Rolly, I know athletes when I see them, and you're a natural-born athlete. I shit you not."

I got used to staying in the big house alone at night while my uncle jumped into his dusty new Cadillac and hit the bars around town. He called it 'honky-tonkin'. Late at night I could hear him stumbling into the house talking to someone, a woman, and it wasn't his cook. Before dawn I heard his Cadillac rev up, and I assumed he was escorting his lady friend back to town.

After several weeks, one Friday night Hank said, "Boy, get cleaned up. We're going to town and have us some supper at my favorite café—Slim's Diner."

As soon as we stepped inside this greasy-spoon joint, sad western music moaning from a jukebox, I spotted a perky little waitress coming toward us. She was short with a good body, black wavy hair, a cute round face with a smile and red lips that begged to be kissed. According to her name tag she was Terry. She seemed to eye me and pay me a lot of attention. She even slipped me an extra-large piece of apple pie a la mode after I finished my chicken-fried steak. She was flirting, always winking at me, and saying, "How's that make you feel, honey boy?" I wasn't sure how I was supposed to respond, so I just acted kind of ignorant.

"She's got her eye on you, young fellow," my uncle teased.

After a while Uncle Hank gave me his keys to an old pickup truck and told me to go to Slim's without him and then handed me two bucks. I felt at ease with Terry and her sexy way. "Hey, handsome, 'bout time you showed up without that old buzzard." Then she tweaked me on the cheek. "I'm taking next Friday off. You want to drop by my place? I'll fix you something a lot better than you'll ever get here."

"Gee, Terry, what do you mean by that?" I was still acting dumb.

"You'll see. Just be there by seven o'clock. Here's my address."

Did she live in an apartment or a house, old and run-down or new and neat? Viola Street was narrow; cars parked on both sides made it difficult to see small house numbers for some apartments and some houses. Finally I found house number 354. It had a wood-floored front porch with the porch light lit and front door open behind a screen door. I was nervous; visiting an older woman was a new experience. I didn't want to act like the dumb kid that I was. Would I be able to make some kind of grown-up conversation? When I stepped up on the front porch, the screen door swung open, and Terry pulled me in, excited and out of breath—me too.

Lights were low, music soft and dreamy. She wore a filmy low-cut blouse and gave me a big kiss. I almost lost it right there.

"Come on, sweet boy, dance with me before we have dinner. I've got some sweet wine to go with my sweet boy."

We never made it to the dining table. On the sofa she said, "Bet you've never done this before, have you?"

My answer came out in an uncontrolled rush: "Oh, sure, lots of times."

"Liar, liar, your joint's on fire."

And I was ready again.

I didn't get home until dawn. Uncle Hank was waiting at the door. I felt weak, afraid of what he might say. "Uncle Hank, I can explain."

But Uncle Hank didn't let me. Instead the old man broke out laughing and gave me a hard pat on the back. "You done broke your cherry, didn't cha? I'm proud of you, son."

Next Tuesday I went alone to Slim's. No one seemed to be there except Terry at the end of the counter and the old cook back in the kitchen. I sat at my usual seat at the counter and looked up at Terry standing in front of me, a sly smirk on her lips.

"Hi, Terry, how are you?"

She said nothing as she slid a small package across the counter to me, and said, "Open it."

"What's this?" I said as I picked up a fist-sized box.

"I said open it, damn it!" A big grin lit up her face.

I tore away the brown wrapper and flipped open a small black box. A shiny stainless steel wristwatch was cradled inside.

"Terry? What's this for? Why are you giving me this?"

"It's nothing. You don't have a watch, and everybody needs one. It's no big deal."

I reflected on what seemed to be happening. It feels so—I don't know how to explain it—easy, or natural. People give presents to each other all the time. I should think of a present for her. But, wait a minute, let's not get carried away. We don't mean anything to each other, except sex. Maybe that's my present for her.

After I said good-bye to Terry, she purred in my ear, "I'll see you Friday, honey boy. I still owe you that big steak dinner, you know?"

I showed up at her house Friday night. Her front door swung open before I reached the first step. She grabbed my hand and pulled me inside. I never did get that thick juicy steak she promised me. I got back late to

Hank's place exhausted and hungry—starved, in fact. Fortunately I found two fried chicken legs in the fridge.

Next Friday I made sure to eat before going to Terry's. I stuffed myself with two giant hamburgers to give me enough strength and energy to last through another demanding evening. "Come on in, lover," she cooed. "I got that thick juicy steak for you to devour before I devour you."

Not to disappoint her, with the help of her sweet wine (I wasn't used to drinking except for beer), I managed to gorge every last bit of steak. I couldn't move from the table. "Come, baby, let's dance. The music is slow and dreamy."

I tried to stand. She helped me, pulling my arms. It must have been easy to see distress in my face. And then it started to come up. I made a dash for the bathroom. On my knees, embracing the toilet, I threw up, splashing ugly bits of meat and other unidentifiable objects all over.

I didn't have the nerve to go back to Slim's for two weeks. When I did, Terry was cool to me. I didn't blame her.

The next summer Uncle Hank was amazed at how much I had grown and filled out. I had been big enough to play varsity football and tall enough to play center on the basketball team. That's when Uncle Hank encouraged me to win an athletic scholarship to a university. Beat that poverty trap and become somebody. "What would you do with a college education, Rolly?"

I wasn't sure at that time.

Work was the same as last year, but when I went to Slim's on Friday night, Terry wasn't there. Instead, a new girl had taken her place. She told me that Terry had run off to live with some dude in Fresno. I felt a big letdown. I had looked forward to continuing our romance. It was a big deal. I had some pretty good girlfriends back home, but nothing like Terry. I thought maybe I'd hustle this new waitress at Slim's. That didn't work. She was married and faithful, as well as being too old.

Good old Hank pulled out boxing gloves and kept me sparring with him after work, just the two of us. In the midst of sparring he surprised me by stepping back and giving me a kick, a gentle kick on the side of my hip. "Hey, Uncle Hank, what's the idea?"

"I'm going to teach you a valuable lesson—street fighting. To survive in some parts around here you got to learn to defend yourself from dirty fighting by dirty fighting yourself. That involves using not only your fists but your feet too. I'm going to teach you a few choice moves."

By the end of summer I was quick and accurate with both my fists as well as my feet. Of course, I didn't think I would ever use either.

The summer after that, when Uncle Hank met the bus from San Jose, he took a look at me hobbling down from the bus and shouted, "What the hell happened to you, goddamn it?"

We stood in front of each other unable to speak. A plaster cast covered my left arm. "Uncle Hank, I broke my arm playing pre-season football this year; lost my chances for a college scholarship. I won't be going to college like I'd planned."

That was when the old oil man made me an offer. He would pay for my college education on one condition: that I never waste my time studying to become a pencil-pusher like my father, sitting behind a goddamned desk eight hours a day.

No problem. I knew exactly what I wanted to study, geology, and work in the oil fields. To earn big money was the force that drove me.

One of the guys I worked with at Uncle Hank's attended the University of Oregon in Eugene. He convinced me, after working all summer in hot, dusty Bakersfield with temperatures one-hundred degrees or more and no clouds to act as a shield from the burning rays, to enroll in the U of O. I liked everything about the university and the coeds, especially one in particular named Lois. She was from a wealthy Portland family. By the second year I really missed the heat and dry air of Bakersfield. Oregon's rain and cold convinced me to head south that summer and work with Uncle Hank. He suggested I enroll at UCLA in Los Angeles. They had an excellent geology department. Besides, Slim's had a new waitress, so my evenings were far from boring.

Chapter 2

On a sunny Southern California day in June 1955 I learned of news so great I could hardly wait to share with my friends. Final exams at UCLA were over. At a local beer garden, celebrating students swam through a tide of humanity quaffing frothy mugs of brew to toast the end of another school year. The crowd buzzed like a swarm of bees ranging over a honeycomb. Many, I was sure, had no plans for the future, but I wasn't one of them. I knew exactly what my future would be, for I was graduating with a degree in geology and eager to start working at my new profession.

I stood up from my table and waved, trying to catch Todd's eye as he struggled through the brawl of mindless humanity.

"Hey, Todd, you blind? Over here." He didn't hear me, but he caught sight of my waving arms.

His beautiful, tall, blond girlfriend—the one with those big boobs she loved to show everyone (well, if I were a girl I'd do the same)—clung to his arm as if he might slip away on this hot spring afternoon. They ducked under the large umbrella shading my table and pulled out two canvas-backed chairs to plop down on.

"Rolly Farrington, you old frat-rat, what's all this special news you're so hopped up about?" Todd greeted me as he caught a barmaid's attention and ordered two beers.

"Becky! . . . It's great to see you," I said superciliously because I was giddy with my good news. Sitting across from me, Becky looked me in the eye with her beautiful blues. Oh yes, our eyes locked. It was obvious she had the hots for me. I think she went for my height, and my wavy black hair, and my olive complexion. Then she frowned and looked away—maybe I was premature in thinking she had the hots for me. Then I focused on her red-headed, freckle-faced boyfriend as I said, "Todd, I was just conjuring up—a new word from today's crossword puzzle—some ideas about earning tons of easy money in a land filled with sensuous *muchachas* whose moment of love cost but a few measly *pesos*. While enjoying warm, tropical sunsets high in the Andes by the side of swimming pools at private golf clubs I'm accompanied by gorgeous *señoritas*—virginal daughters of rich coffee growers."

"Conjured up? What the hell are you talking about, Rolly? How many beers have you had?"

I ignored his dumb-ass question. "I've got bitchin' news, Todd. You remember that consulting job with Brocton Geological Services? . . . I got it." The last three words came out as an uncontrolled shout. "That other stuff I was just paraphrasing Leon Seacrest's latest letter to me from South America. It's what I'll look forward to when I go to work for Brocton in Colombia."

"I don't get it. I thought you were going to grad school?" Todd said.

"You remember I applied for a job with that company because Leon said it really pays a lot. But with a bachelor's degree I figured they'd only hire guys with master's degrees."

"What did Marcia say when you told her?" Becky's blue eyes were drained of all humor.

She looked too serious. Where was that sexy smile she flashed before?

I leaned back in my chair, took a swig of beer as I mulled over my answer, and then confessed. "I haven't told her yet."

"You haven't told her yet?" She looked astonished, her voice as sharp as a knife. "Don't you think you should? After all, haven't you been going with her for over a year?"

She was angry, set to attack. What had happened to her beauty? How could she suddenly get so ugly? She was a bitch, a real bitch—I didn't realize before.

"Yes, but I, rather, *we* have made no commitments," I said in defense.

"She's been counting on your plan to go to grad school and then teaching somewhere. Isn't that what you told her?"

"Look, jobs for new geologists with only bachelor's degrees are hard to find, and I need money. This job pays one hell of a lot more than teaching.

In case you don't remember, I come from a very poor family. I can't pass this up."

She continued her interrogation. "You didn't tell Marcia you applied for that job, did you?"

"No." This was getting too serious. I wanted people to share in my happiness for this great job. "I'll tell her. Don't worry. Everything is going to be all right." What's with Becky . . . making me out to be like some cold, ego-driven bastard?

"Her birthday was last Tuesday; did you give her a present?"

I didn't answer. I didn't know how to.

She didn't wait for an answer anyway. "A birthday card, maybe? . . . She wants to marry you, and don't tell me you didn't know that," she insisted.

I had never even told her I loved her. I always wanted to keep our relationship uncomplicated because of my big plans that didn't include marriage.

"How're you going to tell Marcia? The same way you told your little friend up in San Mateo . . . by mail?" Todd smirked, struggling to control his laughter.

Thanks, Todd. your empty head, as usual, has overloaded your mouth. I could feel the fire rise in my cheeks and forehead. I clinched my fist tight. I could have hauled off and beat the crap out of Todd—ha! My best friend. But Becky saved him from a busted nose.

"You wrote that girl a letter? How tacky can you get?" Becky uttered in disbelief.

"I was in L.A. and I didn't have her telephone number in San Mateo."

"Wasn't there another gal also? Wasn't she from California, too? How'd you drop her . . . the same way, wrote another letter?" Todd said and then added, "What a cocksman!"

"Cocksman? I'd call him a chickenshit lowlife. My God, Rolly, you think you're God's gift to women, that girls can't resist you?" Becky chided.

"No, I'm no gift to anybody, and I don't lead girls on, as you are implying."

"Not leading a girl on, what about all the money Marcia has spent on you?" Becky hissed, looking me square in the eyes again. "That flowery Hawaiian shirt, those faded blue-denims, and loafers—weren't they her gifts to you?"

"Yes, she has paid for a lot of things for me . . . Look, she's rich; I'm poor. If she wanted to go out, I didn't have money, so she paid." And then I added, "You've obviously never been poor, have you, Becky?"

"No, my family's not rich, but we are comfortable," she admitted indignantly. "All a girl means to you is someone you can use, and you don't care one iota how that affects her . . . you are cold."

"Look, like I said, I'm poor. My family never got out of the Depression of the 1930s. My father's company went broke. Growing up eating practically dog food and wearing clothes from Goodwill or Salvation Army or someone's hand-me-downs is about as low as you can get."

"She gave up her religion just to please you."

"I didn't make her do that."

"No, but you nagged her about it."

I stood up, counted out the exact amount I owed for my two beers, and dropped it on the table.

"What about the tip?" Todd asked.

"You take care of it." I slid my chair under the table and wound my way through the boisterous crowd on my way out. *I'm not anything like what that bitch says I am.* I had no illusions about my looks. I considered myself maybe fair looking, nothing special. I was slender and over six feet tall (it surprises me the respect tall people seem to get from shorter people). I had a natural tan complexion, a wide forehead, a thin, straight nose with a slight bump along the bridge from a football mishap (people told me just rub it a lot and it'll go away). In spite of any shortcomings I may have had, a few girls seemed to like me and my impoverished condition because they wanted to mother me, not because I was some hunk. I never tried to impress anyone. True, I didn't have a problem showing my date a good time. One girlfriend swore my best feature was my smile; another commented on my sexy hazel eyes. My teeth were my main attraction, according to a dental hygienist I once romanced. She gave me free teeth cleaning.

Later, back at the fraternity house, Todd asked, "You sure you know what you're doing?" "Yes, I'm sure, Todd." *Damn, my voice sounds weak.* "Hell yes. I know exactly what I'm doing. It's a great opportunity."

"I'm sure oilfield geology might be great, but this bullshit about going to South America, I don't get. Do you know anything about South America? Revolutions break out every two or three days; people get killed, American people especially. And besides, it's a lawless place—robbery and murder are common, everyday occurrences."

"Todd, *that's* a bunch of bullshit. You don't know what you're talking about." I could feel my face redden again.

Chapter 3

A COWARD'S WAY OUT

One ring, words and phrases peppered my mind. Two rings, be cheerful, make her feel my good news is for the better. Three rings, don't cause her to break down and start crying—you'll just start making big promises you have no intention of fulfilling. After the fourth, Marcia's voice came on from her answering machine in her apartment. I felt relieved when her message ended with "I'm at my parents for the week. Something happened and I have to be there. Sorry . . . I'll miss you, Rolly."

Thank God she didn't leave their number. "Hi, sorry I missed you. I wanted to tell you that I got a surprise. Brocton Geological Services offered me a job that I didn't think I had a chance of getting. So you can imagine I'm a little pumped right now. Marcia, I had to accept this job and forget about grad school because my uncle's cut me off. He's had some bad luck. He's strapped right now. Hit dry holes drilling his last two wildcat oil wells. He just sent me six hundred dollars to buy a car, an old 1948 Ford, so I can go to work." *That was partly true. Uncle Hank did hit two dry holes but never threatened to cut me off. He's still rolling in dough.*

I met Marcia's parents once. They invited me to dinner at a fancy upscale restaurant. She bought me new clothes for the occasion. Her fifty-something father was five feet ten, stocky, a college wrestler, and a very successful businessman with neatly trimmed graying hair that added to his features as an arrogant, wealthy son-of-a-bitch. Marcia's youngish mother—right out of a ritzy beauty parlor, her little finger poised, slightly hooked in the most high-fashioned way as she raised her salad fork—didn't say much.

With a slight smile and cold, piercing blue eyes, Marcia's father, Louis Basset, inquired, "You're studying geology, I understand. What does a geologist do besides look at rocks?"

I wasn't going to take his condescending crap. "Search for oil, gold, uranium, stuff like that."

"Must mean you have to travel to mostly God-forsaken environments."

"Well, Louis,"—I took a big leap by omitting to call him Mr. Basset— "if that's where the goods are, that's where I'll be."

No one said much as we finished our salad, sipped our white wine, until Louis said, "Seems like a big gamble. If you don't find what you're looking for, you don't gain a thing."

"I'll be working for a big company. They pay very well, especially overseas."

"Still it'll be in some God-forsaken place and foreign languages to put up with, and food that's probably not edible by any means."

The women saved the day by entering in with inane chatter about the weather and such.

That was my first and last encounter with the Bassets.

There was one more call to make. Maybe she wouldn't be home either. I didn't feel like explaining right then anyway. But then . . .

"Hello," whispered a mournful voice.

"Hello, Mom."

"Rolland . . . is that you?" Her voice perked up although slurred; it was so early for that. "I've got good news, Mom."

"You've been accepted into grad school?"

"No, not that. I got a great job—oilfield geologist for a consulting company near Sacramento." I neglected to say I would be working in a foreign country. "The pay is fantastic."

"Well," her voice dropped an octave, "your father might be pleased with that." That lilt of sadness crept back into her unsteady slur. "When are you coming home, dear?"

Should I tell her not for a very long time? No, I'll tell her that some other time.

TRAINING

I rumbled along 55 miles an hour in my 1948 Ford sedan on Highway 99, a few miles past Bakersfield on my way toward Sacramento as summer sun scorched flat yellow-brown earth; a hot, dry wind energized whirling dust devils as tumbleweed danced across the meandering two-lane road. I recognized a much traveled, rutted dirt road off to the west. Uncle Hank's spread loomed in the distance, seen through haze and dust like it was a ghostly monument—distant memories of that past.

A few miles South of Sacramento open grassland gave way to high cyclone and wood fences fronting stacks of earth moving machines, oilfield drilling rigs with stacks of pipe and other rusting equipment. Two small house trailers squatted side by side in the middle of an acre-sized lot with Brocton Geological Services printed on both sides. This is where I would meet Brocton's company owner, Ray Sutton. Was I nervous meeting him for the first time? Nah, curious maybe but not nervous or intimidated.

A middle aged, short, plump, oval faced man strolled out of one trailer marked "Office." He wore sun-tan pants and a short-sleeved white sport shirt, loose around his ample belly. As he approached, his sunburned face broke into a big smile that eased our meeting. After handshakes, introductions, and small talk—kind of like sparring, neither one trying to land a blow—Ray said, "You'll train on a well north of here with Al Fischer. He went on tour at four o'clock, about an hour ago." I must have looked puzzled because he explained, "In the oilfield we use the word 'tour' meaning 'Shift.' You'll hear it pronounced 'tower' or 'tar' depending where the roughneck is from. This will be your first day of training, so you're on the clock now. As far as where to stay, you can use that other trailer over there until you've finished training and are ready to ship out to

South America. Al just got back from Colombia. He'll tell you all about life down there. You should find life very inexpensive that is if you don't blow all your money on women and booze down there."

"That won't be a problem. I plan to save as much money as possible."

"Good idea, Rolly. Don't see why you can't do that and enjoy life while you're at it." Ray chuckled as if some secret I'm not aware of. "Here, I've got this little booklet for you: Spanish expressions translated into English. It'll come in handy for getting around. You're not going to find many English speaking people there."

That didn't bother me; I'll adapt, I can handle any situation.

It was a short drive over some pave and unpaved roads to my first well. I kept a view of the rig's mast in sight over hills and oak trees. As I drove into the drilling area and stopped, a man shuffled toward me. He was tall and thin, like me, hair coal black; thick bushy eyebrows that emphasized his ivory white face and piercing eyes. "Rolly Farrington I presume. I know all about you from Bulldog, that's what they call your friend Leon Seacrest." He broke into an easy chuckle.

"You must be Al Fischer."

"That's me."

After that introduction he took me around the rig explaining operations. "Simple, rock bits grind up rock formations, pumps send drilling fluid called mud down the drill pipe and rock fragments are carried to surface. Rock cuttings are separated from mud on that shale-shaker. Its vibrating screen separates sediment from mud. You'll study and name the minerals and then test for petroleum gas and oil. Mud is then pumped back down the hole. Your work is more complicated than that. I'll be teaching you everything. It's real interesting, especially when you drill into an oil sand . . . You'll see."

"I'm really looking forward to working in Colombia. I've heard all about the bitchin women there." Damn, maybe I shouldn't change the subject so fast. He's giving me a questioning look.

"Well, I'll warn you right now, it's not all just analyzing geology and whoring around. You'll find your share of rough situations. I bet Seacrest didn't tell you about close calls with snakes, bugs, alligators and bad *hombre*s.

Unaffected by his stories, I said, "That sounds like quite an adventure." We continued our tour around the rig,

"Not another Goddamn rock-hound? Dang, another prune picker, I'll bet." The voice was like an old Chevy with a blown muffler followed by a gravel crunching rasp of laughter from a bear-like man standing on the rig floor, twenty feet above us.

"That's Floyd. He's a tool-pusher for the drilling company." Al said, and then shouted up to him, "That's right, Push, another California boy.

I stared up at this hulking frame and decided I have to learn to stand up to rock hard men or I'll be an outcast.

"Okay, it's time to learn the routine about being a well-site geologist. You scrape up a sample of cuttings from a drilled up formation, examine it under a UV-lamp for any visible oil, put two scoops in a blender, add water, beat it up in the blender, read how many units of gas is given off if any. Wash your sample then study it under the microscope; describe what type of sedimentary rock and name mineral content. If you've got, let's say, sand and shale, write down percentages of each. Last, record all your findings on our log. Got it?"

"Got it."

After two weeks training I was assigned a well on a desolate mountain top. I worked from 4:00 PM until midnight. On my first night I stood shivering outside the trailer-lab—no moon for light and wind gusts threatening to blow me over the mountain edge—I watched two distant jittery pencils of light creep slowly uphill towards where I stood shivering in front of a oil drilling rig. Engulfed in swirling dust from an unpaved oilfield road my replacement two hours late already, Ben Willis crawled out of his VW and was almost knocked over the edge by the wind. "Sorry I'm late. Won't happen again." Which I doubted. "Why are you standing out here in this goddamned cold wind? Did our kerosene heater crater on us?"

"No, just tired of sitting cramped up in that trailer with no work to do except watch the depth gauge needle creep down to three feet per hour."

Just as Ben shut the trailer door we heard rig motors change pitch and the drill penetration rate indicator jump from 3-feet per hour to over one hundred—a drilling break, possibly indicating a formation change from shale to sandstone that could contain oil. I followed Ben dashing out of our trailer-lab, stumbling over drilling equipment hidden in blinding shadows, climbing a steel ladder to the rig floor. He shouted over a grumbling chorus of rig motors for the driller to stop drilling, pull the bit up off bottom, but keep circulating mud and wait for us to study the drilling break. When that fast drilling section surfaced, Ben scooped up muddy ground up rock cuttings. On its mucky surface we could see a filmy scum of crude oil with little bubbles of gas popping up. Under a UV-light, a bright golden sheen of oil appeared. Then another washed sample in a Petri-dish a dropper full of solvent added thin streams of oil ooze from sandstone fragments. Under microscopic inspection, sandstone fragments containing, gray, white, black, and clear minerals. He splashed dilute HCL (hydrochloric acid) on them. Tiny carbon dioxide bubbles surfaced, telling us that calcium carbonate—the mineral of limestone, marble, our teeth, bones, and soda pop— cemented these sandstone minerals together. Minerals we could identify were glassy quartz, tabular hornblende, gray-white feldspar, shiny iron pyrite, and hematite.

He filled out that information in the log and gave it to Myron Alden, the oil company's petroleum engineer.

With training over, I was ready to leave for Colombia. Not too sure where Colombia was, I consulted a map of South America. Then came my most difficult task: I had to call my parents to tell them I was leaving the country and wouldn't see them before I left.

"Hello, Mom."

"Rolland!" she gasped. "Are you coming home? Will you be here in time for dinner?" Her unsteady voice depressed me. I could tell she had been drinking.

"Mom, I've got a problem." I paused to mull over several ways to explain it to her. Best way was to make it short and sweet. "I just got a call from my boss. I've got to leave right away."

"But, you haven't been home for months. How can you leave and not see us first? Are you really going to work in South America? You never told us about that."

"How did you know that I was going to South America?"

"Because we got a letter from an insurance company saying that your life insurance policy was being cancelled because you're going to South

America and the company wanted to know how to contact you to tell you. We didn't know anything about a life insurance policy."

"I know I wanted to tell you myself. But what's this about holding up my policy?"

"They think your life is in danger going there, too wild, too unstable, and the likes."

That was a blow I wasn't expecting. I remembered what Al Fischer had said about dangers there. I couldn't think what to say, except, "Don't worry about that, Mom. I'll straighten that out with the insurance company. There is nothing to get upset about."

After a long silence Mom said, "There's a letter here from a girl named Marcia. What do you want me to do about it?"

Oh God, what does she want? "Look, Mom, when I get settled I'll let you know where to forward it." I would have liked to tell her to tear it up.

Mom was silent. Was she crying? Her tears always got to me. It wasn't that I didn't love my parents. Their sad life makes me dread being around them. I always walk away and try to forget how bad off they are.

Chapter 5

FROM LOS ANGELES TO BARRANQILLA COLOMBIA

I was late. The airline called my name as I entered Los Angeles International Airport. Airline personnel hurried me out across a concrete runway and through the gaping door of a DC-4, a four-engine, propeller-driven airplane, into a confusion of passengers settling into cramped seats. At first glance, all seats looked occupied until I spotted one along the aisle in back. I could make out a woman sitting in the seat next to it, head down, probably reading instruction sheets on how to get out of this death trap in case of a crash. Maybe she was young and attractive, I hoped.

I slid into the empty seat, and a middle-aged, but attractive, woman looked up. Oh, well, I thought, I can get caught up on some missed sleep. I had spent the day before partying with some of my old fraternity buddies.

We greeted each other politely, then she asked, "What is your destination, if I am not being too forward?" she spoke with an almost indiscernible accent.

"Barranquilla, Colombia. . . . My first trip out of the States. Uh, are you going there too?"

"No, Bogotá. That is the capital of Colombia."

The pilot fired up his engines, igniting an explosion and then a roar from four beasts eager to soar into a star-lit sky. The noise was too loud for conversation. Everyone seemed to push back as we raced over the runway. Then I held my breath as screaming engines battled gravity to fly away. My seat companion and I were silent for a long time until the stewardess offered passengers refreshments.

That seemed to break the ice. "You speak Spanish?"

I wasn't sure if that was a question or not. "No . . . well, I mean, I had Spanish in high school and in college. And I had a Cuban girlfriend who liked to seminar me in Spanish when we dated. Well, yes, I can speak some Spanish."

"Well, I hope you learned enough, young man, because I don't believe you will find many English-speaking people in my country."

I wrestled with that warning. "Oh, I think this company I work for will have English-speaking personnel." *Or will they?* "I'm a geologist and I'll be working on sites drilling for oil. There are a lot of Americans in a lot of oil fields." I had been staring straight ahead but turned to look at her face. She was probably in her forties, very well dressed, hair done in a beauty parlor, no doubt, and really quite attractive in a high society sort of way. "Are you Colombian, if it's okay for me to ask?"

"Yes, yes I am." She extended her hand for me to shake in the narrow space between us. "My name is Doña Adelina Marcos Botero de Ortiz." She studied my face. "You look perplexed . . . I guess you are not used to such long names."

"You're right, I'm not . . . why so many?"

"Adelina, my given name; Marcos, my father's last name; Botero, my mother's last name; and Ortiz is my husband's last name—de Ortiz. But I use my first name and my husband's last name—Adelina Ortiz."

"I've got an easy name to remember—Rolly Farrington—and I'm pleased to meet you. Your English is very good."

"Thank you. I studied here in California when I was a young girl. Since you've never traveled to South America I am going to give you some important advice. You are young and a bit naïve, I think. There are people in these South American countries looking for young people like you. You must take care. Pickpockets are all over; some taxi drivers are thieves, if not murderers. In cantinas people will try to take advantage of you; women love to seduce *gringos*, as they call you. Kidnapping is not uncommon, holding a person for ransom. It happens every day, Colombia, Venezuela, Brazil, all over." She paused and seemed to be thinking about something. "My brother was kidnapped by a group of revolutionaries. They wanted a lot of money for his release."

"Is that right?" I was a bit uncomfortable with that news, but I let it pass. *I won't have any trouble with thugs.*

"That was some time ago. He had been a prisoner for several months. When they finally released him he was not the same man: extremely emaciated, skin and bones, and very weak. He had been a big, healthy man, robust, full of energy. But now I don't think he'll ever be the same."

I was silent. Then all I could think to say was, "I can take care of myself." But her voice with its warnings lingered. "I have an English-Spanish book to help me with useful expressions." As if that would protect me from danger.

After twenty-four hours in the air, I felt like a caged animal. Joints stiff from sitting long hours. They didn't respond to my walking up and down the aisle. Well, if I looked on the bright side of things, I had earned one day's pay yesterday after leaving Los Angeles and another day's pay today for not doing any work. In my mind, I added the two days plus two days' living allowances. At least that made me feel better. After all, money was the reason for me going to South America.

At last the DC-4 approached its final destination, Barranquilla, Colombia. The most northern city on the Caribbean Sea, South America. I grabbed my carry-on bag and staggered up the bouncing and rolling aisle to the washroom. After brushing my teeth and splashing water on my face, I combed my recently cut hair, short for the first time, and then studied my reflection in the mirror. A few strands of hair always stuck up in back, giving me that Dagwood Bumstead look. Oh well, I'll never pass for Tony Curtis.

The DC-4 made its final approach for landing in the fading afternoon sunlight, a spectacular crimson and gold sight. We floated over slender mop-topped palm trees flourishing along the sides of many white plaster buildings with dried blood-red tiled roofs. Popping sounds stung through the cabin as the pilot lowered his landing gears. In those final moments before landing, I had studied a map to see how far Barranquilla was from Chanara, the location of my first oil well in Colombia. I was beat from this all-night flight and looked forward to the oil well site to get cleaned up, eat a real home-type meal, and then sack out. I was hungry and weary. Oil companies always have first-class accommodations for their oil field people. At least that's what I'd always heard.

Then the plane suddenly plunged, slamming hard onto the tarmac, and all hell broke loose. Passengers screamed; books, purses, and litter flew into the air as the plane violently tossed everyone around. I suddenly felt the first pangs of helplessness, losing all sense of control. *Is this my introduction to life in Colombia?* I tried to brush aside this bad experience, this omen. I didn't want to admit that sometimes omens come true.

Chapter 6

ALONE AND FORSAKENED

We bumped along over a rough, thumping landing strip with a scream or two from a few freaked-out passengers. Our plane spun around, and from our little window, I could see propellers blowing dust and debris on a crush of people waiting at the terminal gate, women's hair flapping like rags and men's hats sailing in turbulent wind. Joyful faces beamed smiling and laughing as they struggled to contain their excitement.

The door popped open. I turned to Doña Adelina as she said, "Rolly, thank you for your company. It was a long, tiring flight, but you made it enjoyable." Then she asked, "May I?" and took my right hand in hers and made the sign of the cross. From her purse she took out a small, shiny medal. "This is St. Christopher. I want you to carry it with you always. It will keep you safe."

I didn't know what to say. I certainly didn't want to tell her I wasn't religious. So I shook her hand, thanked her, and wished her well.

As I exited the plane, I buckled under Barranquilla's heat and humidity. I searched the crowd for a tall, light-complexioned, blond man about fifty years old named Brett Vickers, the manager for Brocton Geological Services in Colombia. There shouldn't be a problem picking him out in this throng of mostly tan faces, I thought. But after scanning the people milling about, I saw no one who matched his description. In fact nobody appeared to be taller than five feet five. Short must be the norm here.

I was stunned when I realized that I was stranded in a foreign country not knowing what to do next. Screw it; I'll just wait till he gets here. This guy Brett has got to show up soon. The company wouldn't expect me to find my own way around here, would they? Time passed, the crowd thinned, and no tall blond appeared. "That son of a bitch is not going to show up. Damn! What kind of a screwed-up outfit did I hook up with?" I shouted to the astonishment of hustling people around me. "Well, they probably don't understand me anyway."

One couple stopped, and I thought they looked like they might speak English—their skin was lighter than most and their features were more Anglo than what I considered Hispanic. But what the man reeled off in Spanish sounded more like gibberish than any language. The letter *r* rolled off his Colombian tongue like a machine gun. I was speechless. I couldn't think of one word in Spanish to reply to this gentleman. But even his friendly voice was no help to me. With a shrug, the couple strolled off, leaving me racking my brain for a Spanish word, any word.

In all this hot and humid Barranquilla air, I felt a chill. I tried to speak to anyone still at the gate. An employee in coveralls sweeping up cigarette butts and trash gave me only a blank stare. Others nodded and seemed to apologize. I didn't understand them. "Why the hell didn't I pay more attention in my Spanish classes instead of flirting with Barbara in the desk next to me—two years in high school, another two in college, and my little Cuban girlfriend?" *What a Godforsaken place I've got myself into. What do I do next?*

With suitcase in hand, I made my way along a poorly lit corridor toward the main lobby of the airport. Someone there must speak English. In a row of service counters I spotted a sign that said LUFTHANSA AIRLINES. Three uniformed women employees were just closing up for the day. I eyed them approvingly. One was tall, blond, and good-looking; another was brunette, short, a little plump like her round, cute face; and the last one was middle height and thin, with black straight hair and a kind of stern or sarcastic look. I was proud of my ability to size up women at a glance. "Pardon me, but I bet you speak English?"

With a jaded, glassy stare, they all announced in a stern German accent, "Of course we do."

"Wonderful! That's wonderful!" I beamed. My worried frown must have melted to a wide grin, because a feeling of relief swept over me. "Could you possibly tell me how I can get to a good hotel? You see—"

"Certainly. If you wait a moment we will take you there," the tall, good-looking blond said with a smirk, as if she were really saying, "Is the young *gringo* lost?" Not only serious but also good with the sarcasm.

"You know, mister, you had better learn some Spanish quickly if you plan to be here long."

"Oh, I'll get by. I catch on quickly."

Their smiles told me, *we doubt it.*

"What does 'I'll get by' mean? I don't understand. 'I get by,' meaning I get by what?" the blond one asked.

"It means I'll get the hang of it."

"What? Are you sure you speak English?"

"It's English all right, American English."

"We speak only English English. The Queen's English."

"And very well, I might add. You three speak beautifully; that English accent sounds good."

After I picked up my suitcase, the three *fräuleins* marched me out the front lobby door and halted before an ancient Ford sedan. I walked around it, checking out its dents and scratches, and declared, "She's a beauty. What color did she used to be?" This brought out peals of laughter from all three young ladies. They seemed to be loosening up with my droll sense of humor.

"We don't know. We just bought it."

In the weakening glow of early evening, the ride from the airport opened my eyes to a drastically new world. Waves of ragged peasants with dusty burros and horses carrying cargo made their way to hovels they must call homes. Some horses pulled carts made from rear axles of cars or trucks and roughhewn wooden flatbeds. An occasional overloaded, mud-spattered truck or car honked as it sped by our rattling Ford making its way over a sinkhole road. With the car windows wide open, I caught some unfamiliar odors—wood-burning cooking fires, cow dung, roasting coffee, and rotting garbage.

"What's that stink?" I asked as we passed several shanties.

"From that fruit stand; it's papaya you smell. It has a strong aroma," one of the girls answered.

"It must be rotten. Smells like it."

"No, not necessarily. It may not please your untutored nose, but papaya is delicious."

The rough road finally gave way to a palm tree lined street with sumptuous homes surrounded by luxuriant, large, leafy plants in riotously blooming gardens. It led to a curved driveway heading up to a white-stucco arched structure for cars to enter and drop off hotel guests. "Wow! It looks like someplace out of a movie. Will I see Humphrey Bogart when I go inside?"

The girls just laughed.

"I'm impressed." I wasn't kidding. I was out of my league here. "What's this we drove into, a canopy or something?" I asked.

"It's a *porte cochere*," the plump girl in front explained.

"Yeah, that's what I thought," I replied, awed, not knowing if she was speaking Spanish or German or something else.

The three German girls snickered. Obviously, they figured I had no idea what she had said.

As I crawled out of their car, I told my three young rescuers, "You know you have saved my life, and I want to pay you for your heroism. How much do I owe you?"

Almost as one they replied, "*Nada*."

"Nothing? No, no, I want to pay just like I would have had to pay a taxi driver."

"*No problema*. We live very close," the tall blond said as they left me standing alone again to fend for myself.

Chapter 7

EL HOTEL DEL PRADO

A maroon-uniformed, brass-buttoned doorman took my suitcase and opened a massive front door on the way into this grand hotel. In the lobby a slender, young *señor* dressed in a brown suit, crisp white shirt, and matching darker brown tie politely welcomed me with a big, white toothy smile and outstretched arms, *"Bien venida, señor."*

"Huh?" I said, confused. "Pardon me, but do you speak English?"

"No, lo siento mucho, señor." And he then held up his hands, indicating for me to wait as he dashed through a side door, returning quickly with a shy, slender girl.

"I speak a little English," she whispered in an accent I thought intriguing. Her eyes were downcast as if afraid I might bite her.

"Oh, good! Can you put through a call to Los Angeles, California? I must talk to my boss. It's urgent. Nobody from my company met me at the airport, and I don't know what to do."

"I shall see what I can do," she uttered demurely, still not making eye contact.

I handed her a business card with the company's telephone number that would be answered day or night, seven days a week. She then retired into a back room. The hotel clerk and I stood facing each other, silent as if neither knew what to say, the Colombian with a slight smile on his face. I wondered, *are you laughing at me? I know you have to be careful with these foreigners.* "You sure you don't speak English?"

He just gave an "I'm sorry" look and shrugged his shoulders.

The girl returned after what seemed an eternity, shaking her head. "I tried the best I could, sir, but no one answered at that number."

"That bastard Morgan's probably at some bar getting smashed instead of taking care of business." The young lady's eyes flared with shock and excused herself to return to her safe haven. "What the hell do I do now?" Register, naturally. Of course I didn't understand a word I was signing, but I did make it clear I wanted an air-conditioned room. A bellhop carried my suitcase and led me up a curved, beautifully tiled staircase to the second floor. Along an open, wide terrace smelling of flowers, maybe orchids from gardens, a chorus of crickets and frogs welcomed me to early evening. "How about you, *¿muchacho, hablar Español?*" I realized too late I had said "to speak" instead of "you speak."

"Sí, señor."

Of course he did. What a stupid question. *"Muy bueno."*

It was a first-class room: spacious with a high ceiling, two beds, good-sized dresser, desk and chair, and a large window overlooking a wide patio below. Lights illuminated bright red, green, yellow umbrellas over tables and chairs spread out along an Olympic-sized swimming pool. Couples enjoying cocktails occupied several tables. They all looked like well-to-do Colombians, women in high-fashioned dresses and men in white ruffled shirts or lightweight jackets. Musicians played softly to blend in with the warm, quiet evening. The word *alluring* fit here.

Next, I checked my private bathroom. "Oh, look they goofed. The *C* for cold is on the left-hand faucet." I twisted the handle, put a finger under a flow of water, and quickly jerked it back. "Damn! They should have an *H* for hot." On the right a faucet handle was labeled with an *F*. "Ah ha! *F* for *Frio* and *C* for *Caliente*—high school Spanish!"

After showering and sporting a brightly colored short-sleeved shirt and creased suntan pants, I had to find some English-speaking people or I would go nuts. I needed to contact Brocton Geological Services here in Barranquilla. Even though it was evening, maybe somebody was on standby and still in their office.

Descending the multicolored stairway into the lobby again, I confronted a new desk man, a haughty attendant with a wild, sweeping black pompadour.

"A sus órdenes, señor," he said condescendingly.

I knew that meant something like "I'm at your service."

"The telephone *señorita*, please."

"¿Teléfono?"

"*Sí,* that *señorita.*"

"Ah, ¿la señorita Consuelo? Lo siento, no está."

"She's not here? . . . Ah damn! Must have finished her shift. What should I do now?"

"*¿El bar, señor?*" the clerk suggested and pointed down the hall.

"Of course, there's always an American or someone who speaks English in a bar."

Chapter 8

A NIGHT TO REMEMBER

Leaving the oppressive humidity of the hotel's lobby, I entered an air-conditioned bar that lifted my spirits with its inviting atmosphere and familiar whiff of booze. Low, cool lighting illuminated several small tables where couples sipped cocktails and chatted. Subdued music mixed with murmurs of Spanish and occasional laughter. I made my way over to a small bar with six stools, one occupied. Then a bright-eyed, dark-skinned bartender with a beaming grin asked in accented English, "Welcome, *señor*, what may I serve you?" *I wonder how he knew I spoke English.*

"A beer, make it a nice, cold beer. Glad to hear someone speak English."

"And I'm glad you speak English, too, *señor*," he said emphatically, that beaming grin never leaving his face.

"Oh, why's that?" I asked. His friendly voice was relaxing.

"So I can practice my English. I want to speak perfect, without an accent, make Americans feel at home here in Colombia."

"Just get here?" a man two stools away asked me. He was dressed like me, short-sleeved, modestly patterned sport shirt and light brown suntan pants. An American, I figured—tanned face, sun-bleached blond hair, with that confident, easy-going air that you find around beaches in L.A. He looked to be in his mid-thirties.

"The name's Clayton, Andrew Clayton, but just call me Andy. People here call me *Andrés*. That's my Spanish name."

"Pleased to meet you. I'm Rolly Farrington." We shook hands. His were rough and callused.

I decided to unload my problems. "Yeah, I just flew in this afternoon and I'm completely screwed. No one from my company met me at the airport." I went on to explain my predicament.

"Not to worry. You have your company's name, so it shouldn't be hard to locate."

"Hope you're right. I've had a strange feeling ever since I got here that I've been forgotten." I took a long draw on my beer. "Tell me, Andy, how long you been down here?"

"I've been working for an oil field supply company here in Colombia and Venezuela for seven years now."

"How do you like it?"

"Fine. You get used to a slower lifestyle here. It's nothing like working in the States. Sure, there are inconveniences, like you want to do things in a hurry but find out businesses are closed midday for *siesta* time. You have to learn how things work around here." He studied my face for a moment. "I know you just got here, but do you think you'll adjust to the life here?"

"Well, I'll confess I'm not sure I'll fit in here. Never been in a foreign country before, and I miss California already."

A slender man—dressed in a beige tropical suit, white dress shirt with a tie that featured wild, brilliant tropical flowers—took the stool next to me. He was Colombian, I was sure—olive complexion, jet black hair, and a thin, neatly trimmed mustache. Mustaches seemed to be the in thing here.

"Good evening, gentlemen. Are you by chance saving this seat for anyone?" He spoke English well with a slight accent. After a short exchange of the usual, he said his name was Raul Pacheco and stated, "I'm in an import-export business. What do you fellows do?"

"I'm with an oil field supply company," Andy said.

"And I'm an oil field geologist."

"That's interesting. I assume you look for oil in big holes in the earth here in Colombia?"

"No, not in big holes. Usually oil is found between sand grains in thick beds of sand or sandstone deep in the earth."

"Now there, you see I've learned something new already," Raul said.

Soon we were buying each other rounds of beer. Time slipped by and finally Raul suggested we should think about dinner, a nice dinner and a little entertainment.

I wasn't sure what he meant by entertainment, but I had an idea. It sounded good to Andy, but I was hesitant. It might be smarter not to rush into this new environment; I didn't know what I would be getting into.

After all, this Raul was a complete stranger. I remembered the warning *la señora* on the airplane gave me about con artists being dangerous, if not life threatening. It might be better to stick close to the hotel until I get to know more about life in Colombia.

After more rounds of beer we were getting along like three old buddies. Raul stood up and announced, "Come on, I want to take you guys to a real nice place you're going to really enjoy."

"Well, why not? What do you say, Rolly? We don't want to miss that, now do we?" Andy said with a wide grin and a nudge in my ribs.

"Well, I'm game if you are, Andy." *Although I didn't feel game.*

Our cab took us for a long ride, making many turns through dimly lit narrow streets, past houses with animated people outside trying to cool off in the hot and humid night air. Naturally, I was completely lost. I imagined Andy was, too, although I could see in the darkened cab that he had a happy expression on his face.

Finally we stopped in front of a dimly lit house; shadows made by tall trees with far-reaching branches blocked the faint glow from a streetlight. Curtain-covered windows allowed a sliver of light to escape around the edges. To me this house and the whole area looked ominous.

Raul paid the taxi driver, who then sped off like he had to flee or suffer something bad, very bad. I wondered if I should have left with him. "Come on, gentlemen, don't look so hesitant. You're going to like this, I swear," Raul encouraged.

He knocked on the door, and we waited in a dank cove of the entry. Finally a huge black man opened the door and looked us over before Raul said, "*Buenas noches*, Abraham. I am an acquaintance of *la señora Lorena*."

We were ushered into a parlor and then into a more secluded alcove. I noticed four men with four women in bright party dresses huddled around a small cocktail table. Their voices were low except for an occasional burst of masculine laughter along with a high-pitched titter from one the ladies.

"Looks like this is going to be expensive," I said. Damn it, I said to myself, I came down here to make money, not spend it. I just got here and now I'm going to blow my whole wad on my first night.

"Not with your dollars. You'll find they go a long way down here," Raul said with a knowing smile.

The waiter asked something in Spanish. I understood only one word—*caballeros*. Raul said something that sounded like whisky. A bottle immediately appeared; the waiter broke the seal on the bottle to show, I was told, no one had tampered with its contents. He poured it into three glasses. Ice and water were added if needed.

We toasted each other with "*Salud*" and drank our first glass, followed by two more, and then sat back for conversation.

From shadows in a recessed hallway, three ladies in bright high-class cocktail dresses emerged. The tallest one made her way to me. That was understandable; she was taller than Andy or Raul. She sat very close to me and whispered something. I understood "*Buenas noches, mister,*" but the rest I missed completely. However, I did catch her name, *Elena*.

The whisky made me feel loose and in control. I remembered to say, "*Mucho gusto,*" several times to give the impression I knew what I was talking about. Our conversation contained a lot of "*¿Qué?*" and "*¿Cómo?*" and unending chatter on both our parts, like we seemed to understand each other. I admired her unique ability to make me feel at ease and as if she really went for me. That was okay even though we had just met. It was an illusion; I didn't mind because she sent my male juices surging.

When music started to play, she stood and took my hand and put her arm around me. We danced, or at least that is a generous description of what we were doing. I marveled how well she could follow me even though I had no idea how to dance to Colombian music. It was fun. I was having a ball.

After several dances, I looked over at our table and noticed it was set up for dinner. When I was served a plate I asked what it was and was told *arroz con pollo*. "What's that mean?" Rice and chicken. It tasted unusual; different herbs, I imagined. But I was too hungry to let it bother me. I hesitated with the tossed green salad. Maybe it could be contaminated with germs. But Raul reassured me that salads were okay here.

When Andy and Raul and their ladies finished eating, they stood up and went to other rooms. I looked into Elena's smiling eyes, and once again she took my hand and then led me across the dance floor to her bedroom. The lights were low; the air, warm and humid. Perfume from Elena and flowers filled the atmosphere. She led me to the foot of her bed. I wondered if she heard my pounding heart. She dropped my hand and embraced me and then smiled, looking up into my eyes. Her words were lost to me, but the sounds she uttered in my ear sent erotic chills down my neck and shoulders and back; never before in my life had I experienced such sensations. Love making had never been as exciting as this. She began to unbutton my shirt. I didn't move, letting her have her way. She was in control and I loved it. My shirt came off. I kicked off my shoes. She undid my belt, unzipped my pants. I thought I was going to explode with desire. I wanted to hold her, slip her onto the bed, but I resisted. This was her show. She studied my naked body and said something with a coquettish grin. It didn't matter that I didn't understand her words. She glanced at her shoulder strap once, twice, then I got the message and eased each strap slowly off her shoulders and down to her waist. Her pert breasts round and firm, made me gasp slightly. Then her dress quickly slid to the floor. Her black laced panties were next. She took my hand to feel her smooth, firm thighs. She slowly rotated, not shyly but boldly and without shame, letting me appreciate the sight of her body, a body she seemed proud of. She shuddered as my warm palms stroked her supple upright breasts, waist, and hips.

A gentle push and I slid back, my head resting on a starched white pillow. She crept on top of me. I was ready for her. She rolled me on top and guided me into her, our breaths, slow and rhythmic, gradually becoming feral-like panting. Then I could hold back no longer. A divine explosion surged throughout my body, leaving me exhausted, exhausted passion.

Still breathing hard, I felt her roll out of bed. Placidly, I watched her sit naked before a vanity mirror slowly combing her ruffled hair. I started to rise to put on my clothes, but she swept over to stop me and pushed me back down on the bed. She whispered a few indiscernible words then motioned me not to get up, to lie quietly. She rushed through a side door that must have been a bathroom because I could hear water running. She returned with a warm, damp washcloth in hand and gently washed me. That was a new sensation, and it felt relaxing. She finished and returned the cloth to the bathroom. I remained on the bed. After a short period, she returned and mounted the bed and caressed me. I didn't expect to make love again, but she made me want to. After a while I lost count. It wasn't like I had expected—one time, maybe two at the most. But she did not let me leave her bed. I would spend all night with her, and when she felt I was ready, she would test me with her soft fingers. Sleep didn't come until early morning.

They were following me, menacing ragged people; now chasing me. I didn't know what they wanted, what I should do. They shouted. I didn't understand them. The dirt road snaked around thick vines and bushes and trees. I didn't know where I was headed, but I knew I had to find someone or I would lose everything I had hoped for. But who did I have to find? I didn't know who he was, what he looked like, or where to find him.

I woke startled, sour taste of old whisky and beer coating my mouth. I was sweating. Slowly my mind cleared and my breathing eased; my heart slowed. It was only a dream, but why such a nightmare? Then it struck me. I couldn't relax now. I was in Colombia in a high-class whorehouse, and I didn't even know what it was going to cost me. Elena emerged from her bathroom wearing a flowery silk kimono. I was tired and felt ill at ease. *What do I say to a lovely prostitute on the morning after?* She spoke in a low, husky voice; I didn't understand her (she probably knew that). She slid a business card from her sleeve and handed it to me. I glanced at it, a telephone number, an address in Bogotá, and her name in large sweeping letters. I knew I had to ask her how much I owed her, but how do I do that? I was afraid the night's activity was going to cost me my total salary. Three Spanish words popped into my head: "*Cuánto la noche?*"

In a hushed voice she murmured, "*Cincuenta pesos.*"

Fifty pesos? That's a lot of money, I thought at first but then realized it was only five dollars. I gladly paid her, gave her a quick embrace, and bid her a fond *adios. Damn, I wish I could express myself.*

A cab parked curbside patiently waited for anyone who needed a ride. On the way to my hotel I agonized over whether Vickers had been searching for me, not knowing how the hell to find me. *Got to get back to my hotel fast.* But it was still early; the sun was barely up.

Chapter 9

MEET JOHN TURNER AND WELCOME TO CHANARA

A hotel maid had hung up my clothes and straightened the room. Fluffy white towels replaced yesterday's wet ones that I had left on the floor. My bed looked inviting since I hadn't slept much since leaving L.A., but I was hungry, so I made my way down to the dining room. If Vickers was looking for me, that's where he'd find me.

A short, stocky waiter with tight, crinkly black hair handed me a menu. His cheeks lit up with a smile, exposing his piano-keys teeth. "*Bien venida, Señor Farrington* (how'd he know my name?). "*Me llamo Héctor, a sus órdenes.*" His jovial face put me at ease, lessening my anxiety about being stranded since I arrived, like a deserted rat on a sinking ship. He babbled something in Spanish I didn't get. His white, starched serving jacket and white serving gloves reassured me this was a high-class hotel.

"I'll have two eggs, bacon, toast, fruit, and coffee, please," I ordered.

"Dos huevos, tocino, fruita, y café," he translated.

"Sounds about right." I remembered *huevos* and *café* from high school Spanish. I waited, playing with my fork while glancing around the half-empty room. People eating and chatting, some dressed in lightweight tropical suits, others in dark, heavy ones—they must come from cold territories, wherever that might be. A warm breeze wafted in through open French doors.

Hector set a heaping plate in front of me. The smell of coffee and bacon alerted my senses. "What's this?" I asked, pointing at my plate.

"Plátano frito, señor. Muy bueno."

"Looks like fried banana to me. I don't think I'm going to like it."

"Your waiter's right," a loud voice behind me interrupted. "That's fried plantain, or cooking banana. It's sweet and delicious. You've got to try it."

I turned around in my chair to stare straight into a stranger's face: a lopsided grin showing an irregular row of teeth that reminded me of partly eaten white corn on the cob appeared right under his bent, rippled nose, like maybe he should have led with his chin instead of his nose. This sunburned, unshaven stranger with aqua-blue eyes wore dusty denims and a sweat-stained, short-sleeved tan shirt. With darting eyes, he surveyed the room like a boxer quick to avoid a punch, never losing that grin. He was, I figured, either an odd-ball character or a con artist, or my savior.

At a loss for words, I could only squeeze out, "Do I know you?"

"The name's Turner, John Turner. Just drove in from Chanara, that oil well you are supposed to be working with me and Banks. Didn't Vickers tell you?"

"Vickers? I haven't seen him. Nobody met me at the airport when I arrived. I was stranded there. Couldn't talk to anybody. No one spoke English except for three German girls working for Lufthansa . . . how'd you know I'd be at this hotel?"

"This was the first place I looked for you. Have you tried to call him?"

"I don't even have his number; don't know what he looks like, except for being tall and blond."

"Well, that sonofabitch was supposed to get you a *cedula* and all that shit and then take you to the well out in Chanara." Turner thought for a moment. "Hell, I'm in charge if Vickers isn't around, so I can do that for you," he chuckled before continuing. The idea of him being in charge seemed to have just popped into his head. "And then I want to get laid. Don't suppose you can help me there. You wouldn't happen to know a good cathouse, would you?"

I thought about last night, pondered whether to tell this guy about it. "I just got in last night, remember?"

To a passing waiter Turner said, "Hey *muchacho*, bring me a plate of assorted fruit, pancakes, bacon, and three fried eggs and coffee." With a self-satisfied smile, he went on. "I could say that in Spanish, but why bother? These people need to learn English, anyway."

Turner's loud voice and screw-the-world attitude bothered me as well as the people seated at the other tables. He didn't give a damn if he pissed people off or not. But, I had to admit, I was glad to have someone show me the ropes.

I ate silently, eyes on my eggs and *platanos*, while Turner continued with what he seemed to like to do best. "I worked all over this goddamn country, know it better than most of these Colombians you see around us, even that bunch laboring in gardens beyond those open doors you see. Been in plenty of tough spots—bandits, rock slides on mountain roads, wild animals, you name it, I've been there," he bragged as he churned away on a mouthful of bacon and pancakes. "Hey, help yourself to papaya. It's delicious," he offered, pointing at a plate overloaded with fresh fruit.

"No, thanks."

"No? Why not? It's good for you."

"It's putrid . . . smells rotten, and these eggs taste different."

"That's because they're fresh. Chickens here live on the ground and eat bugs and worms. That's what gives them that real taste eggs should have. Lots of food will taste different to you at first. Meat's not aged, always fresh. You'll get used to it."

"I doubt it," I said in a low voice with a slight snarl, shaking my head.

The waiter approached with two breakfast bills. Turner interrupted his chatter and chewing to speak softly in rapid Spanish to the young waiter. Then the waiter departed. Turner returned to his plate and monologue.

When the waiter returned, he set one bill next to my plate. My frown caught Turner's eye. "Hell, it's easier this way. Don't worry; I'll make it up to you next time. I didn't bring much money with me when I left Chanara this morning. Anyway, I'll need extra money if I'm going to get laid. Shit, I had to leave camp there at five this morning so I could find out what happened to you." I noticed some people getting up to leave, their plates with uneaten food on them.

I figured he was like a boxer—spar, dance around, and then POW! He lands a haymaker on me. "You pay the bill, Rolly, ole buddy. What's the matter? You look pissed," Turner stated with a grin full of teeth.

I just hunched my shoulders as if to say "forget it."

"Shit, man, slack off. You've already got paid for two days plus living allowance without doing a fucking bit of work. What do you do, count your pennies, too?"

Neither of us spoke until Turner said, "We got to *vamos* out of here and *dale clavo* down to the federal offices in downtown Barranquilla and get your paperwork out of the way."

I gave Turner a tight grin and said, "I know you said, 'Let's go' in Spanish, but what's the rest?"

"Means we got to shag-ass fast before *siesta* time. Every goddamned place shuts down for two to four hours. No business dealings, so we've got some things to attend to before noon. Have you got enough *pesos*?"

"I planned to exchange my dollars for *pesos* here at the hotel."

"Wrong, you get a crappy exchange here. We're going downtown. I'll take you to a money changer."

"Shouldn't we go to a bank?"

"Listen, this money changer will give you the best deal for your bucks. Don't worry, it's all legal."

The race started. We flew in John Turner's company jeep, dodging traffic, scaring pedestrians—some even carrying huge bundles on their heads—and going through stop signs before reaching our destinations: a business building down town. A line of people waited for their number to be called. Turner grabbed my arm and dragged me to the front counter, elbowing a customer away from it. He leaned over and whispered into the attractive clerk's ear. She smiled and quickly helped us file papers for a work permit. As we rushed out, people in line gave us hostile grimaces . . . not surprising. We zipped back to the hotel to settle my bill. In front of the hotel Turner spotted a tall, thin creep, about my age, with notably ashen skin, like he never spent time in the sun. He shouted over the buzzing crowd, "Hey, Jesse Logan, what the hell are you doing here?"

Logan returned a loud greeting: "Turner, you old crock-a-crap, I'm doing business here." The two shook hands like old buddies.

"I want you to meet Rolly Farrington. He just flew in from L.A. yesterday."

We shook hands. "I got a good deal for you, Rolly. How does twelve *pesos* for a buck sound instead of ten *pesos*?" I exchanged five one-hundred dollar bills.

"Let's go, cracker-ass. It's hotter here than Hades," Turner shouted, typical Turner, always hyper. "Hey, Rolly, I can hardly wait to dive into that Olympic-sized swimming pool at our drilling camp. This evening when it cools off, we can hit the courts. You play tennis, don't you?" Turner added in all sincerity. "It's really a beautiful place."

I couldn't tell if he was bullshitting me, so I changed the subject. "Who else is working this well with us?"

"Brian Banks. You're replacing a dead man."

"Dead man? What happened to him ?"

"Climbing the mast he didn't fasten on the safety belt."

"Well what happened?"

"His foot slipped on one of the rungs of the ladder; he couldn't grab the side of the ladder so he fell a hundred feet head first. He was dead by the time we got to him," Then Turner added, "Look, Rolly, you got to be careful around drilling rigs. You never know when something goes wrong and catches you off guard; you can get killed.

We bounced along in Brocton's jeep toward Chanara on unpaved gravel roads rumpled like washboards. A cloud of billowing dust in our eyes and a noisy engine made conversation impossible. As I expected, Turner barreled along like a mad man in a destruction derby. I hung on with hot wind in my face and occasional swarms of bugs bouncing off my cheeks and forehead or nestled in my hair.

We started traversing farmland—green sugarcane spreading out on both sides of the road. Cattle grazed on grassy slopes. Our scenery quickly changed to vine-covered jungle followed by a thick forest on rising mountains. After several hours we approached a row of adobe shanties with palm frond roofs—a village. Turner skidded to a stop at a roadside stand selling fruit, vegetables, and meat hanging over a smoky fire pit. I chose to stay in our jeep under the burning sun until a mouthwatering smell of meat sizzling on a grill roused my appetite. I had to be careful with what I ate, for fear of food poisoning or parasites, but I figured cooked meat should be safe.

"Welcome to Chanara. I don't know about you, but I'm having some of those *salchichas* and a *cervesa*," Turner said.

He pointed to some sausages as he grabbed a beer out of a wooden tub filled with tepid water. "As you can see, there's not much to Chanara— just three or four streets, a police force and a couple of whorehouses down by the river. Not bad. Gals start looking pretty good after a few rum and cokes." John Turner chuckled.

It was late afternoon. I could see over the top of distant hills a steel drilling rig derrick towering above tall trees. The jarring ride would end soon. "How are conditions at the well-site camp?" I asked.

"Bitchin'! You'll love our swimming pool, tennis courts, and golf."

"Are you bullshitting me?"

He smiled but didn't answer.

Maybe it was true. I relaxed as Turner veered off the main gravel road onto a narrow, dusty lane with deep ruts. "There you can see our camp." I saw a flat bulldozed area the size of a football field and an oil well drilling rig in the center of it. Turner pointed to three structures at the edge of the bulldozed plot on higher ground: one was the Americans' sleeping quarters, next to it a prefab cooking and dining unit, and then a cabin. Every building was mounted off the ground on foot-high posts—to keep out snakes and other unwelcome pests. The walls were a little over six feet high, bottom half made of clapboard and top half open screened windows. The roof was covered with palm fronds.

"Who gets the cabin?" I asked.

"Boots Delaney, chief engineer for Hendren Oil Company."

"How does he get along with geologists?"

"He doesn't," Turner answered. "Well, I mean he's always looking over your shoulder ready to jump all over you for the smallest infraction. So you always have to watch your step."

"Thanks for the warning."

He opened the screen door to our sleeping quarters. A voice shouted from somewhere in the darkened room: "Close that goddamn door before you let in all them goddamn bugs."

"I will, I will, Curly, just as soon as I show our new man his bed." A single unlit light bulb hung from the thatched roof. Wooden flooring creaked, and a few bugs clung to outside screened windows scratching to get in. "Put your suitcase under that bed. It's yours," Turner ordered. I could see the bed wasn't long enough for my long legs. I looked around: no closets, no chest of drawers, just a room full of single cots. Two buzzing fans in opposite corners made the place somewhat cooler than outside.

"I know you were kidding about a beautiful camp with swimming pool and tennis court, but I was told we would each have a private room."

"Rolly, this is the oil field, not some fancy resort. Come on, I'll introduce you to Curly."

Curly lay sprawled on top of his rumpled bed in his underwear. "Curly, I want you to meet our third geologist on this well. His name is Rolly Farrington." Then John said to me, "Curly is the bull pusher in charge of three American tour pushers who run the crews of Colombian roughnecks."

Curly's white beach-ball-sized belly matched his white bald head that, when he was outside, was protected from the sun by a hardhat that didn't protect his beet-red face. He sat up from his cot and put his feet on the floor and squinted at me. "You ain't from California, are you?"

"Yes, I am. Why do you ask?"

"No particular reason. You'd better be ready when we start drilling again. It's going to drill fast like in a snow bank."

We made our way down a gentle slope on foot from our rustic living place through scattered low bushes and dusty grasses.

"Aren't there a lot of snakes in places like this?"

Turner didn't bother to answer me. I had been warned to watch where I stepped and to search between my sheets for scorpions, reptiles, and spiders. We reached Brocton's trailer-lab next to the rig where John Turner, Brian Banks, and I would study the geology of drilled-up rock cuttings.

Turner beckoned me to peer in the trailer window. I saw someone's legs stretched out on a padded bench. Turner jerked the door open and shouted, "What the hell's going on in here? Why aren't you working?"

Up bolted a gasping man from the bench, face as pale as a sheet. Turner rolled with laughter and said, "Scared the shit out of you, didn't I, Brian?"

"You stupid bastard! You could have given me a heart attack."

After the man calmed down, Turner introduced me to Brian Banks, third member of our geology team. He was in his early twenties like me, a little taller than John Turner but thinner. His brown hair cascaded over his forehead to the top of his steel-rimmed glasses. He seemed shy, like a threatened animal.

Turner explained he would take the daylight tour from 8:00 a.m. to 4:00 p.m.; I had the afternoon tour from 4:00 to 12 midnight, and Brian the morning tour from 12 midnight to 8:00 a.m.

A booming roar from dueling rig motors outside our door drowned out our voices. I could hear heavy metal tools being dropped on the rig's steel-plated floor twenty feet above our heads. "The hole is only 500 feet deep. They just cemented casing in the well and are now waiting for it to set before hooking blowout preventers on top of the casing and then testing them before drilling deeper," Turner said. "So they won't be ready to drill out until after midnight, which is good news. So after we eat we can go back to Chanara, have a little booze and get laid. We'll be back way before they're ready to drill."

"Shouldn't we stick around and check out all our equipment and have everything ready? We're in for some fast drilling for the next few days," I suggested.

"Naw, I checked out all our shit just the other day. No problem," Turner boasted.

After a hot, dusty ride in failing daylight to Chanara, Turner pulled up to a series of adobe riverbank *cantinas*. The weak lights mounted on the sides of a few *cantinas* glistened in scattered mud puddles. I spotted what looked like a black concave rock the size of a hardhat in As I stepped from the jeep onto that hard rock that turned out to be soft and squishy. I lost my balance but was able to grab the side of the jeep, saving me from falling flat ass in muddy water.

"What the hell was that?"

"You just stepped on a humongous toad, you asshole," Turner couldn't stop laughing.

This trip to a whorehouse was not a good idea, I reasoned.

With flagging interest I accompanied Turner and Brian into a darkened open air *cantina*. Humidity must have been 100 percent. It was crowded with drunk, loud, sweating people. Cigarette smoke burned my nose and eyes. The dance floor was full of gyrating bodies that resembled a well choreographed riot. A small group of musicians wailed away on trumpets and saxophones while an animated drummer tried to beat holes into his four drums. This place epitomized honky-tonk. We found an empty table.

The top was etched with cigarette burns and wet from spilled booze. Beer bottle caps, beer bottles, and flattened cigarette butts littered the cracked cement floor. A flashy bar girl dressed in a short skirt and bulging red bra asked to take our orders. I ordered a beer. And so did Brian.

"Bullshit! Bring us a bottle of rum and coke. Forget the beer."

"Rum? What the hell are you talking about, Turner? We've got to go to work in a few hours, so forget about rum, especially a whole bottle. Brian and I want two beers," I said, but Turner insisted on ordering a bottle of rum.

Three young *muchachas* dressed like our barmaid and with cheeks daubed with pink rouge, lips coated with blood-red lipstick, and eyelashes ladened with mascara sat down at our table and proceeded to put their arms around each of us. Not one of them was bad looking, but their brazen approaches didn't turn me on. They were too loud, too tough, and not in a sexy way. My girl jabbered in my ear and stroked my arm, then my shoulder, and finally my left leg. Our ladies were drunk, and one bumped Turner's rum bottle. It broke on the cement floor. In a flash he slapped her face, knocking her flat. Brian grabbed his arm and yelled, "We'd better get out of here before you start a brawl!" Turner brushed off the warning and started to talk vigorously in Spanish, making the girls laugh. But when he pinched another girl's nipple, she stood up and whacked him across his face. He doubled over with laughter and tried to pinch another one's tit, but she saw it coming and moved away quickly.

Turner banged on the table and shouted at Brian and me: "Hey! Why don't you candy-asses do something? If you're not going to screw these whores, at least dance with them." And then he grabbed another barmaid by her arm, lifted her on his shoulder, and carried her off to a bedroom. We drank our beers and waited for Turner to finish with his girl. Suddenly a loud shriek soared above the frenetic music. At first I thought it was a trumpeter going wild, but then a naked girl darted from Turner's room, across the dance floor, bumping into sweating dancers, and out through another door, leaving everyone wide-eyed and in shock. Later Turner sauntered up to our table with a stupid grin on his face.

"What the hell did you do to that girl?" I shouted.

"Not a fucking thing. So forget it."

I couldn't forget it. Now I understand now I understand Turner's depravity.

"John, we'd better start back to the well. It's getting late," Brian said, trying to look calm, but failed.

"Yeah? What time is it?" Turner asked.

"About eleven thirty," I answered.

"One more and then we'll go," Turner insisted.

Brian didn't like it but gave in.

When we finally left and were on our way to the car, a ragged old man scampered up to us and startled me. It was dark and I couldn't see his face under his wide-brimmed straw hat.

"What's he want?" I asked.

"Give him a couple of *pesos*, Rolly," Turner slurred.

"What for, for Christ's sake?"

"No one stole our car or tires or seats, did they?" Turner said, laughing.

"You gotta pay for protection here or they'll rob you blind," Brian explained.

I was having second thoughts about putting up with this kind of life just to get rich. I could always return to California oil fields.

Turner insisted on driving. With no streetlights to guide us, he sped along blindly over dark, unlit roads until I warned him: "John, slow down, you can't see shit." Then we banged over something in the road. The three of us were bounced off our seats. Turner, shaken, said, "Just something in the road, piece of metal maybe."

"Well, goddamnit, you'd better stop and see what's wrong." I was at the point of losing my temper. "Does this heap have a flashlight?"

"Yeah, sure." Its weak batteries gave off a feeble glow.

"We've got a flat tire, boys," Turner announced. He held the flashlight while Brian and I worked on the flat. We lost precious time before getting back on the road.

Brian and I were panicking. We had no idea how soon they would be drilling. "If they start drilling and we're not there we'll miss hundreds of feet of formation that could be a sand body with high pressure gas and we would miss it. The oil company would send all three of us packing. Turner didn't seem to care about losing his job.

When we finally saw the brightly lit rig, it looked like an island surrounded by a black sea. Randomly scattered scrub brushwood caught defused light from the rig making a picture of frozen turbulent waves.

"There are a lot of men on the rig floor!"

"Must be midnight. That's the crew change. Don't worry, Rolly, they're not *banditos*," John Turner laughed.

John Turner drove up to the rig to drop off Brian. "Okay, Brian, you can handle it from here. Rolly and I are going to hit the sack."

"Don't you think we should stick around for a while? Make sure Brian gets started okay?" I asked as I got out of the jeep.

"Suit yourself, Rolly." With that John spun around and headed to our sleeping quarters, leaving me behind.

The trailer was dark. Brian clicked on a switch, but no light came on. For a moment both of us were stunned. It was pitch dark inside, and we found that nothing worked—no electricity for our equipment and no water for washing rock cuttings. The crew on the rig was ready to start drilling.

I dashed outside in the dark and found where our trailer's thick, rubber-insulated electric cord ran toward the rig. I yelled to Brian that I would follow it to where it plugged into the light plant. Brian called back that he would find a way to reconnect our water system.

I followed the cord but lost it where it dipped into a muddy puddle. I searched the other side of the swampy mess and located it in obscure muddy drilling debris. It snaked along the side of the rig until it rose up over I-beams that supported the rig's motors, draw works, and everything else. I crawled along under the rig, with out light and with rig motors over my head roaring in my ears. I searched in utter blackness until I located the cord again. With it in my hands I found an open space I could crawl out from under the rig. I stumbled over piles of drilling gear. I continued following it around mud pumps and storage tanks to a metal structure mounted on skids—the light plant. I could hear a diesel motor running a generator inside. I unlatched the steel door and stepped into a buzzing maze of thick, coiled, snake-like, electric cords weaving around on the floor, their ends plugged into connections on two walls. I grabbed it and I searched both walls for an empty socket. There it was, like it had been hiding from me. I jammed our connection into that empty socket and then dashed outside where I could see our trailer. And there it was, all lit up. We were in business again.

Brian and I hurried to make sure everything was working. Then the rig let out a deafening roar, and the crew started drilling. It was obvious that the drilling was going too fast for one geologist to keep up with catching drilled-up rock samples, processing them, and then recording his findings in our geologic log—the written record of the geology—so I volunteered to record Brian's data as he worked on the rock cuttings. By the time drilling slowed, it was four in the morning. Brian could work alone now. Before I left the trailer, I asked him, "Tell me, Banks, what's with this guy Turner?"

"What do you mean?"

"I mean does he always think he's king shit? Looks to me he pushes all the workload on us. Why do we have to put up with his bullshit? And what about what he did to that poor screaming whore?"

"I've gotten used to how he operates."

"Does he always make you pay the bar bills?" Brian hesitated. "No, he seems to pay sometimes."

I was getting ready to leave Brian and the trailer when lights swept through our window from a jeep that had just pulled up outside. A tall, ramrod-straight man stepped into our trailer. His close-set eyes and the mean frown stitched to his eyebrows could only mean trouble. His first words exploded in our ears: "Why are there two geologists working here tonight?" There was no humor in his voice.

We had no idea where this guy came from so early in the morning. I piped up. "No, there's only one working the morning tour. That's him, Brian Banks. The first night of drilling we wanted everything to go right, so I stuck around for a while."

"Boots Delaney is my name. I'm chief engineer for Hendren Oil Company. Let me tell you two right now, if you've got one of those refrigerators in your trailer, there will be no beer or booze in it. And that's final. Next thing I want to tell you, this is a NO DOPE HOLE. Do you know what that means?"

"Sure," I answered.

"Well, tell me goddamnit, what's it mean?" He grew impatient.

"Dope means information. A no dope hole means we don't give out any information to anyone except you and anyone from your company."

"That includes nobody is allowed in this trailer except me, you geologists for Brocton, and engineers from Hendren Oil. You see anyone hanging around here, you notify me. Do I make myself clear?"

"Yes," Brian and I answered in unison, like puppets.

"Next, drill 20 feet into a drilling break; analyze your cuttings from that break. If there's oil and gas, call me, but don't resume drilling unless I tell you to. If there is no oil or gas, you can continue drilling. You understand what I'm saying?"

"Yes, but what is your definition of a drilling break? I've heard several in the past."

"Well, let's say you're drilling about 15 feet per hour and suddenly it increases to 40 feet or there about."

"We understand. You can count on us."

"I'll see you boys later." He climbed back into his jeep, gunned his motor, and was gone.

"Kind of a salty old buzzard, isn't he?" I said to Brian.

"He can be tough to work for. I've worked for him before. Doesn't have much respect for geologists." It was predawn when I left the drill site and hiked uphill to our camp. As I opened the door, I heard the now familiar refrain, "Close that goddamned door! You're letting those goddamn mosquitoes in." That voice rang out above snoring and wheezing from other sleeping Americans.

Before I went to sleep, I wondered about John Turner. He helped me a lot in Barranquilla. But he's a different guy out here, and this place is nothing like he said it was—tennis court, pool. Lying bastard.

Chapter 10

DRILLING

After a couple of weeks our drilling rate of penetration had slowed down to three or four feet per hour. Boots Delaney drove up to the trailer while I was working. First thing he checked was our refrigerator for beer.

Without any introduction or asking how everything was going, he asked me, "Why does your daylight geologist, Turner, call this formation we are drilling in clay when you know goddamn well that clay drills fast like one hundred to two hundred feet per hour? If anything it's got to be hard rock we are drilling in. Look at your drilling rate chart; we're only drilling about 3 or 4 feet an hour. If it was clay, we'd drill right through it in no time."

He caught me off guard with his question, so I took my time and thought it out. "We're grinding on a hard compacted clay formation. The bit just spins on this claystone because it's too hard. The bit's teeth have to grind it to a powder so when it comes to the surface it is soft, mushy clay, so that's what we have to record on our log. There are different kinds of clay. Some, like this one, are made up of clay-sized grains called argillaceous clay; other clay is cemented together with calcium carbonate that's called calcareous clay, which is hard and brittle; and then there is siliceous clay cemented with silicon dioxide, like quartz, and that would be harder yet and would come to the surface as brittle chips. If we saw any chips we could name it, but since it comes up soft clay, that's all we can call it."

He gave me his stern, unreadable stare and then turned and drove away. We were getting used to Delaney's questions and quizzes, as if he would love to catch us making a mistake.

At lunch the next day the only seat open was in front of Boots. Several men were there enjoying fried chicken with french-fried potatoes. Boots broke the silence. "I've got a few rocks here in my little bag I would like you to identify." He looked at me with piercing eyes.

Suddenly I felt he was going to pull a trick on me. "Sure, let's have a look at them," I managed to say, acting as confidently as I could. He rolled out a thumb-sized, six-sided, tabular-shaped, clear and glassy crystal. I said, "Boots, that's silicon dioxide, better known as a quartz crystal." I held it up between my thumb and index finger for everyone to see.

He smiled and said, "If you didn't get that one, you'd be a lousy geologist." He pulled out four more minerals.

I picked up each one seperately, hefted them, and then rolled them around in my hand. I picked up the quartz again and scratched it against a flat, rectangular white stone. "This one is calcite—calcium carbonate. See, the quartz is harder and can easily scratch calcite. This next metallic sample is pyrite—iron sulfide—commonly called fool's gold. And this next one is selenite, which is sodium sulfate and water, also called gypsum. It's very soft; you could scratch it with your thumbnail."

"Here's one I'll bet you won't get." He handed me a long, black, prismatic crystal.

"How much do you want to bet?"

"Ten *pesos*."

"Tourmaline . . . pay up."

He looked at me, not taking those stern, cold eyes off of me, while others shouted out, "Is he right? Did he get it right?"

He gathered up his rocks without any change of expression and flipped out a 10 *peso* bill. He couldn't have picked easier minerals for me to identify.

For the next several weeks the three of us worked together without personality or geological problems. Delaney continued to make unscheduled visits while we worked. That kept us on our toes at all times. I came to work one afternoon as usual to replace John Turner promptly at four. I had noticed a different jeep parked next to the pipe racks but didn't think anything about it. I entered the trailer as usual. "Is everything running smoothly, I hope?" I suddenly sensed something different but didn't know what.

"Don't look so stiff, Farrington. Everything is going as smooth as cat shit," Turner answered.

Then I noticed a tall blond man standing in a corner of the trailer, his back to me as if he were studying something on our desk. He turned and said with a big smile, "Hi, Rolly. Remember me, Jesse Logan?"

"What the hell is he doing in our trailer, John? Delaney is going to go fucking ape shit if he finds him in here. What the hell got into you, Turner?"

"Don't get your balls in an uproar, Rolly. Delaney won't be checking on anybody until late tonight."

"But why is Logan in our trailer when no one is supposed to be here?"

"He was in the neighborhood, so he decided to stop by." Then he abruptly changed the subject. "Look, you'll have to get our log up to date and then run off ten copies."

That's when I noticed *aguardiente* on his breath. "What do you mean I have to get the log up to date? That's your job during your tour."

"I was busy." And, as if an afterthought, he said, "We hit some fast drilling, jumped from 20 feet per hour up to 100, got some gas and some oil fluorescence in our unwashed sample. Looks like we're in sandstone. Nothing to get excited about."

Before I could ask him why he hadn't recorded his findings, he left. That son of a bitch hadn't evaluated any of the oil we drilled into. Would it be good enough to rate it as a show, or would it be a minor trace of oil? I had to work fast, check how fast they were drilling when the oil first came to the surface. I studied a cuttings sample that was sand. "Holy shit! Look at that oil." It wasn't jagged, ragged like dead oil. I watched little round pops spread out on the surface as a sheen of good oil with rainbow colors. I checked the gas recorder when Turner first got this oil: 120 units of methane gas. "My God, that's an oil show, a goddamn good oil show." I had to see Turner's write-up in our geologic log. "Nothing! He hasn't put a word in the log for that depth. That sonofabitch!"

I wanted to find Turner, grab him, and drag his ass back to finish his job, but he was gone, and now that judgment was up to me. If I was wrong I would screw up everything, including my job. Testing an oil show is expensive and could take several days. I hurried up on the rig floor and told the driller to stop drilling and wait for orders. After I quickly evaluated oily cuttings and wrote down my findings, I rushed over to Boots Delaney's trailer.

Cigarette smoke filled his room. Boots was seated at his table smoking, drinking whiskey, and talking to the afternoon tour pusher, who was drinking coffee.

"Listen, Boots, we got a good oil show about 40 feet up the hole. Maybe 40 feet of good oil sand."

He sprang out of his chair like an exploding volcano, shouting, "What the goddamned hell are you talking about? What do you mean 40 feet up the hole?"

"Well, I just came on tour. But that sand looks awful good to me."

"You stupid bastards just committed a cardinal sin. You know goddamn well you're supposed to notify me as soon as you get a drilling break. I ought to run your no-good asses out of here, you understand me?"

I shouldered the abuse and then attempted to quench the flames. "I know. It was a mistake. But I don't think any damage was done. Maybe it's better it happened this way. Now we know we have at least 40 feet of oil sand, and it looks good. The overburdened shale is a good, dense cap rock. And all I know is we stopped drilling at 40 feet, so maybe this oil sand is a lot thicker yet," I said, feeling my face flush after being chewed out for something I had no control over.

"Good enough to run a test?" Boots asked, as he forced a slow, contemplative movement of standing up and stretching his crackling and creaking arthritic bones, adding to the fire in his eyes.

"It's worth a try."

"And if it's nothing, it'll be your ass."

As I stewed over my judgment in my chair in the trailer waiting for Brian to relieve me at midnight, I wasn't sure if I had overreacted by calling that iridescent sheen an oil show. That oil occurred on Turner's tour. He should have evaluated it. My mind was so full of hate for Turner's leaving his responsibility on my shoulders. But maybe he had seen the oil and knew it wasn't anything to get excited about.

Brian tramped in at midnight on the dot, eyes as big as an owl's. "What's going on?" I explained the situation and waited for his experienced opinion. He only said, "Oh, then I don't have to work tonight."

When I reached the sleeping tents, Turner wasn't there. I waited until next morning to confront him, but he was ignoring me. He sat at the far end of the breakfast table with a couple of oil field hands. I was damned if I was going to let him off the hook so easily. I knew I had to be careful around these men. They loved to see a confrontation. It put some life into their mundane lives. "You left me holding the bag."

"Over nothing," he shot back.

"Over nothing? You're wrong. Putting all those pieces together makes an oil well."

"Bullshit! I've seen more oil than you'll ever see." He threw his napkin down on his half-finished breakfast and stomped away.

The others in the room looked puzzled.

I was dying to tell them all about Turner leaving his tour early and missing the oil show, but I realized it was a problem between Turner and me and it would be better to keep it that way. Turner continued to keep his distance from me. The only thing Brian said was that I had better be right about that oil show because we would be under the gun the next day with that open-hole test. If I was wrong, Delaney would run us off.

Chapter 11

DRILL STEM TEST

The testing assembly was scheduled to arrive from Barranquilla the next day. Turner took that opportunity to suggest taking a run into Chanara and getting laid. "We got until tomorrow and no work to do. What do you say?"

"I might go for a beer," Brian muttered in his reluctant way.

"How about you, Rolly?" That was the first time he had spoken to me since our confrontation.

I couldn't get it out of my mind that I might be wrong about this oil show. "No, I'd rather stick around here."

"Suit yourself," Turner said as he and Brian took off.

I hardly slept that night. I rolled out of bed in the morning with a splitting headache. How was I going to make it through the day? With my bloodshot eyes I could see the rig and drill pipe standing upright on the rig floor. The hole was filled with carefully controlled mud, heavy enough to keep the sides of the hole from caving in and keeping high pressure gas from causing a blowout.

The morning grew hotter and muggier. Drilling crews were making up the tester and were ready to connect to the drill pipe and then lower it to the bottom. After a few minutes it started to rain, a heavy rain. Roughnecks on the rig were slipping and sliding dangerously, but they kept working. They had a job to do.

I joined Brian and John at a dining table out of the rain while we waited for the test to start. I didn't feel any better even after a big breakfast of steak, eggs, and pancakes.

"Shouldn't take long before we see if you stuck our necks out and they get chopped off or not, Rolly," John Turner said with a leering grin.

"We'll soon see if you fucked up. I warned you there wasn't enough oil to make a show."

It was taking forever to put the tester together and start the test. Nothing seemed to be happening on the rig floor. The three of us met with Boots Delaney, who introduced us to three big-shot engineers from Hendren Oil Company in Barranquilla. We shook hands. No one had much to say. I could feel cold insecurity creeping down my spine. If I was wrong about the oil, I knew no one would shake it off and say we all make mistakes now and then, so don't worry about it; you're young and have a lot to learn.

We stood near the rig so we would be present for the test results. The waiting was unending for me. I was responsible if this test was a failure. I could see these big shots were becoming impatient.

Finally the tester a mile down at the bottom of the hole was opened. Everyone expected to see crude oil come surging to the surface. The waiting dragged on. Everyone checked his watch. One of the big shots said he wanted to wait another half hour. My anxiety increased; my legs grew weak. I looked for a place to sit down but gave it up. I could sense their enmity. There were no smiles on any faces. Boots declared in disgust, "We're wasting our time. If there's oil down there, it should have been up a long time ago."

"Well, have the crew pull the pipe out so we can see if any oil was captured in the tester itself," one of the engineers suggested.

The three of us retreated to our trailer-lab to wait for the test assembly to come up out of the hole. "Something's wrong here. That was a legitimate oil show I recorded," I said in my defense to Turner and Banks.

"You sure you know a legitimate oil show when you see one, Farrington?" Turner snorted.

"Hell yes, I've seen oil shows, and some not even as good as this one."

"What are they going to do now?" Brian asked.

"Run our asses off," Turner quipped.

The tester was pulled to the surface and checked by the engineers; the three of us were with them. "See there, the tester is closed, so when we open it now we should at least see some oil," Boots said.

After it was opened, one of the company men declared, "Not a drop!" Then he looked at me. "I want to see you, Farrington, in our trailer right now."

Boots Delaney and the big shots from Barranquilla glared at me as I entered their trailer. Even with the air conditioner buzzing cold air, I was sweating.

"You know how much this test cost our company? Shit, you don't want to know."

I could either shut up and accept being fired or defend myself. I chose to defend. "I tell you, I tested for oil and I found oil popping up in unwashed and washed cuttings. Rainbows of live oil surfaced all over washed sandstone chips with 120 units of gas associated with crude."

"Might as well put on another bit and go back to drilling," said one man halfheartedly.

"Let's think about it for a minute. If it's true what this man says, then there's got to be an explanation for what happened," another reasoned.

"Yes, since there was not one drop of oil in your tester, then maybe it was a faulty tester. Maybe it jammed and never opened," I suggested.

Minutes passed, everyone was deep in thought. I was about to explode and start talking gibberish.

Boots cleared his throat and uttered, "Take that first tester off and run a new one in the well." He looked at me after he spoke but didn't say a word, just left me with more to think about.

I didn't sleep that night chewing on what might happen if we got another negative test the next day. I just didn't see how I could be so wrong when that oil looked so good. It wasn't until the third day that they were ready to run the test another time. I didn't have much appetite thinking what they would do if they got the same results as the first test.

"We're on the bottom with the tester," the driller yelled down from the rig floor to the engineers standing by the sump where crude oil would flow if the test was positive.

"We're all set here. Go ahead and open the tester up," Boots called.

"She's open now," the driller called down again.

We all stood anxiously waiting for negative or positive results. Seconds ticked by. I fretted. *Not again! I better get ready to pack my suitcase.*

Suddenly we heard a loud hiss that became a screaming whistle and then a roar as crude oil shot out of the conductor pipe into the large dugout sump. Gas blew out at the upright stand pipe. Boots with a bow and arrow shot a diesel-soaked rag into the escaping gas; it caught fire and threw red hot flames straight up into the air. Everyone stood for a moment like paralyzed zombies and then gave a loud cheer. Relieved, I felt something like an electric shock. A broad smile beamed on Boot's crinkled old engineer's face as he said to me, "You done okay, boy. Glad we listened to you."

John Turner didn't look too happy and walked away toward our trailer-lab. *He's pissed because I was right and he was wrong. Well, fuck 'im.*

Boots Delaney called the three of us into his trailer. "We're going to be busy completing this well and moving the rig to a new location. You guys head home. We'll call your company when we're ready for you on the next well." He paused for a moment. "Farrington, I'd like a word with you. You other two can head on out." Turner gave me a curious look as he and Banks filed out the door.

"Farrington, I'm not sure what went wrong between you and that fellow Turner, and I don't really care, but I warn you not to turn your back on him."

We packed up all our equipment in Brocton's trailer and left the location. Turner asked me, "Are you going to Barranquilla with Brian and me or go to Medellin to see your buddy Leon Seacrest?"

"I want to go to Medellin but how do I get there from here?"

"Get in; there is an airport on our way to Barranquilla."

The airport was an hour away. When we got there the ticket line was long; I thought it would be hopeless getting a ticket. But according to Turner: No problem. He pushed me ahead of patient travelers to the counter, giving everyone some excuse in his rapid Spanish. He told the male attendant that he had to speak to Anita Alfonso. Excited, she hurried over to us. He easily charmed Anita to make arrangements for me to fly to Medellin.

"You can take this flight leaving right now for Barrancabermeja and from there catch the next flight to Medellin. It should get you there in a couple of hours. What do you say?"

"What about a flight straight through to Medellin with no stops along the way?"

"There isn't any. This is the only way to get to Medellin today. Let me warn you. Your Spanish stinks, so stay at that airport. Don't venture into town and get screwed up."

"Okay, but shouldn't I call Leon before I leave?"

"Don't worry about that. I'll take care of it. Now get on that plane. Remember when you get to Barranca you stay at the airport. Don't go into town. You know just enough Spanish to get yourself into big trouble."

I don't get it . . . . John Turner can be a ruthless tyrant at times and then be like a big brother to me.

Chapter 12

MARISOL IN BARRANCABERMEJA

Strong winds batted our airplane around like a toy. If this flight lasted much longer, I was prepared to throw up. I looked for a barf bag but there wasn't any. I toughed it out until we landed at Barrancabermeja's airport. In scorching heat I faced a long wait for my flight to Medellin. I had neither reading material nor anyone to talk to. How was I going to kill time alone in this near-empty, sweltering air terminal? The only air conditioning was in the bar, but there wasn't anybody inside, not even a bartender. I was bored, so I made up my mind to forget Turner's advice and take a taxi into town. I was a tourist at heart and liked to see new places. I could go for a couple of cool beers in one of Barranca's *cantinas* and practice Spanish with a local bar girl. But I had to be careful about getting back to the airport in time to catch my flight. I wouldn't want to get carried away with some sexy barmaid and get stranded in town. I found a cab outside the air terminal. Its driver was napping, so I startled him with "*Hombre necesito ir a Barranca.*" But before I got into the cab I made sure this taxi driver understood that I wanted to go into town and come back. I used an old standby—I finger-pointed here, *aeropuerto*, and then pointed out in the distance, *Barranca*, then back here, *aeropuerto*. I think he understood when I said, "*Dos hors aquí.*" Two hours should give me plenty of time for a few beers, or else it wouldn't be worth going. He acknowledged that he understood by saying, "*Yo intiendo.*"

During a dusty fifteen-minute ride into town, I tried to make conversation with my driver. Normally I could have spent this whole trip talking—in English but not in Spanish. I was handicapped by not being able to say exactly what was on my mind. Over these rough roads I couldn't study my handy *Spanish for Travelers*. I did my best but ended up listening more than speaking and understanding only about a quarter of my driver's Spanish.

The cab stopped at the best *cantina* in town, according to my driver. It didn't look like much to me. If this was really their best, I could only imagine what the others looked like. It was a chore, but I explained again to my cabby that I had to be back at the airport in two hours and not a minute later. With that made clear, I proceeded into the *cantina*. It was open-air, with a high roof to keep the sun out. At that early hour, it was not very busy, music not too loud, and weather not too humid. Ceiling fans cooled the air like a morning breeze. A slinky, dark-haired *muchacha* took her time sauntering over to my table, giving me plenty of time to appraise her stuff. She was flashy, as one would expect, and had a smile that made language no problem.

"*¿Qué quieres, mi amor?*" she asked, what did I want, and added "my love," which sounded like an open invitation.

I figured I knew the answer to that one, "*Tú,*" I replied, using the intimate *you* form instead of the formal *usted*.

"It is not too early for that, my love?" and then she laughed that hearty party girl cackle as she gently stroked my hair. "My name is Belita," she offered, speaking Spanish slowly so I would understand exactly what she said, not like the taxi driver, who spoke like he drove—taking no heed of stop signs or periods, running so many words together that a sentence sounded like one long word.

"Or perhaps it is too late?" My answer didn't make much sense, but I realized that when you are attempting sexy conversation, sense isn't as important as enthusiasm.

I ordered beer. She brought back two from the bar: one for me and one for her. She knew what she was doing and so did I. She sat down and we tried to talk. Not getting anywhere, I pulled out my *Spanish for Travelers*. She took it out of my hands, skimmed through it. "This is good," she said in slow Spanish. So we practiced. I read, she corrected my pronunciation. She picked out important words and phrases. She asked me if I understood. Of course I did; the English translation followed the Spanish.

The *cantina* was filling with people as time slipped by, but I didn't pay much attention. My attention was held by this perky little bar girl with gold-colored bows in her dark, wavy hair. I hardly noticed a tap-tap on my right foot, then a tap-tap on my left, as if my feet had fallen asleep and started to tingle. I paid no attention until the tapping grew more intense; then the table erupted, spilling our beer. We spotted the cause: two ragged *gamines*. Two street urchins were vying for the job of shining my boots. Belita pulled them apart, ready to throw them out into the street. I intervened and settled their argument by having both boys shine my boots, one boot for each. They snarled at each other like two little street curs over a bone.

An aroma of fried meat drifted over odors of rum, beer, and *aguardiente*—Colombia's anise-flavored brandy—making my gastric juices flow, so I ordered a large *fritanga*, which consisted of thin slices of fried pork and potatoes, topped with raw green tomatoes, then eaten with toothpicks. I even gave toothpicks to the two shoeshine boys, but they dug in with their hands, picking out meat first with their dirty fingers. I had to order another one for Belita and me. Through the growing din of music, laughter, and voices one word caught my attention—*hora*. The word *hour* made me realize time was all important. A quick glance at my watch launched me out of my seat. "I've been here almost two and a half hours! Where's my driver? I've got to get to the airport right now." No one understood a word of English, but they got the idea when I shouted, "¡*Avión*! ¡*Avión*! ¡*Necesito avión*!" The other bar girls started running around looking for taxicabs, buses, jeeps, horses, or anything that could get me to the airport. Amid this confusion I suddenly noticed someone familiar standing like a shadow in one corner of the *cantina* sipping beer as he conversed with another bar girl. *That's my taxi driver*! He seemed to have appeared out of nowhere.

Belita took up my cause and yelled in Spanish at the top of her lungs: "Where have you been, you worthless *hijo de la grande*? You're a half hour late!"

"I don't have a watch" was his only response, given so innocently.

"I'm going to miss my plane." I was still in English. Belita and the cab driver looked at each other questioningly. I asked for the tab for the beer and food. I was shocked when I saw it but managed to sputter in Spanish, "What's this seven here for? Why so much?" and pointed at the total on the bill.

"No, my love, that's not a *seven*. That's a *one*," Belita replied.

In English I said, "Oh, that's right. Here a *one* looks like a *seven* and a *seven* has a horizontal bar through it." I gave Belita a healthy tip, about what I would have paid her if we had gone to bed together, and then I kissed her cheek. The bar girls and the other folks in the *cantina* cheered.

In the jeep, heat and dust from unpaved roads didn't bother me. I was too concerned about missing my flight. *I've really screwed up: spent too much money and missed my flight to Medellin.* When I couldn't see any airplanes on the runway my worry changed to panic. I was convinced I had missed my flight. What was I going to do now? I didn't have much cash left.

The driver slammed on his brakes, and we both rushed into the terminal. No crowd was waiting for my flight. I panicked more, convinced I had missed the plane. My driver frantically pointed up at a flight schedule board on the wall, but I couldn't understand what it said. I hadn't mastered airport Spanish yet. He read aloud as slowly as he could but ran words together, as usual, trying to get through to me. I still didn't understand him, so I just chewed my lower lip and hoped for a miracle. I was ready to give up and go back to Barrancabermeja and see about working something out with Belita. She seemed like a good-hearted gal I've always read about in paperbacks. Maybe I could hitch a ride to Medellin by road instead of flying.

My alert taxi driver took my arm and steered me over to a ticket counter to a girl who knew how to speak Spanish slowly. She explained very carefully, as if I were a small child, about the flight to Medellin. It was delayed two hours because of weather problems in Barranquilla. Luck was with me, but then I always believed in luck and always counted on something turning up at the last moment to save me. It always did.

The taxi driver and I pulled away from her counter and went outside so we could settle up. Happy now, I managed to ask my driver how much I owed him. "*¿Cuánto . . . ir . . . Barranca . . . y . . . aeropuerto?*"

He put up five fingers. I couldn't believe it. Five *pesos*. Wow! That's cheap. Almost with disbelief I said, "*¿Cinco pesos?*"

"No, *señor*," he retorted. "*Cincuenta pesos.*" Not even a hint of a smile. He was serious.

"Fifty pesos?" *He's trying to screw me. That's too much. I'll bargain with him. After all, that's what you do in foreign countries.* I held up three fingers and said, "*Treinta.*" Thirty.

He shook his head and said, "*Cuarenta.*"

I said okay to forty. "*Está bien cuarenta.*"

Out of nowhere a velvet voice broke my concentration. "*¿Tiene problemas, señor?*" she asked in slow, clear Spanish. I was amazed I understood her.

Brain dead, I turned to get a better look at who was producing these warm and wonderful sounds that had kindled my interest with her charming tone, but all that came out of my mouth was "Huh?" The word should have been "Wow!" She was beautiful as well as charming.

She realized my Spanish was zilch, so she tried the simplest words possible. "*¿Dificultad en pagar el hombre?*"

Her beauty left me speechless. Her dark eyes sparkled with self-confidence. They could, I imagined, peer right into my soul. She controlled her world and maybe other men's worlds as well. Her dark hair seemed to flow in waves around her smiling face. Words didn't come freely until I took hold of my senses, and then all that surfaced was "*¿Qué?*" A stupid thing to ask, especially since I had understood exactly what she had said.

"*¿Es usted Americano?*" she asked with a coquettish twinkle in her eye. She knew what a startling effect she had on men.

"How'd you know I was American?" I asked in English, without knowing if she understood me.

She just smiled with a knowing grin. She turned and spoke for a few moments to the driver and then pulled back thirty *pesos* from the driver's hand and left him with ten. The driver didn't look happy but accepted it.

"*¡Gracias!* . . . *¡gracias!*" I gushed, though I couldn't hide my disappointment. I thought I had negotiated a fair deal with this man, honesty on both sides. I filed this information away for further reference when dealing with taxi drivers. "*¿Usted Medellin?*"

"Sí, voy a Medellin."

"*Bueno. Mi nombre* Rolly Farrington." I managed to ask her if she would like a Coke or beer in the air-conditioned bar.

She accepted my offer and we entered the bar.

"*¿Su nombre es?*"

"Marisol." Her smile changed to a quizzical frown.

Was she upset with me? Was I being too forward? As we passed through the lobby, I could see a few perspiring people napping as they waited for their flights. The chilly bar—separated from the stifling main lobby by thick glass doors—was completely empty except for a bartender who appeared to be hoping for patrons to give him a reason for being there. Large picture windows bordered by lush green vegetation looked out onto shimmering heat waves rising from the asphalt runway. We found a comfortable booth and gave the bartender our order.

"*Cervesa*," I said.

"And for the *señorita*?"

"Coke, *por favor*."

With my hands folded on the table in front of me, I sat back in the leather-cushioned seat and readied myself to charm this beauty with my winning, but limited, conversation. I aimed to make up for my pitiful performance in the scene with the taxi driver.

The bartender brought our drinks, but before we could drink them, we heard the roar of an approaching airplane. She rose from her seat and thanked me for the untouched Coke, and as I was paying, she got in line with the other waiting passengers. When I got to the line, she was already boarding the plane. By the time I boarded, she had found a seat next to another lady. I had to sit several aisles in back of her. I was disappointed she hadn't waited for me. We could have sat together and really gotten to know each other, but I guess I hadn't impressed her.

Chapter 13

ON TO MEDELLIN

As we flew out of Barranca, I thought about Marisol. In fact, I couldn't stop thinking about her: the way she handled that cabby, her voice strong and firm but filled with humor, as if to say the incident was no big deal. She was sitting with an older woman, chatting and chuckling. They didn't know each other because I had seen them introduce themselves. As I watched them enjoying each other's company, I guessed Marisol had already forgotten me.

Our smooth flight over green jungles ended as we climbed higher and away from trees and vines to be challenged by the sheer rock walls of the Andes. Winds bounced us around. Cabin walls creaked and crackled, and people groaned. Our young flight attendant, offering refreshments, staggered up the aisle, then suddenly down the aisle, stumbling like a drunk. She managed to reach me after spilling half of my beer.

We followed a narrow cut through jagged granite mountains with tumbling white-water rapids far below. It was hard to enjoy the beauty because my roiling stomach threatened to throw up.

"Is this normal . . . this jousting about like a Ping-Pong ball?" I asked a man seated across from me. He turned toward me. His face was ghostly gray-white. He opened his mouth to talk but no words came out. I shrugged it off. He probably didn't speak English anyway.

The pretty attendant struggled up the aisle again with another beer for me. This one was foaming all over her hands and floor. I tried my Spanish, but she didn't understand a word I said. *How am I going to make out with señoritas if I don't know enough Spanish to make simple conversation?* But the noise and bumping around made it impossible to communicate anyway.

As the pilot announced our approach to Medellin we began to lose altitude, mountains appeared sprinkled with farm shanties and pastures. Farther along, more buildings separated by a network of roads came into view. Then taller buildings towered over congested traffic and bustling pedestrians— this was the city of Medellin.

Crosswinds made the flight rougher. We lost more altitude circling this broad valley. I tensed when I looked out my small window and saw a car on a mountain road higher than our plane. *Were we going to crash?* My hands clamped my armrest like vises. I turned to face the man again seated across from me. "Eets alwhase like deese, *señor*," he commented and then drew back, staring ahead into space, lips moving in prayer, and crossed himself.

On our last low circle, our wing tips seemed to almost brush a lush green golf course where little figures of men waited for another golfer to make his putt. Just at that moment our pilot roared his four engines louder and caused him to miss his putt. All he could do was shake his fist at us.

We landed safely on firm tarmac. I unbuckled my seat belt and stood up. I could see Marisol standing as she waited for the door to open. Before I could get my bag out of the overhead, she was gone. My last glimpse of her was of her hugging and kissing people at the gate, and then she melted into the crowd.

I made my way out of the plane and inhaled fresh, cool mountain air that confirmed Medellin's reputation as being the "City of Eternal Spring." I scanned the crowded air terminal looking for Leon Seacrest. It would be hard to miss that thick-shouldered, happy bear of a man; his turbulent sandy-blond hair and freckled face nailed him as a *gringo*. But I couldn't see him anywhere. In his letter to me he wrote that his size labeled him a celebrity here. He was in his late twenties and looked tall compared to this crowd. "Goddamnit! Just like arriving in Barranquilla. Where are those Lufthansa angels when I need them?" I searched through swarms of excited people, without success. "No, he's gotta be here, someplace." Then I reasoned where the most logical place would be and made a beeline to the bar. There he sat, his broad ass covering a barstool, his thick arms flailing as he jabbered with a barmaid, in Spanish, no less. His baritone voice boomed out over the ambient noises.

"Bulldog! Ya big ape, why weren't you outside waiting for me? Thought I was abandoned again like in Barranquilla."

"Rolly! I've been here guarding this beer for you while I learned about the fascinating life of a barmaid. Drink it before it gets too warm." We shook hands and punched each other. "We got a few errands to run before I take you up to our *finca*."

"*Finca*, what's that?"

"A villa, or a hacienda, where me and three other geologists from Brocton live."

Leon maneuvered a 1939 Lincoln through thick traffic. His horn cleared a path through scattering pedestrians.

"This your car?" I asked.

"It belongs to the four of us. She's a beaut, isn't she?"

"She's bitchn'; dents and rust add to her charm," I said with a chuckle.

He pulled into an unpaved, dusty parking lot. "Gotta park here so old Pedro over there can keep an eye on her. Some bad people like to steal from us good folks."

I was struck by the humanity around me: streets and sidewalks teeming with people rushing about. Some elegantly tailored women chatted with companions as they hurried along, paying no attention to the impoverished peasant women dressed in rags toting heavy hemp bundles of merchandise on their heads. Men in suits acknowledged those women of wealth by bowing and tipping their hats while they ogled alluring younger girls. The only stationary people were lottery ticket sellers. Barefoot, shirtless five-to-ten-year-old kids in torn, dirty short pants guarded parked cars so no thief could steal hubcaps or windshield wiper blades. If car owners didn't pay these *gamines,* thieves would steal whatever available. Bulldog brushed away open hands of beggars, their pleading eyes having no effect on him, but I, an easy mark, gave out several coins. I kept my eyes on gorgeous, smiling girls: some well dressed; others in faded outfits that didn't hide their natural beauty.

"So this is Medellin, the land of beautiful women." Shifting my gaze away from the dark, seductive eyes of *señoritas* or *muchachas*, I asked, "Are all big cities here crawling with mobs of people?"

"Just around this time of day. In a few hours these streets will be deserted—*siesta* time. You've heard about that; businesses close for two or three hours. After that everything comes alive again. It's great! You've got to get used to this Latin American way of life."

"I'm not sure I can."

"Sure you can. Just give yourself a little time."

We ducked into a small electrical store. Leon bought extension cords and light bulbs and a speaker. Next, at a small *tienda* selling produce, bread, fruit, and rice, he bought a big hemp-fibered sack to hold his heavy load. Then he whistled for a young, shirtless beggar to heft the load and follow us back to the car to dump everything into the trunk. He paid the child a few coins. Happy now, the youngster's face lit up. "*Gracias, mister gringo.*"

"Are we ready to leave now?" I asked, anxious to escape so many people and get to his *finca*.

"No, now we'll go over to that *tienda* over there," pointing down the street.

Leon bought big jugs called *garafas* of *aguardiente*—the anise-flavored brandy that was a favorite of Colombians—and bottles of rum, beer, and colas.

"Are you going to tell me what all this is for?"

"Didn't I tell you? We're having a big *fiesta* tonight; more like a *paranda*, which is a really big *fiesta*. It's to celebrate a German friend going back home for a vacation." We put stuff in the backseat and then locked the car again. "Now let's go over to Hotel Nutibarra and have lunch."

It was a short walk through a few narrow, winding streets, on which I could easily get lost, then to a park-like plaza with grass and flowering bushes in front of a handsome brown stucco hotel. "First class," I uttered as I looked around its high-ceilinged lobby. After a short walk through the hotel we entered a covered patio with white-jacketed waiters serving fashionable patrons. We ordered a couple of beers while Leon translated the menu for me. As we sat back waiting for our meal, I asked Leon, "You know John Turner?"

"Yes, but not well. Never worked with him. Lives in Barranquilla near Brocton's office."

"Seems like a hell of a guy. He really knows his way around, busts in front of everybody in line and gets what he wants with nobody hassling him. He knew exactly where to go to get my visa and *cedula* and everything. What would I have done without him?"

"Yes, I know. I've heard a lot about him."

"He introduced me to a guy named Jesse Logan."

"You mean Spider Logan."

"Yeah, that's right; he kind of resembles a spider with two legs. I thought he looked strange."

Leon agreed. "What did you think of Brett Vickers?"

"Haven't met him yet. I expected him to meet me when I arrived in Barranquilla. Isn't he one of the owners?"

"He sure is. He hangs out with rich folks at his club, plays a lot of golf. He's supposed to be lining up wells for us."

I wanted to know more about Brocton Geological Services. But then our food arrived, ending our conversation. Even though Colombian food tasted foreign to me, I cleaned my plate so fast I didn't notice its taste.

"Let me tell you what I fell into when I first arrived in Barranquilla. Some Lufthansa girls gave me a ride to the hotel—"

"Hotel Del Prado, no doubt," Leon added.

"Yeah, that's right."

"After you checked in, you went to the bar."

"Yeah, how'd you know?"

"You met a guy by the name of Raul, and he took you and another *gringo* to a luxurious whorehouse."

My mouth was agape; how'd he know what happened? "Raul supplements his income as a Colombian coffee exporter by supplying that whorehouse with a lot of business."

Chapter 14

LA FINCA

As we drove out of the city, Leon asked me, "How'd your girlfriend, Marcia, take you going to work in South America?"

"Okay . . . no problem." Leon and I met at UCLA and had been good friends for two years before he graduated a semester before I did. He dated a lot of girls but never went steady with anyone. He was like me, not wanting to be tied down.

"No problem? . . . That doesn't sound like Marcia."

"She took it okay. I'm telling you, there was no problem, and that's the end of it." *So shut up about Marcia.*

We sped along a winding, thinly paved road just wide enough for two vehicles to squeeze past through almost vertical mountains. It seemed impossible for anything, especially corn, to grow on such steep terrain, but it did. I wondered how farmers harvest it.

A truck like a huge elephant belching black smoke labored slowly up the grade ahead of us and started to go around a blind curve. Leon swung over into the left lane and floored the accelerator. As we drew even with the truck, suddenly around the curve a car came toward us. We were going to crash head on. Leon stomped on the brakes; the other car did the same. The truck veered up against the mountainside. In a chorus of horns blasting all at once, our hearts pounding, we missed each other by inches. After that close call, neither of us said a word.

I felt like cussing Leon and punching him in the nose for almost getting us killed. Instead I could only say, "Sure is beautiful country, and air so fresh and clear. I can see why you guys take your days off in Medellin."

"It's God's country."

Even on the sharp curves Leon kept the gas pedal floored as we zipped past several big, heavily loaded Dodge or Mercedes trucks. Cars were less frequent, but they always seemed to be driven on the wrong side of the road. I doubted I would ever be able to drive in Colombia.

We peeled off the main road onto a long gravel driveway; it wrapped around to the front of a house built in the style of a Swiss chalet, freshly painted white with red trim and blue shutters. On level ground in front of the entry, I could see a wide veranda with white wooden railings. "It is kind of like being in Switzerland," Leon explained.

Lush grounds: thick green lawns, palm trees, bromeliads, and ferns. In the middle of all this a large swimming pool with flagstone decking surrounding it. An open-sided cabaña housed a huge patio barbecue. I looked back at the house as the ornate double front doors swung open and two young girls emerged smiling graciously, one tall and slender, the other short and stocky.

"Rolly, I'd like you to meet our cook and young maid, Florencia and Matilde. Matilde is a wonderful cook, and Florencia is just wonderful to look at. But she works hard helping her sister."

"I agree, she's a knockout."

"So keep your hands off unless you want to knock her up and have to marry her."

After a round of handshakes, both *muchachas* bowing, I said casually, "*Mucho gusto.*" They bowed again, giggled, and then flew back into the house. "What a life!" I marveled. "They're knockouts. Do they speak any English?"

"Not a word, and don't try to teach them any, either. Let them teach you Spanish."

Inside the house, rustic, tan leather couches, cushioned chairs, and dark wooden tables were spread around a great room. Off to the left was a room with a polished wooden bar complete with brown leather barstools. "Cozy, or maybe comfortable is a better word," I muttered in total amazement. "This must cost you guys a fortune."

"Yeah, sixty bucks a month split between four guys, or make it five if you're going to kick in with us." The voice came from behind me.

"Oh, Walter, I didn't see you," Leon said.

"I was down by the pool sunning myself in preparation for our *paranda* tonight . . . Hi, I'm Walter Gillespie, and you must be the new man from California." He had brown hair, a round coconut head, easy smile, average height, average build, and was dressed in a bathing suit and T-shirt.

I introduced myself and we shook hands. He looked like he might be a hell-raising guy with that wide smile. I asked, "You guys only pay sixty bucks a month for all this? How come so cheap?"

"As long as the dollar stays strong, you'll find your money will go a long way here in Colombia."

Florencia came into the room and tugged at Leon's shirt sleeve as he was talking to me. She was explaining something to him, but I didn't understand much other than the words *necesitamos* and *comer* (*we need* and *to eat*). "Come on, we gotta go down the hill and buy a few things I forgot to get in Medellin."

I followed Leon down a narrow dirt path through tall grass brushing against our pant legs toward a quaint building along the other side of the road from *la finca*. Ahead of us, I noticed what looked like a twig lying across the path. Closer, that branch was smeared red, glistening in the sunlight partially shaded by tall trees. "Leon, is that a snake?"

"You got it. Look, its head's been hacked off."

"You mean there are snakes around here?"

"Looks that way. The head's over here. Check out those fangs. Must be a *mapaná*."

I was more careful now going down to the road and across to a red and white and green stucco building, the bottom half of its walls painted red, top half white. Windowsills and shutters were green. Moss and algae covered part of a russet tile roof.

Strong-smelling hemp sacks were filled with potatoes, corn, some kind of long brown root (they call yuca), *platanos*, and regular bananas. This was the local store, *la tienda*. Leon went about conversing and picking up cigarettes, some kind of sugary-looking pastries, and butter wrapped in green banana leaves.

He finished shopping and suggested we sit at a small, rough wooden table and have a beer.

"How do you like it?" Leon asked.

"What?"

"Colombia . . . Barranquilla, Medellin, or what you see here away from the city. Peaceful, no?"

"I don't know yet. It's going to take a lot more adjusting before I can say I like it. That whacked-up snake I don't like. Must be a lot more around in these steep mountains. So much vegetation, you never know what you'll run into. . . . Who killed that snake?"

"*Mapaná.* Probably one of the *mayordomos*, you know, those caretakers or gardeners." Leon stood up and said, "Come on, we'd better get back; people will be coming soon."

"Which way are we going?"

"Same way we came."

That was what I was afraid of. "What about snakes?"

"Forget about snakes."

We climbed back toward *la finca* with the sunlight low in the west. A fully packed jeep had just bounced up to the house. Right behind it, a station wagon slammed on its brakes, followed by other cars. Men dressed casually, whereas *señoritas* dressed in party dresses. A few people with children and folks of all ages mingled in a boisterous group, chattering with words I didn't understand. Everyone greeted each other, hugging, kissing, and shaking hands. I stood alone, looking out of place and embarrassed. Leon put an arm around my shoulders and started introducing me: Adolfo, a short, slim *amigo* sporting a thin mustache over a loud voice was an engineer eager to show me a bridge he helped design and build; Gustavo, a tall, robust pre-med student with a great sense of humor, invited me to watch an appendicitis operation the next day; Juan, who didn't work because it was against his religion (his joke), wanted me to take him to Hollywood to meet actresses. According to Leon, he was from a very wealthy family; and Federico, owner of a *finca* on which he raised cattle. He wanted to show me his prized bull. Some names I didn't get or couldn't remember.

I was trying to talk to three *señoritas* when I noticed the back of a girl whose hair was like a sea of shiny auburn waves. Without seeing her face, I was sure I knew who she was. How could I be so sure? She seemed to be keeping four people amused by her animated conversation. They burst out laughing several times but quickly leaned in again to hear what more she was saying. Then someone said something to her, and she was the one to double over with laughter. I still hadn't seen her face.

"Hola, amigo. Do ju spick Spanee? I yam Bruno, mucho gusto en conocerle." He was a short, tan-faced man with a wide grin stretching beneath a bushy black mustache sauntered up to me with an "I own the world" attitude in his humor-lit eyes.

"Mucho gusto, tambien. I don't speak much Spanish, but I think I'm going to learn fast. *Mi nombre es* Rolly Farrington."

After shaking hands, he told me he would help me with Spanish. He took me by the arm over to where everyone seemed to be talking at once. Bruno said in slow Spanish, "Rolly, I'd like you to meet—"

"Marisol," I said softly, not blurting out something inane as I did at the airport in Barranca.

"What!" Bruno uttered in total amazement. "How'd you know my sister-in-law, Rolly?"

"Long story," I tried to say in Spanish.

"Ni tan largo, (not so long)" she corrected me. *"Como está,* Rolly?"

I couldn't think of an answer in Spanish.

"You got a lot of explaining to do, mister," Leon said, standing in back of me.

I just gave a slight nod while I tried to think of what to say. She was swept away by others before I could squeeze another word out. Musicians had arrived and started playing on the veranda. People moved there and into the house to dance. Marisol broke away from an animated conversation to dance with another young Colombian.

I turned to Leon and Bruno to explain how we met that morning, and then asked them, "Is she going with that guy?"

"Not that I know of. But I know others who've got an eye on her. They all speak Spanish better than you," Leon chided.

Bruno must have sensed my letdown because he brought over a bottle of *aguardiente* and shot glasses. *"Salud!"* he tossed down a jolt, then handed me a shot glass full. It was my first taste of this clear liquid. It burned all the way down to my stomach. Leon quickly handed me a slice of pineapple to put out the fire.

"*Gracias,*" I uttered feeling heat all over. "*¡Bueno, muy bueno!*" I could barely speak. Three more *Colombianos* gathered around and gave a toast. I was feeling right at home now.

Bruno began conversing with everyone. I couldn't follow his Spanish, so taking Leon aside, I asked him, "Just who is this smooth talker Bruno anyway, besides being Marisol's brother-in-law?"

"I don't know much about him, really. Says he's got a *finca,* a big spread of land up in the mountains. I don't know if he's got cattle, or a gold mine, or grows coffee, or likes to bullshit us. Seems to be a big shot, though."

I watched him mingle; giving young *señoritas* big hugs and kisses. He chatted with his other friends and made them howl with laughter. But I was mainly interested in keeping my eye on Marisol.

A short, dumpy man with "Made in America" written in his I-got-it-all demeanor, sauntered over to me and barked at me: "You that new guy from California? Not that we need another arrogant Californian!"

"Yes, I am. Rolly Farrington, another arrogant Californian." I stuck out my hand to shake. He reluctantly extended his limp-fish grasp.

"Then you'll be working with John Turner."

"That's right. He's quite a guy, like he sort of rescued me when no one met me at the airport in Barranquilla."

"Really? I have an entirely different take on John Turner."

"How is that?"

"I'll just say I cannot fathom the depth of his depravity."

"Ah, so you met Thirsty here?" Leon said, as he walked up to join us.

"Wise ass," the American retorted. "That's Thurston, not Thirsty. Thurston Thornton, for your information. I'm the first geologist Brocton hired, and the best one they'll ever have. These other jokers would be lost without me. I'm revered for my acerbic wit, as you will no doubt come to appreciate."

"Aren't we lucky to have such a great icon? You thought you knew a lot of geology, but wait till you have the honor of one of his lectures, whether you want it or not."

"Aside from this fellow's misguided humor, may I ask you, as a university-educated geologist, can you explain how these tall mountains came to be?" Thurston asked me.

I wasn't expecting to be tested on my first visit to Medellin. "Diastrophism," I blurted out.

"And what does that mean to you?"

"Mountain building," I answered.

"Some people have coined the phrase 'continental drift,' but that doesn't explain any of the energy that causes that drift, the energy that could push these mountains to their stately height," Thurston continued.

"And you can explain it?" I asked.

"That's what I'm going to devote my studies to explain, just as soon as I have saved enough money to pay for my doctorate. I give myself one more year before I'm ready to return to the States and resume my studies. It will be different this time back—better by a long shot. I will be married then. I shall miss this place, though."

"He's marrying Marisol's cousin, Dora," Leon explained. "What do you think of that, Rolly?"

'Well . . . that surprises me." I didn't know what to say. To me it would be strange to marry a foreigner, especially one who doesn't speak English. Colombian customs, I imagined, were different from ours.

The sun had set and a great orange pumpkin moon had risen, its rays turning our faces golden brown in waning light. A plump, smiling girl shorter than Thurston hurried from the terrace toward us. Thurston saw her and purred, "Through the prism of moonlight I can see my love seeks to rescue me from these depths of banality."

As she approached, he reached out and turned her around to return to the party without introducing me to her. All I gleaned from that glimpse was around face, an engaging smile and encompassed in short black hair.

"Well, what did you think of our company dork?"

"He's a dork all right."

"Yes, Thirsty is a whole different breed of cat. To me, it's surprising he found someone who can put up with him."

"Bet he was a loner in the States. 'Through the prism of moonlight,' that's a new line. I'll try to remember it."

Roasted pig was served with a mountain of rice, fried *platanos*, roasted ears of corn, green salad, and other things I didn't know the name of that were scooped up by everyone and carried to tables and benches. Beer, *aguardiente,* rum, and whisky flowed like water. The only visibly sober people were some ladies. They seemed to be used to men boozing. When Juan, humorously, tried to speak English, I tried to answer him in Spanish. Everyone laughed. These men were regular guys, full of good humor, although I understood only part of what they were saying in Spanish. I was becoming more familiar with the language, and they gave me an incentive to learn more. In all this confusion I hadn't lost sight of Marisol, and if I wasn't mistaken she was ignoring me. I didn't seem to make an impression on her. I noticed she was helping to sweep up cigarette butts and trash while a few other young *señoritas* cleared the tables of empty dishes and glasses. *Señoritas* helping servants impressed me, very democratic.

"You know, Leon, this is the best way to learn Spanish."

"How's that?"

"Drunk. Your mind's wide open, no hang-ups about making blunders because, I guess, they expect you to blunder. When you're drunk, your brain absorbs language like a sponge."

"We'll see what you say after you sober up in the morning."

"Hell, it is morning."

Chapter 15

WALTER'S WALL

"Hey, Rolly, wake up, goddamn it! It's almost noon," Leon's voice from downstairs was like a foghorn. "We've got plans for a full day's outing." I opened my eyes and couldn't remember where I was; a pounding headache reminded me of last night's *paranda*.

After breakfast, Leon, Walter, and I jumped into their old car and took off toward Medellin. Walter weaved through clouds of black truck smoke. Suddenly he jagged to the left and barely missed an oncoming car by a few inches.

In town we pulled into a parking lot next to Club Medellin. "We'll get you a guest pass like ours. It's a good deal. We can go for a swim, have a few drinks, and then eat."

"And after that, what's our plan?" I asked.

"How about either a movie in Spanish or a visit to the girls?" Leon offered, emphasizing *girls*.

"I've seen all the movies I want to see," Walter put in.

We swam for a couple of hours and then had an early dinner, the club chef cooked up Colombian-styled charbroiled steaks— thinly sliced and marinated with an indefinable taste, a blend of onions, cilantro, tomato, and a tangy sauce. Conversations revolved around young women.

"Rolly, do you understand there are only two types of women in Latin American countries?" Leon asked me.

"Probably, but go ahead. I'd like to hear your description."

"There are *señoritas*, and there are *muchachas*. *Señoritas* are virgins, and *muchachas* aren't," Leon briefly explained.

After dinner it was still early. Walter drove through narrow streets with block-long walls with doors that, when opened, were shown to be homes. Leon called out, "Stop at that door with the light hanging over it. That's the place."

This command seemed to jolt Walter because as he turned sharply toward the door. He didn't slow down enough. We bumped up against the front of a house, knocking down part of its wall.

A very red-faced Walter blurted out, "I thought there was a curb there!"

Shrieks from terrified females alerted us to be prepared for a machete attack or worse. Out came a large, angry woman charging over a pile of rubble wielding a huge machete glinting in the glare of a few streetlights. Five girls tried to stop their madam, but to no avail. One ferocious swoop of her weapon crumpled part of the car's roof.

She was hysterical, as were her girls. Soon doors along the way popped open and more excited people with drawn machetes scrambled toward us. No time for us to flee. Our motor was dead. By this time the madam was in the arms of her girls, sobbing as if mortally injured.

We were surrounded by scowling *hombres* ready to take the law into their own hands. It was the action of some women, mothers with babies straddling their hips or clutching mama's protecting leg that calmed the situation. Everyone's adrenalin seemed to wear off so we could negotiate Walter's way out of this catastrophe. Going inside what was left of a parlor, we assured the madam that Walter would pay for all the damage. Fortunately, there lived a mason down the street. He agreed to do the job of repairing the crumbled brick and cement block wall.

Finally, when everyone settled down, one girl—I took to be about eighteen or nineteen, a *muchacha* no doubt and not a *señorita*—smiled with a smile that was neither provocative nor disinterested. She had straight black hair and dark eyes that looked up from her slightly downturned face, which was flashing a devilishly seductive grin. Whatever she murmured I didn't understand, probably not important anyway.

My two companions drifted past fallen rubble into a small living room with two sofas behind two cocktail tables laden with full ashtrays and half-empty glasses of melting ice. No men were present. Two more girls followed, echoing each other with *"Buenas noches,* Leon."

I could feel another party coming on when Leon and Walter put their arms around the girls and bubbled forth with lively Spanish. The *muchachas* joined in with laughter and chatter. They ordered a bottle of whisky, which in Colombia is Scotch whisky (bourbon must be unknown here). I tried my best to make conversation with my temptress with the seductive eyes. She seemed to know how to handle non-Spanish-speaking people. Music came from a vintage 78 rpm record player. I figured it was better to fake my way through a few *cha-cha-chas* and *merecumbés* than try to murder Spanish conversation.

Dancing wasn't getting me anywhere, so I came up with the one word that would do the trick for changing the routine: "*Cama*" was all I said. The word for "bed" did the trick. Leon and Walter had already disappeared with their friends.

The bedroom was lighted by a small lamp with a red-and-white-striped lampshade. A large wooden crucifix hung on one wall, and a portrait of Jesus Christ stared down at us from over her bed. The only other furniture was a dark wooden dresser and a frail stiff-backed chair. A white sheet and two pillows covered her bed. The bed looked clean. I didn't want to catch crabs or anything like that. She spoke in hushed tones. Low light glimpsed her beguiling smile. I started to undress slowly, my eyes on her as she slipped her dress down enough to reveal tan breasts just large enough to fill my palms. She giggled and slid her dress past her pink panties on to the floor. She scooped it up and hung it on a hook near the door. She pushed down my jockey shorts. She studied me for a moment and then uttered an approving sigh. She gave me a gentle shove. I fell back on her bed and she jumped on top. We rolled over. I wanted to take it slow to savor the moment. She didn't want to savor. Afterwards I lay back relaxed while the feeling lingered. For me the ride was good. I couldn't tell how or what she felt.

From that day on, this place was named Walter's Wall, or The Wall That Walter Rebuilt, in honor of Walter Gillespie.

THE DATE

The next morning Leon got a call from John Turner telling him that he and Walter and another geologist would start a new well the next day. Leon asked, "How come you are calling me instead of Brett Vickers?"

Turner told Leon that Vickers is in Bogota so now Turner is calling the shots.

"We got things to do today, Rolly," Leon told me. "I want to make a date with Raquel. Maybe go to a movie and then a little dinner at Alfredo's afterwards. You feel up to speaking Spanish with one of Raquel's friends?"

"Why? Don't you want to be alone with her?"

"Yes but I can't take her out without at least one other couple. *Señoritas* always need to be chaperoned."

"Sure, how about having her fix me up with Marisol? I would like to find out if she really doesn't like me or if it's just my imagination."

Leon and I had a beer at an outside bar on a corner in downtown Medellin while we waited for our dates. We caught sight of them down the street walking quickly in a stream of pedestrians. I watched a young guy bow as he passed the two girls. He must have muttered something because both girls covered their faces and laughed.

"Did that guy say something out of line to them?"

"No, he's just some glib young stud whispering a flowery compliment in passing. That's what you've got to expect here in Medellin," he said. "I sure wish I had that gift of glib. Girls really go for it."

"Leon, I bet you could become the 'glibbiest." He laughed. "Tell me, what do those guys say to be glib?"

"Just a bunch of flattering stuff called *piropos* that gets females all hot and bothered."

"You say *piropos*. Is that more glib than glib?"

"I'm saying when you are clib it's because you are saying *piropos*."

Raquel and Marisol were still giggling when they met us. In rapid Spanish they confessed they were thrilled by the guy's poetic *piropos*. I couldn't think of anything to say. Marisol still had that effect on me. There was something about her I couldn't explain. She captured my full attention. I wanted her to realize that I was not just a tongue-tied dummy. She did help me out by speaking slowly in Spanish and got me talking. She was so at ease. She had a way of making me feel like we had been friends for a long time. I could tell she enjoyed helping with words that I had meant to say. I actually wanted to put my arm around her, but didn't dare.

The movie was American, for which I was grateful. After we were seated, the lights dimmed and the picture came on. It was in English with Spanish subtitles. That was great. I could learn what English words were in Spanish.

We shared a bag of popcorn, and when our hands bumped in the bag, we both tittered like a couple of teenagers. We laughed hilariously at the film even though it was a pretty low-grade comedy.

Toward the end of the picture, I wondered if she had this good a time with other fellows. I remembered how spirited she was at the *finca* party. Nevertheless, she seemed to accept me for what I was, a little stupid but not a bore.

After the movie the girls thanked us for the nice time, but it was getting late—although the sun hadn't faded yet. It was only four in the afternoon. "It's early. Plenty of time for a little dinner," Leon said.

"Oh, we're sorry, but we have to be home," Raquel answered.

I learned something—etiquette, Colombian etiquette. We shook hands and the girls thanked us for a nice time, and then we thanked them for allowing us to take them to a movie. I never thought to do that in America.

Just the two of us dined at Alfredo's. I couldn't stop talking. "I can't believe what a great time I had with Marisol. I want to see her again, Leon."

"What are you getting all excited about? What do you want to do, marry her?"

"No, don't get me wrong. I just want to see her again, that's all." His comment calmed me down.

"Tell me, Rolly, are you Catholic?"

"No. What's that got to do with anything?"

"She is, and that's important to girls here, and their families."

Chapter 17

MOMPOS

"*Buenos dias.* Brocton Geological Services, Miss Consuelo Uribe speaking." I could tell she was smiling; anyone with a cheery voice like that had to be smiling.

"Consuelo? What happened to Dorotea?" I thought Dorotea was happy at Brocton.

"I don't know. This is my first day."

"Okay, good luck. I'm Rolly Farrington. Brett Vickers left a message for me last night. Could I speak to him please?" I could hear men's voices in the background.

"I'm sorry, he is in Venezuela, I'm told," she answered, her voice uncertain, a slight quiver. "Would you like to talk to Mr. Turner?"

"Yes." I clearly heard John Turner's voice in the background but couldn't make out the other voice until a high-pitched giggle erupted; it was Jesse Logan. He seemed to be with Turner everywhere.

"Hello, Rolly. Good that you called early—"

"What happened to Dorotea?"

"She went with Vickers to Venezuela. He's trying to drum up business besides having fun with Dorotea. Listen, you've got about thirty minutes to catch a flight to Mompos. You must get there to supervise loading our unit onto a barge and then off-load at our new location. Eastmont Oil Company is pretty rough on our equipment. They've damaged a couple of our trailers moving them to new locations, so we've got to have a man there to supervise and also start work on the well as soon as they spud in. We work from grass roots to total depth. Brian Banks and I will be out by then."

I couldn't believe he hung up before I could ask for more information. I turned to Thurston, who had just come downstairs for breakfast. "Goddamned Turner just told me to fly out to a place called Mompos and load a trailer onto a barge; then he hung up. What exactly am I supposed to do?" I could feel a sinking feeling creeping down my spine. "And where the hell is Mompos?"

"You don't have to know where it is," he said, his face screwed up like he had just eaten a lemon. "Avianca's pilot will know the way, for Christ's sake." He thought he had popped up with a funny because he laughed so hard he choked. Under control once again he went on, "You'd better pack your bag quickly and get to the airport. If there aren't any flights to Mompos, you'll have to hire a jeep."

"I don't get it. Shouldn't one of you guys do it? You're experienced and I'm not. Anyway, what's the big deal loading a trailer?"

"You never know how long these things take. Nothing works like it should. You may be out there longer than you plan. Better take your toothbrush and clean underwear. Get in the car and I'll drive you to the airport."

I had heard about Thurston's driving inability. I had to accept his offer: I had no choice. I jumped in next to him. He stomped on the clutch like he was killing a dreaded scorpion, rammed the gas pedal to the floor, and then popped the clutch. The car lurched twice then stopped cold. My heart stopped also, but I managed to paste a patient smile on my face in contrast to Thurston's glare.

"This goddamned cheap Colombian gas!"

The motor burst to life on a second attempt, and we charged down toward Medellin's airport. He dropped me in front of the airport and took off before I could ask him for help getting an airline ticket. However, I found my Spanish good enough to get on a flight.

I accepted a beer as we took off on a roller coaster ride out of Medellin Valley. After an hour and two beers, we started to circle. Through my cramped little window, a thick, brilliant emerald forest dominated the view. Ahead a pinch of pale green appeared. Cows grazed on pasture grass that was bordered by tall conifers. Through the dappled vegetation below, I could see brown-gray mud puddles reflecting silvery sunlight. We circled once more, and then our flight path straightened. We lost altitude. Not far away I saw a wide muddy river coiling around a village crammed with squat tile-roofed buildings and narrow streets bustling with cars, trucks, people, and horses.

Bang! I heard landing gears pop out ready for landing. We made one low pass over grassland. The calm grazing cows panicked as we made our pass over them; they hightailed it in all directions. We circled again, making another low pass but this time no cows. Finally, we bounced and jarred straight in on hard green grassland.

Our cabin door swung open and tropical heat hit me like from a blast furnace, probably twenty degrees hotter than in Medellin. I gripped a metal railing pipe on a short flight of stairs but quickly jerked my hand away—the metal scorched my hand.

Stepping out onto mud and cow shit, I could feel my ears burn in the piercing sun. I had to get under shade in a hurry. I made my way to a small, concrete block air terminal, its white paint turned weathered-gray. Inside was like an oven.

My suitcase, which I had forgotten, was lugged to me by a shirtless, barefoot boy of about ten. The boy stretched out his palms for a tip, which I gave him, probably too much because he sprang away shouting with glee and with a bunch of ragged kids trailing after him.

I didn't know what I was supposed to do. Would Brocton have a taxi waiting to take me to a loading barge by this river? *Ah, here comes a guy who must be looking for me.* I understood his first words in Spanish: "Do you want a ride to town?"

"Are you from Brocton?" I asked in my ragged Spanish.

The swarthy man's sweating brow wrinkled into a frown. He probably didn't understand me because he repeated what he had just said: "*¿Quiere que le llevo al pueblo?*"

"*Sí, sí,*" I muttered, unsure of my Spanish, so I repeated in English, "Take me to town."

He was short and stocky like the other sinewy, tank-topped men working and milling about the airport, their leathery feet strapped inside thong sandals. His jeep's canvas seat cover was hot, warning me not to touch the glistening handrail inside the roofless vehicle. He floored the gas pedal, spraying gray mud and dust over people walking along the unpaved road next to the river Cauca. It must have rained recently because there were mud puddles in low places and dust billowing from higher ground.

My driver asked me, "*¿Donde?*"

How do I know "where"? I asked myself but then pronounced, "*Barco, planchon,* boat." I hoped he would understand my pronunciation for ship or boat or barge and take me there.

Hot and dusty people scrambled to unload heavy burlap sacks that had been hoisted on their heads and shoulders. Shoppers pecked away on produce and fruit in open markets like scavenging crows. Horses, burros, jeeps, and dirty mud encrusted trucks crept through narrow, winding streets. These people were probably considered poor, but to me they seemed to be rich in food and work.

We pulled up along the river where more workers were busy loading or unloading livestock, merchandise, and more people on or off flat bottomed river vessels. Ahead, I spotted a rusty barge, big enough to carry an oil drilling rig. I looked for our company's trailer-lab, but it wasn't there. What could have happened to it? A chunky man stepped out of a cantina across from the brown river and waved his *sombrero* for our jeep to stop.

"Are you Rolly Farrington?" the stranger called out, his English thick with a Colombian accent.

"*Sí, sí,*" I blurted out.

"My name is Abelardo Zuniga. I'm the main man, troubleshooter, and English speaker working for Eastmont Oil Company." His thick black mustache matched his straight black hair like so many others in the street. I imagined my face glistened with sweat just like his. "*Por favor* follow me."

"What about my suitcase?" I asked.

"That *muchacho* will take care of it. Don't worry." And then added, "Just flip him a few *centavos*." The boy said *gracias*, grabbed the money and ran.

My driver from the airport drawled, "*Seis pesos, señores.*"

"Did he say *six pesos?*" I asked Abelardo.

"*Ladron!*" bellowed Abelardo, calling him a thief and then to me, "It should only be four *pesos.*"

We paused, staring at each other until I got his message; I peeled off four *pesos.* I was hoping Eastmont Oil Company was paying all my expenses. The driver drove away clutching pesos in one hand and his hot steering wheel with the other.

"Come on, *señor* Rolly, let's have a drink and I will explain what's going on here."

I scanned the river for a tugboat. A barge partially loaded with drilling equipment bobbed in the slow current upriver, but no tugboat.

"Where's the tugboat and where's my trailer that I'm supposed to supervise loading?"

"I'll tell you after we have a drink. Come on."

Lively music drifted from a cantina. We entered, pushing away strings of beads that were intended to keep flies out. To my surprise we had to step down a steep flight of splintery wooden stairs to the bar, surprised because the ground floor seemed to be lower than the river. Then I noticed other steps leading *up* to an open trough urinal, where I could see a man pissing. That was a little out of the ordinary, I thought.

I felt uneasy in this dark, burrow-like bar with its earthen floor littered with cigarette butts. But after a couple of beers and Abelardo Zuniga's lively conversation, these unusual surroundings didn't matter anymore. "We wait for a tugboat to push a barge upriver, where our equipment and your trailer are on a riverbank," Abelardo said in rough English, searching my face for a sign of understanding.

Anxiously I climbed upstairs to check outside for a sign of a tugboat. No such luck. My host suggested we have something to eat. He must be kidding if he thought I'd eat anything served in this dive. For sure it wouldn't pass health department inspection. He ordered *carne asada—bien, bien asada*—meat expressly *well* done—so if it is so definitely charred, all the bugs that live in it will be killed. That savory smell struck my nose and made my digestive enzymes flow. I couldn't resist. I ordered the same. It tasted so good I ordered more. Abelardo picked up a slip of paper from our table, the bill for beer and lunch, and then set it down so I could see it. "Brocton gives you geologists a very good living allowance, I believe."

"Yeah, sure. How about your company?"

"*Nada,*" replied Abelardo, his forefinger tapping the bill for the lunch.

Without a word, I peeled off a few *pesos,* got up, and climbed the stairs to leave, Abelardo right behind me.

Stepping outside, we saw a tugboat maneuvering behind a barge. Noisy music inside the restaurant had drowned out the boat's low-rumbling engine. Abelardo said *El capitán* wanted to hurry upstream to avoid darkness, too dangerous to navigate at night.

"If I have to go upriver, how am I going to get back to Medellin this afternoon?" I asked Abelardo.

"You're not going to Medellin. You're going to accompany your equipment upriver to your next drill site," he said, grinning like he enjoyed telling a guy he had to jump off a cliff.

I was speechless for a moment before growling, "What do you mean? No one said anything about going upriver after loading the trailer."

"Mr. Vickers often replies to such complaints as yours with his phrase, 'Tough shit.'"

"How come you know what Mr. Vickers says? You work for Eastmont Oil Company and not Brocton Geological Services."

"I know Mr. Vickers very well. Our two companies work together a lot. Brocton even has a desk in Eastmont's office."

The river tugboat had two decks. The entire lower deck housed a large diesel engine; the upper deck had a pilothouse toward the bow with raised windows looking to the back, sides, and front. In back of the pilothouse I could see several doors. I guessed they were cabins. A galley with a table was located aft. The boat was painted dull green, which peeled in many places, leaving exposed raw gray wood.

I climbed aboard the tug and shouted to Abelardo on the dock: "I bet this was supposed to be your job and not mine."

"You are a very smart geologist, Mr. Rolly," he jokingly replied.

"Captain Eustacio Cova invites you to accompany him in the wheelhouse," a deckhand informed me.

I answered in my best Spanish: "*Con mucho gusto, señor.*"

Even with all windows open in the wheelhouse where three men stood shoulder to shoulder, it smelled of rotten tobacco, sweat, and diesel fumes. *Capitán* Cova stood on a block of wood so he could see the bow. Besides being short, he was stocky with a potbelly hanging over his belt. His bushy, gray mustache beneath his wrinkled walnut-sized nose made him look more like a comedian than a boat *capitán*. I wondered if he was tall enough to navigate his tugboat behind a tennis-court-sized barge around serious bends in the river.

Once under way, the tug's propeller churned up gray river-bottom silt and then struggled to push the half-loaded barge against a strong current. *Capitán* Eustacio Cova spoke in rapid Spanish, with a *costeño* accent, marking him as being from a coastal province. "*Bien, señor,* now we can turn the helm over to Mateo while we go aft and enjoy an afternoon coffee with a splash of rum."

The diesel engine vibrated under our feet, causing my teeth to chatter. We made our way aft to the cooking and dining area. A rectangular table, about eight feet long and three feet wide, stretched out in the middle of the deck several feet from a stove and sink. We each pulled out a chair and sat down. With nervously shaking hands, a young kitchen helper served us filmy mugs of coffee and then hefted a liter bottle of tea-colored rum to top them off. Everything was set on the table in front of *el capitán* Cova. Sipping the fortified coffee gave me confidence to chat with my drinking partner. The cook served us crisp, salty, fried *platanos* for us to munch on. *Well, this might be an adventure I hadn't planned on—a river cruise.*

Before we finished our drinks the tugboat slowed and angled toward an embankment. I could see Brocton's trailer-lab among scattered drilling equipment. Mooring lines were stretched out and secured to majestic *ceba* trees. Deckhands muscled a wide platform linking the barge to the river embankment. A tractor towed our trailer-lab up onto the barge. I didn't have to do anything.

Other drilling equipment was loaded aboard as a red sun began to set over western mountains. I smelled sizzling meat frying in a skillet over an old electric stove; I was ready to eat again. I hadn't thought about how safe it was to eat in such questionable sanitary conditions. Where did they wash their eating utensils? Maybe they're not clean.

A meal of fried meat, white rice, and brown beans was served on cracked plates of unrecognizable faded patterns. Hunger overwhelmed my willpower as I clutched an ancient knife and bent fork to dig into tender meat bathing in juices that tinted a pile of white rice. "This is delicious," I exclaimed in Spanish, muffled by my chewing.

El capitán Cova and two deckhands devoured their meals like starving panthers. Their glistening foreheads and cheeks reflected light from a dwindling sun setting against a fiery-red cloud bank that hovered over jagged western mountains. A soft breeze helped lower the temperature and keep mosquitoes away.

After eating we sat picking our teeth and waited for the cook to bring out a large bottle, called a *garrafa*, of *aguardiente* and a plate of fruit. Pineapple (*piña*) and coconut (*coco*) I recognized but none of the other squishy, colorful fruit.

Skylight grew dim. The flickering flames from four candles mutated the men's shiny faces into grotesque masks. I imagined I looked no different and laughed as I searched my brain for the Spanish word for ghouls, but I could only think of the word for clowns, *payasos*. We drank until the four candles wasted away to a guttering glow.

In the morning I awoke with a roaring headache in a small, dimly lit cabin. "Where the hell am I?" I lifted my hand and tapped empty space next to my cramped bunk where I thought a nightstand should be. My eyes grew used to the murky morning light as I recognized the gauzy haze of insect netting around me. In an open round window—porthole—a small fan buzzed like an irate mosquito. I became more aware of the temperature in this bug-infested cabin and wondered how in the world I could have slept in such heat! I must have passed out. Something I didn't do frequently.

The only things I could recognize in this darkened room, or cabin, were a chest of battered drawers, a porthole the size of a dinner plate, and a large hand-carved crucifix hanging on one wall. Popping sounds from maybe a light generator plant throbbed like the beat from a monotonous phonograph record. Through filtered light I could barely see my wristwatch. It was 5:30 a.m. I had a sour licorice taste in my mouth, a reminder of too much *aguardiente*. That's right. I'm on a river tug that's going to unload my geological trailer onto a riverbank somewhere.

I swung my feet over the side of my bunk, hitting the steel floor, and instinctively jerked them back. No, there wouldn't be snakes on a river tug, would there? How about scorpions or spiders? I scrutinized the floor in the fuzzy light before setting my feet down again.

My head ached. *What happened last night? Did I drink all that aguardiente by myself? No, our captain and his cook drank, too.*

To make sure there were no foreign crawlers hiding in my boots—flopped over on the floor like a couple of drunken roustabouts—I shook them out.

I stood up and felt stiff all over. On my way out of the cabin, I stumbled, forgetting the low doorway, and hit my head. Outside, I bellied up to the railing. A quiet morning mist surprised me and felt refreshing, the only time the air smelled really clean since I had left Medellin. I only hoped it would stay that way all day but knew that as soon as the sun came over that green horizon the place would be like a steam bath. I stared out across a broad tableland on the other side of the river. *Everything looks so green and washed.*

A door creaked open two cabins down from me, and a young blossom of a barefoot girl escaped quietly along the deck, down a stern ladder onto the main deck, then over boarding planks to a wet, sandy riverbank. Even though she made several furtive glances back at the river tug—contrasted against a vaporous sea of green—her eyes never seemed to fix on me standing motionless as if I were a part of the boat. Maybe to her I wasn't really there, or maybe *she* wasn't really there. I couldn't believe that this wasn't just an alcoholic dream. Then she turned and faced a dense jungle that swallowed her up in an emerald tide slowly engulfing what little open land existed. Is this an indication of what kind of day this was going to be—full of illusions?

I cleared my mind of that evaporating girl. Instead I thought about my responsibilities for the day. Simple, all I had to do was wait for rig hands to finish loading equipment safely onto that barge moored up ahead of us.

Our sleepy cook staggered along the narrow deck from his galley carrying a cracked bowl of what looked like brown river water but was actually *café con leche*—coffee with milk. It smelled good. I picked it up from his nicked and scratched wooden tray and immersed my thumb in the thick, oily infusion. If my thumb could take the heat, it must be just the right temperature to drink. It tasted sweet and syrupy, which I was growing to like. I gave the cook, Oscar, a pat on his hard hat—it was said he wore it even while he slept. He gave me a big toothless grin. *What a thoughtful guy*; in fact, the whole crew seemed happy and friendly.

"*¿Mucha lluvia anoche, no, Señor* Rolly?"

I didn't understand him at first. The cook's Spanish was like a machine gun. Did he say it rained last night? No wonder this land looked so wet and clean.

"*Sí, mi amigo, mucha lluvia.*"

Right below me three ragged men squatted on a plank, short towels draped over their brown bare backs, and scooped up river water in *totumos*, hollow gourds, for washing their faces and brushing their teeth. Besides threadbare pants cut off at the knees, they wore T-shirts with various sized holes, or no shirt at all, and leather thong sandals. Sometimes they looked up at me, flashing broken-toothed grins.

El capitán sidled up to me and uttered, "You're looking at poverty at its lowest level. But you know, they are good, honest people, trying to do the best they can." He leaned on the deck rail and muttered as if he were delivering a sermon. "Well, that's why you *americanos, gringos,* came down here in this hot and sweaty jungle in the first place. You're here to show these *compesinos,* these peasants, right out of the cornfields how to handle machinery, how to drill an oil well. If they already knew how, there would be no reason for you to be here."

"Will these men follow us up to our next drilling location?"

"Maybe not. I'll pay them off when we finish today, and they can follow us or go back to their cornfields."

"Instead of working, I've heard these people are cutthroat bandits. Some of the geologists I work with told me about bandits raiding drilling camps and chopping off heads."

"You're not talking about these people here. These are *costeños,* people from the coast. They are peaceful. You're talking about *bandidos* from the mountains. They are the killers; that's where all the trouble is."

I thought over what he just said. Of course I was convinced nothing would ever happen to me. "I guess Americans have nothing to worry about."

"Don't kid yourself. A big boss, *un jefe grande,* didn't want to cooperate with one gang of bandits in the mountains of Tolima, so they dragged him out in front of all his fellow *americanos* and chopped his head off. Mountain people are a different breed entirely. People you're looking at here are peace-loving people."

Smoke drifted from a grass hut at the edge of the jungle where workers slept. That hut was also home to a cook and her helper, two ageless women with small, naked, potbellied kids laughing and playing with makeshift toys.

The women wore gray, threadbare dresses that covered their own potbellies and dark skin. Their joyful voices and laughter amazed me. How can people be so happy if they have no future, no security in their old age? Maybe they will be able to depend on handouts from their grown children, or other relatives. The captain said their hut will disappear, along with the women and children, after all the drilling equipment is loaded and carried upriver. For all I knew they would dissolve in this jungle like diesel smoke from the river tug.

As men filed back from the river through a clearing to their hut for breakfast, I heard Oscar's dinner bell clanging. Breakfast was served at the stern on the worn and stained wooden dining table. *Capitán* Cova, head mechanic Emilio, and deckhand Teodoro—Cova's son—sat waiting for me before starting to eat. We exchanged spirited salutations, "*¿Cómo amaneció, hombre? ¿Durmió bien, eh?*" My Spanish was good enough to join in their cheerful greetings. I felt we shared camaraderie. Oscar served the captain a large bowl of white rice, followed by another bowl of brown beans, then a platter filled with *arepas*—white flat buns made from corn or hominy served at Captain Cova's every meal. After the captain heaped his plate full, he passed everything on. Next came a large platter of fried eggs—crispy around the edges with dark yellow yolks—thick, greasy bacon, and *platano frito*. This type of banana fried seemed to accompany every meal. It was partly charred and golden brown but as sweet as honey.

It was a feast. I tried to comment that this must be like having breakfast on your own private yacht. What I got was a blank stare. My Spanish still needed more refining. But who cares if dishes were washed in muddy river water? Who cares if the cook might not have soap for scrubbing plates? I was too hungry to worry about insignificant details like germs.

From my seat I could see the rolling flow of the river, bordered by embankments, and then a flat floodplain the size of a football field cleared of jungle. "You've got a good life here, *capitán* Cova. I think I'd like to sign on as one of your deckhands."

"And I would hire you and make you my first mate. Yes, it's a good life, but it hasn't always been that way. Not too long ago I had a loving wife and eleven kids. Now I have only my one son left."

I wasn't expecting to hear tragedies. "Well, I'm truly sorry. What happened to your family, if you don't mind talking about it?"

"No, I don't mind. They're gone now, and you know what the strange thing is? I always benefit from my misfortunes." *Capitán* Cova frowned and hunched up closer to me. "Soon after I lost them I got this boat, and business on this river has been good, very good, ever since."

"Sorry about your loss. How'd they die?"

"No, no, they didn't die. She just ran off with a rich landowner from Cordoba and took all of my kids with her except for Teodoro here."

I didn't know if I should laugh or say I was sorry or congratulate him, so I changed the subject. I asked Emilio, sitting next to me, "Was that your little sweetheart I saw sneaking out of a cabin early this morning?"

"Was she a tall blond with blue eyes and red lips and big *tetas*?"

"Well, I wouldn't say that."

"Then she wasn't mine. My women are all blond *gringas*. She must belong to Teodoro!" he laughed heartily as if it were a great joke.

"I only wish it was true," Teodoro said, his dark eyes wide and excited.

"Well, then whose girl was she? Or was she just my hallucination?"

"Well, my son here has girlfriends all up and down the river, and pretty soon half the babies you see will be his." His father appeared proud. They all laughed, smoked, and drank more coffee. No one was in a hurry to end breakfast and go to work in the broiling heat.

Everything seemed peaceful. A sudden cool breeze swept in from across the water, and a few clouds hid the sun. This morning was perfect, until we were startled by frenzied shouts from workers a hundred yards away in a dense grassy area. Two men with machetes were flailing away at something, or each other, as two others huddled together. From our chairs, we couldn't see well, but I feared they were fighting.

I dashed from our breakfast table, down a wobbly ladder to the main deck, then across a plank onto the riverbank. When I arrived, out of breath, I saw the two men hacking away at something but not at each other, thank God. Another man was attending to a fourth whose arm was bloody. I hoped it wasn't an artery. I shouted, "*¿Qué pasa? ¿Qué pasa?*" They all started jabbering at once about what happened. "*¡Culebra! ¡Mapaná!*"

I knew from what Leon had told me that the *mapaná* was the most deadly snake in the world. These men claimed that a *mapaná* had struck his arm. The man, Luis, was going to die, a horrible agonizing death. According to stories, blood would ooze from every pore of his body while he turned green or white, or leathery, right before your eyes. There was nothing anyone could do. They all knew it.

Whether this man understood his fate or not, I couldn't tell as I tried to examine his wound. But Luis was writhing so much all we could see was blood covering not only his arm but his chest, too. His face grew ashen, but I couldn't see any actual fang wound. I ordered everyone to hold Luis still so I could wipe away blood to examine his wound. But there was still too much blood to see clearly. "Did any of you see this snake strike him?"

"¡*Sí, sí!*" they all answered excitedly.

"Actually see fangs go into his arm?" I quizzed.

"¡*Sí, sí!*" again they all replied. "That's really what we saw."

But I wasn't convinced they had witnessed anything except a lot of thrashing about and shouting. "Maybe that snake didn't bite him."

"No, no, *señor*. This *mapaná* struck him. We saw it," one of them cried, pointing at the long, hacked-up serpent.

"You've seen snakebites before, haven't you?"

"Oh, sure. Hundreds of them."

"Well, aren't they usually two little holes that don't bleed much?"

"*Sí*," they answered together, heads nodding.

After I put a tourniquet on Luis's arm with an old rag I had in my hip pocket, they could see, instead of two tiny punctures, a deep gash. "Maybe he struck his arm on something, maybe on this piece of sharp steel, when the snake surprised him. We've got to get him back to the boat before he bleeds to death," I said to those much surprised men.

They all praised me for performing a miracle—changing a snake bite to a cut from that sharp piece of steel. I realized I would never convince them that I didn't do anything supernatural. In the meantime, they finished chopping that long, gray snake into little pieces, except for its head, which looked surprisingly small in comparison to its lengthy body. But those fangs were as deadly as anything I'd even seen.

when the excitement ebbed and everyone's nerves calmed, they carried Luis back to the tug. There was a bare minimum of first-aid supplies. They sat him on deck while I cleaned his wound with outdated hydrogen peroxide from a bottle with a loose cap. Luis had a happy smile, either because it wasn't a snakebite or because he didn't have to work the rest of his tour but would still get paid. Maybe he grinned for both reasons.

Chapter 18

DRILLING PROBLEM

We sailed up river against a choppy current; rounding a bend we found a large bulldozed expanse of land in the middle of a thick jungle. A barge with four large house trailers was tied up to a huge ceiba tree. As Captain Cova maneuvered closer to the riverbank and behind the other barge, I scanned the area for the geologists I would be working with. All I could see over the sodden ground were workers busy preparing to set up drilling equipment. I couldn't find anyone even resembling a geologist or an engineer. *Does that stupid bastard Turner expect me to work this well alone?*

After we docked on the river bank I trudged through mud to the barge with the four large housing trailers. A door to one of the trailers swung open; a robust man, probably in his fifties judging from his overhang pot belly, came out and stepped down a short flight of stairs. He shrugged his shoulders and uttered, "Brr, that goddamn air conditioner is set way too cold in there." But soon sweat broke out on his face. He introduced himself as Earl Robbins, head engineer for Eastmount Oil Company." His spotless and scrupulously pressed tan pants matched his short sleeved crisply ironed shirt that made him look like he was in uniform.

I told him I was pleased to meet him and that my name was Rolly Farrington for Brocton Geological Services.

We shook hands. "You must be looking for that other young fellow right inside our dining trailer here. I think he said his name was Brian something."

"That's exactly who I'm looking for; thanks, Earl."

I stepped inside and got a blast of North Pole air that chilled me to the bone. I spotted Brian sitting at the dining table by himself reading a book.

Two other men—I took for American tool pushers—sat five chairs away from Brian. That seemed normal for Brian . . . not being the most sociable type. No one else was in the narrow cramped room. Before I started to walk over to greet him I called his name. He looked up for a second saw me then returned to his reading. That used to bother me.

"Tell me, Brian, When did you get here?"

"I arrived yesterday with Eastmont Oil Company's engineer." He marked the page where he left off reading.

"Who else is going to work with us?"

"I think it might be a new guy. I'm not sure."

"That means if he doesn't show up by tomorrow, we'll be working twelve hour tours."

"It looks like it."

"What's with the four trailers? What are they used for?"

"Two trailers are sleeping quarters for American personnel. The third trailer is for cooking and eating; the last one is an office and storage. The drilling rig and most of the equipment were loaded on the second barge."

It was time to get to work setting up our trailer and prepare for working with just the two of us. I hoped the new geologist would arrive soon. Temperature was already in the nineties. As I worked sweat rolled down my face and back.

Earl Robbins drove up. He could have walked the short distance but that would have meant sloshing through thick mud. "How soon will you boys be set up with your trailer and all your hook ups to the rig?"

"We'll be set up when you're ready to start drilling," Brian answered solemnly. "What's the name of your well?"

"*Arpaca* No 1. We want to spud in as soon as possible." His voice and demeanor were friendly. I was hoping for a good working relationship with Earl Robbins. "Boys, I want to stress that this is strictly a 'no dope hole.' Do you know what that means?"

"Sure, no information to anybody except to your oil company personnel and Brocton's."

"Exactly. Don't let anyone else in your trailer," he had a calm, nonthreatening voice; not like other engineers who like to roar commands. "We cemented casing last night at 500 feet. Start your log at that depth."

After Earl left I pressed Brian again, "What about the other geologist?"

"I told you don't worry, he will be along soon." Brian's answer had a sharp edge. I could tell I bugged him so I volunteered to work the first twelve hours. The first four days were an exhausting nonstop fast drilling. The next day Earl Robbins (in *uniform, of course)* knocked on the door and then climbed into our trailer as I worked on cuttings. "You look like you could use a glass of iced tea." He set a gallon jug on the sink and poured me a glass. "There should be enough to last you boys for a while."

What an unexpected surprise. I drank it so fast it gave me a splitting headache. "Thank you, Earl. That was a lifesaver." Later when I told Brian what Earl Robbins had done, all Brian said was "That so?" Nothing ever impresses Brian. "You boys know I'm in kind of a hurry to finish this well. I'm due to retire right after we're done here." I had notice earlier that Earl Robbins seemed to be skipping drilling rules that are never skipped by other engineers.

Another day while I was catching up with my drilled up cuttings samples I noticed from the trailer window, an outboard launch buzz downriver; making sweeping U-turns, then finally tie up to the dining barge. I paid no attention and kept working. A sharp rap on my door surprised me. It swung open. John Turner stomped in full of energy and grinning like a madman. He grabbed my hand squeezed it with his vise grip. Behind him Logan's unwelcomed face appeared. I was stunned, afraid Robbins might catch sight of him . . . an unwelcome outsider. I could get fired for breaking rules.

"Turner! What the hell are you doing bringing Logan in here?" I grabbed Logan and pushed him passed Turner outside so I could quickly slam the door behind me.

"Hey, Rolly, why so uptight? It's me, your friendly *gringo* buddy."

"You should know the rule here. This is a no dope hole. You could get me fired." I said, standing in the hot sun and hoping to get rid of him and get back into my air-conditioned trailer.

"Hold on there, Rolly. I'm here on business. I brought John so he could get to work."

Turner stayed in the air conditioned trailer while I questioned Logan. "Why'd it take Turner so long to get here?"

"*Yo no sé, Jose.*" That was Logan's smartass way of saying *I don't know.* As usual, he was all smiles and acted like he belonged here. "I'll be leaving after I deliver two bottles of rum for Earl Robbins. He can't function without it. I'll be heading back to Mompos. Is there anything I can get for you when I am back in town? I have connections with anybody who's somebody."

I ignored his offer. He left and started walking towards his tied up boat. He turned and waved back at me with all smiles. Back in the trailer, I confronted Turner. He said, "Look, I'm late because I had no transportation until Logan came along from Barranquilla." I was less than anxious to meet up with John turner again but I'll put up with him.

On the eighth day the drilling slowed to a reasonable 20 feet per hour. Our ground-up cuttings samples consisted of rice-sized grains of sandstone and chips of brown shale. Next, 5 feet deeper, I found a marked increase of half-an-inch to inch-sized platy chips of brown shale and less sandstone. Brian arrived to work his tour. When I showed him my samples he immediately shouted, "We are drilling in running shale. Our mud can't hold it back. It's going to plug up the well and stick the pipe if we don't act fast."

This was the first time I had seen Brian so charged up. "We've got to check the shale-shaker to see how much shale is coming up."

At the shale-shaker, what I saw made me speechless: a cascade of inch sized shale tumbled over the shaker, building a mountain of steaming chips on the ground.

I followed Brian scrambling up the ladder to the rig floor. Earl Robbins was talking to the Colombian driller. The engineer puffed on a cigarette and then took a gulp from a beer bottle.

"Earl, we got a problem."

Earl shot a look of anger at Brian. He didn't like that word *problem*. "What are you talking about?"

Just then the rotary table stopped turning the drill pipe, rig motors stuttered to a stop, along with the mud pumps. Dead silence. Earl's anger suddenly changed from anger to helplessness. The tool-pusher stepped up to the controls reached for starter lever. It let out a deafening scream. We strained to hear the motors start rumbling again . . . but no; only dead silence. Brian jumped fourth knocking the tool-pusher back and pulled on the started lever three but nothing happened. "Your fuel line is plugged, can't you tell?" Shouted John Turner who suddenly appeared out of nowhere. "Your motors aren't getting any fuel. You two stooges (meaning Brian and me) follow me." He spun around, grabbed the ladder bar and slid down to slick muddy ground, with Brian and me on his tail. The race continued until we reached the back of the rig where diesel hoses connected to motors. He ordered an idle roughneck standing by to unscrew the fuel line. "Just as I thought . . . out of diesel!"

"Impossible," Shouted Earl, "That tank was filled the day we got here."

Turner climbed on top of the fuel tank and found a 10-inch-diameter hole used to fill the tank. "There is no cap on this tank," he shouted down to us. He peered inside. "Leaves! This tank is plugged up with what looks like tree leaves." He took another look and reached down into the tank and pulled up a handful. "They're not leaves; these are locusts! Earl, get your hands to hook up to your standby fuel tank. I can see from here that one has its cap screwed on. I'm betting we won't find locusts." They scrambled hooking up the hose, as time was ticking by fast. The pipe in the hole hadn't been moved up or down for almost an hour and that was enough time for pipe to get stuck in place. Finally Earl ordered the driller to try the air starter again. Once again the blast of compressed air let out its deafening scream. Motors coughed twice and then roared. Mud pumps started churning. We dashed over to the edge of the deck railing. A thin stream of mud flowed out. The driller was ordered to pull the pipe up. The pipe wouldn't move. Earl pushed the Colombian driller aside and grabbed the brake handle himself. After revving the motors, he then pulled the brake lever up. The rig squeaked, shuttered, and vibrated violently. He stayed glued to the brake handle and his eye on the weight gauge even though he was exceeding all the rig safety regulations. The tall rig was about to crash down. And no pipe movement.

Earl climbed down from the rig floor and lamented "We're screwed boys. That pipe is stuck solid."

"Maybe not," Turner uttered.

"What'd you say?" Earl's ears were alert as he hoped for a miracle.

"You've got a couple of barrels of crude in the storage shed. We can use them to spot oil at the plugged zone and then try to yo-yo the string of drill pipe up and down. We might be able to slide the pipe through that stuck zone and out of danger. Rolly, go back to the trailer; check the depth where all this running shale came in. We'll circulate crude through the bit up to where the pipe is stuck. We'll start pulling gently on the pipe and then slack off, next pull a little harder and repeat slack off followed by pulling to work the pipe and gradually loosen the shale's grip on the pipe." At first we found negligible movement. Turner encouraged the crew not to give up. He told Earl to keep yo-yoing. Gradually we could see more movement until finally the pipe moved freely out of the stuck zone.

"Turner, you're a genius," Earl crowed.

"You better keep your pump circulating, or else it will plug up again," Turner recommended.

"You did a good job, and if my company has plans for casing off that running shale to drill deeper, we'll let your company know."

Brian and Turner planned to fly to Barranquilla. I planned to go to Medellin and relax before the next well.

Chapter 19

THE BIRTHDAY PARTY

My taxi dropped me at our house in Medellin. Florencia opened the front door as soon as I rang. She seemed more flustered than usual. She bombarded me in her high, worried tone, which made her Spanish harder to understand. With her everything was a crisis.

"Settle down, Frorencia; I don't understand a word. Where is everybody?"

"Oh thank God you're here," she explained more slowly. "All the other *americanos* are working, and *la señorita* Marisol has invited everyone to her birthday party tonight at six o'clock. She would be very disappointed if at least one of you didn't attend."

"Birthday party?" *Did I hear right?* "Did you say birthday party?"

"*Sí, señor, un cumpleaños.* Six o'clock tonight at her uncle *don Humberto's* home."

I checked my watch. I had just enough time to shower, shave, and get dressed, although I didn't have any party clothes, just clean work clothes.

I was out on the street with no taxis in sight. Fortunately, Humberto's house wasn't far, so I double-timed with my long strides past people gawking at me as if I were some towering alien. I weaved my way, bumping into hordes of pedestrians, when suddenly I realized I was heading to a birthday party without a birthday present.

On a wedge-shaped street corner, a wedge-shaped shop caught my eye—La Tienda De Gustavo Navarro. *Maybe they sell something I can buy as a gift.* As I entered, the shopkeeper, Gustavo, I presumed, looked up—furrowing his eyebrows and narrowing his eyes—from a newspaper on his counter and spoke with a curious uncertainty in his voice. "*A sus ordenes, señor*," which meant *at your service*.

My eyes caught sight of open gunny sacks of potatoes, yuca, and corn slumped over like slumbering bodies along one wall. Photos of bullfights and bullfighters, a Colombian flag, and brilliant bullfighter bandoleers adorned a wall behind *señor* Navarro. Through a large window I caught a view of busy traffic. Next to the window, two thin cane chairs were pushed up against a basketball hoop-sized table, topped by two small cups for coffee, called *tinto*, the rings of coffee dregs still in the bottom of the cups. I looked around the shop and was convinced that if more than three people were present, Gustavo would have an overflow crowd. On further search didn't suggest anything that would pass for a birthday present.

In Spanish, I explained, "*Señor*, I need to buy something special for someone very special. I'm going to her birthday party tonight."

My accent must have confused him, or maybe he'd never been asked for something special for someone special, because his eyes bugged, and his mouth hung open. "Pardon me for saying, but I've never met anyone two meters tall before."

"That's okay; I hear that a lot lately." I stood before this waist-high counter and drummed my fingers as I glanced at my watch.

"Do you want me to make a suggestion?"

"Yes, please do."

"A bottle of *aguardiente*."

"That's a good idea, but—"

"If it's a party, everybody likes to drink *aguardiente*."

"But I need something for a gift."

"That's a tough one." Gustavo stood encased behind his narrow wooden counter, gray and lined like his face, and almost as high as his chin. Next to him on the counter a box-like cabinet about a foot wide and a foot tall with dusty, smoke-coated glass sides contained slumping *empanadas* inside. A cigarette dangled and then fell from his parted lips. He steadied his gaze, with his mouth open in disbelief, maybe because he hadn't gotten used to my height. Finally he said, "What are we, the long and the short of it?" He waited for my response to his little jest but got none. "Not everyone appreciates my light humor," he whispered.

He paused as if to find some kind of sign in my eyes that I got it. "This is like coming face to face with a stone face that's not easy to humor." He raised his voice. "I could tie a birthday ribbon around the neck of a *garrafa* of *aguardiente*? It's not really a fiesta without one," he said with a chuckle.

Gustavo Navarro's second attempt at a jest was answered solemnly without a grin. "No, that's not a present. I'm in a hurry. I'm late already." I felt my face flush.

"I have just the ticket. But first you must relax. This will make you more comfortable." From under his counter he came up with a bottle of *aguardiente*. He poured two shots in shot glasses. He handed me one and then raised his arm and shouted, "*Salud!*" He gulped down his shot and motioned for me to do the same. It burned all the way to my stomach. He poured another, and we both downed them together. I felt warm inside and a little light-headed. Then he came up with a little box about three inches square and half an inch thick decorated with a replica of the Colombian flag. He opened it. Nestled on a velvet pad I saw a pale-green crystal the size and shape of half a walnut mounted on a silver surface with a clasp on the back—a broach.

My eyes lit up. "It's an emerald!" I reached for it and took out my small hand lens from the chain around my neck. With my hand lens in place I squinted into the gem. It was clear, not dark-green like expensive emeralds, and it lacked inclusions called *gardens*. I bet he would jack up the price. I hadn't come to Colombia to buy presents for girls I hardly knew, but she was different. "How much are you asking, *señor*?"

"It's very valuable. Been in my family for generations."

"It is too pale to be worth much money," I claimed. I was here to save money, not to spend it. "I'll buy it only if your price is reasonable."

"Good. We're finally having a conversation. I knew I could get to you. Are you sure you know enough about *señoritas*?" As he was speaking, he poured out two shots of *aguardiente*.

"Of course, I know lots of *señoritas* and *muchachas*."

He said, "*Salud!*" We both threw down our drinks.

"What do you think about a little bottle of perfume? *Patuli*, for example. Wouldn't that be appropriate to go with the emerald? After all, most women want to smell good to impress their gentlemen friends." He poured out two more shots. We drank. He poured out another round.

"No, the emerald is enough. I don't want to overdo it." I anxiously drummed my fingers on the counter; my cheeks felt warm and were probably red from that anise-tasting concoction. "Like I said, I haven't been to many Colombian parties before."

"You need *limones* to go with the *aguardiente.* Here take this bag of them."

"So many?"

"Oh! I almost forgot—*mango*; they are in season now."

"That's a lot of stuff."

"No, one more thing—*empanadas* fresh out of the oven." He took out the tired-looking *empanadas* that were slumped over in the cabinet. He started wrapping everything in sections of the newspaper that he had been reading.

"What else?"

"That's all. I'm not going to sell you anything more. All I've got left is a sports page, and I'm going to read it before I sell one more thing." He made a quick list of all the items and then showed it to me. I could hardly read his scribble, and the *aguardiente* dulled my senses, but his sum total I could afford.

"Fine." I took out a roll of *pesos* that always reminded me of play money. Just then the door opened and a man, collar up and hat pulled down low on his brow, slinked in. He paid for his cigarettes while keeping his eyes on me and then left.

I was feeling all warm inside and hesitated before downing my final shot.

"Don't do that. Don't keep your money all rolled up in a wad like that. You don't know who is watching you. Just take a few bills to buy your needs and keep most of it in your boot. There are people around here who will kill just for your loose change. I tell you this as a friend. Do you understand?"

"Sure. I appreciate your concern. But I can take care of myself."

"You probably can." He paused, his words hanging in the air. "Cigarettes? I just thought of them. You'll need cigarettes, won't you? People smoke their heads off at a fiesta. Here, take these, a variety of brands. Maybe you'll meet more than one someone special." He started to wrap the cigarettes in a section of his sports page but then reconsidered. Instead, he wedged them in with the *aguardiente.* Gustavo went on: "Could you ease my curiosity, if I'm not being too bold? You're not from around here, are you?"

"Correct, I'm not."

"Must be Italian or maybe French. Your Spanish is not bad, but your accent is not from here."

"No, not like yours. I'm American."

"I never would have guessed American. Well, for an American your Spanish is okay, although I don't know many Americans, one or two, maybe.

"Well, it's been interesting as well as informative talking to you. I'll be back soon for some more good advice," I said.

At that, Gustavo called his two sons from a backroom. "Come on, boys, there's work to be done. Help our American *amigo* carry his goods."

"It's not far, just up the street. But we've got to hurry."

The boys struggled with my bundles, stumbling over broken slabs of sidewalk. I carried the *garrafa* of *aguardiente* hanging inside a netted rope bag. I walked in the road because the narrow uneven sidewalks were not wide enough for three abreast. Streets were not in any better condition, but it gave me more room to stretch my legs. Potholes in the street acted as speed bumps to slow traffic. It wasn't until later that I realized I had no idea how much I had paid for that emerald.

At the front door to *tío Humberto's* home I heard a rumble of happy voices as well as music and laughter. All were welcoming sounds. I knocked and waited. Nobody opened the door, so I knocked harder. The door swung open, and *don Humberto's* eyes lit up when he saw me; a broad smile creased his chubby cheeks. He grabbed me in his arms, almost making me drop my *aguardiente*, and gave me *un fuerte abrozo.* "¡*Rolando*! I am so glad you came tonight." He ushered me in to meet his other guests. The two young boys carrying my bundles followed. I saw older, parental types and young teens conversing with each other around the room. They anxiously gave their attention to *don* Humberto as he introduced me to his guests. I searched for that one familiar face I came to see in this passel of unfamiliar faces.

I had met Humberto—this short, round man, his smile hidden under his black bushy mustache—on my first visit to Medellin at *la finca.*

"But what is all this, *don Rolando*?" he asked as he eyed my assorted bundles.

"Something for your party." In a way, he made my name *Rolando* sound worldlier, with a roll of the *r*, than just plain old Rolly. And in English, I've never liked my name Rolland.

"But we have more than enough of everything for our party."

"I got carried away. Colombian parties are new to me. I just wanted to show my gratitude for your invitation." We deposited our load of newspaper-wrapped packages on a table.

Humberto's wife, Amparo, rushed to greet me; her eyes reflected a happy welcome for me. She gave me a kiss on the cheek, while Humberto's brother, Guillermo, poured out another large shot of *aguardiente*. Men raised their shot glasses. Light sparkled through the clear liquid as I toasted in my best Spanish: "In honor of being invited to your home." Someone added, "¡*Salud*!" Then we downed two more shots.

As I scanned the group looking for Marisol, I became aware that this was a dressy affair. I must have appeared as an example of Americans' lack of class. Just another *gringo* wearing boots and clothes suited for *la selva* — the jungle— with long, unruly hair needing a trim. I came to this party for the express purpose to meet Marisol again. Where was she? Maybe she was intentionally avoiding me. I thought I might slyly leave. But how does a guy my size do *slyly*?

Humberto asked if I would like to see the rest of his house. I said yes. He took my arm and led me through a large open-air patio in the middle of his house. Because of Colombia's tropical climate, all rooms had high ceilings that allowed fresh air to circulate in through open windows high up on the walls. For me, coming from California—with its cold winters—I was surprised to see no furnace to heat their home. He explained that their weather was warm year-round. I was led down a hall past bedrooms to a kitchen located in back of the house. It was a typical Colombian kitchen open on three sides, under a roof that kept rain out but allowed smoke and heat to dissipate into fresh air. Beyond the kitchen I could see a garden with a few banana trees and a large guava tree loaded with tart fruit. Walls of neighboring houses enclosed this whole area. A waist-high sink set in solid cement had a large round boulder in it. The rock was used for pounding meat or mashing corn for making *arepas—cornmeal buns.* Delicious aromas wafted from steaming pots on an electric stove. Ana, their highly celebrated cook, had her own small room next to the kitchen. It housed a narrow cot and a small chest of drawers. An adjacent room, a little larger than a closet, housed a seat-less toilet, a one-faucet shower, and a tiny sink.

On our way from the kitchen, I noticed there were enough bedrooms for all five children and one for parents. Each bedroom had religious pictures or mementos, including a cross over each bed. One main bathroom had a shower with no curtain, so when in use everything must get drenched.

If Marisol hadn't arrived by now, it must mean she wasn't coming. Humberto noticed I was uncomfortable. "Rolando, I want you to meet my Uncle Enrique," he announced. "He is our oldest family member." Enrique was dressed in typical clothes of this region: a small brimmed felt hat and a white cotton *ruana* (similar to a Mexican poncho) with thin blue stripes. A large leather purse, called a *carriel* and used exclusively by Colombian men, hung on a strap over his shoulder. He wore a starched, white shirt and tan pants with balloon legs, and leather sandals called *alpargatas.*

"*Mucho gusto, señor.*" Then I told him my name: "*Me llamo* Rolando Farrington."

"You speak Spanish?" Enrique spoke slowly in Spanish so I would understand.

"Better than I do, uncle," Antonio, Humberto's oldest son, interjected.

"He exaggerates," I corrected.

"We all tend to," Uncle Enrique laughed and then eyed my size. "You must be over two meters. Antonio, if your friend *Rolando* here isn't a living exaggeration, I don't know what is. You can't be from here."

"That's right. I'm not. I'm from America."

"So is everyone here. Which America?" Enrique inquired.

"Yes, of course, you're right. North America, California," I answered, my face flushed, a little embarrassed.

"I've heard of it." he said smiling, as if to say, who hasn't? "Yes, I have. Berkeley. University riots. That's California." He grinned and then with pride said, "I'm from Retiro. Have you ever heard of it?"

"Sure, I've even been there. It's near Rionegro. Are you still living there?"

"No. I left Retiro about fifty years ago. I started a little funeral business in town there, but business wasn't good. There was already one funeral parlor, and that was all they needed. Not many people live in Retiro. Too quiet there. No problems. So naturally not much business. That's why I came to Medellin. I got started in a little place on *Juan del Corral.*"

"And business was better here in Medellin?" I asked.

"It was fantastic! You wouldn't believe how good it was. I had to turn business away, so I moved closer to *Junin*, in a bigger place, right next to *El Hotel Santa Margarita* on one side and a furniture store on the other. Besides tables and chairs, they made boxes, great boxes, and I needed a lot of them, those long narrow ones. You know what I mean. I used to get a lot of business from that hotel, by the way. In fact, I used to have more business than he did, so at times they rented me rooms for storing my customers. That hotel owner preferred my customers to his because mine were not noisy and dirty like his. Sometimes people, mostly drunks, would get my place mixed up with his hotel. They nearly died when they found out their mistake."

"That's mostly exaggeration, isn't it, Uncle?" Antonio asked.

"Only slightly, but the funeral business is good in this town and always will be. Our generous public makes sure of that. They are so obliging. You know how crazy they get here, not only on Saturday nights, but every night. People might be poor, but they always manage to get drunk. And you know how ones with money drive, drunk or sober, in these narrow streets. Nobody watches where they're going whether they are walking or driving. I'd be making a fortune right now if I hadn't retired. Best thing that ever happened to our funeral business was alcohol and the automobile."

After Enrique finished his story, my attention switched to the music and people dancing on the parlor floor. Suddenly the music stopped. I heard a commotion at the front door. People crowded around the entry. I wondered what was happening. And then to my surprise, Marisol appeared. Even at that distance I could see happiness in her face. She had to throw her arms around everyone and kiss. The party suddenly seemed to come alive. What attention or influence this one person radiated! When she finally came up to me, my mind went blank. My Spanish deserted me. She looked more beautiful than ever. As a record started to play, she grasped my arm and we began to dance. I tried to dance without stepping on her toes. I had no idea what I was supposed to do.

After the music stopped I wasn't sure if this would be the right time to give her my present. I hadn't seen anyone else giving her presents. Maybe that wasn't a custom here. I decided to take the small package from my pocket. "Marisol, I have something for your birthday." I hoped my hand wasn't noticeably shaking. I handed it to her. She seemed not to know what to do or say. "Open it, please."

She fumbled, almost dropped it. When she saw what it was her voice was soft, unusually soft, and rather unsure. "Oh Rolando, it's beautiful, so thoughtful of you. Thank you." She gave me a kiss on the cheek.

I could feel my cheeks redden. "It's just a little gift for your birthday." With the family and friends all around, she tried to be her normal self, chattering and laughing, entertaining everyone, albeit in a calmer voice and demeanor. The music started again. I suddenly felt bold. I took her hand and led her to the dance floor. I regained most of my composure. I held her very close. Her cheek touched mine. I don't know if she felt the same sensation I did, but I was completely confused, torn between the irrational me—*love*—and the rational me—*don't fall in love*. I don't remember how many records we danced to. I know I didn't want to stop. I wanted to keep Marisol close to me, her soft arm on my shoulder. I whirled her around, looking into those dark smiling eyes, those tempting lips, and then she placed her head on my shoulder. For the rest of the evening we both must have been quietly thinking about what was happening to us; at least that was what I was thinking. We both seemed to be having difficulty speaking. I felt a little weak. I never had this strange feeling before.

When the party broke up I thanked my hosts and hostess, all their friends and relatives, and realized that at Colombian parties, saying good-bye can last forever. Humberto's wife asked me if I had a key to my home. When I confessed I didn't, she suggested I call home and tell Florencia to let me in. Most Colombians are aware of thieves, especially at night. After I said good-bye to everyone, I looked for Marisol. She must have slipped out before I had a chance to ask if I could see her again.

When I knocked on our front door, a drowsy Frorencia opened and let me in and then she said goodnight. I didn't see anyone, so I went right to bed. I couldn't sleep thinking about what I'd gotten myself into. I desperately wanted to see Marisol again, but I didn't understand how I felt about this lovely young *señorita*. I hadn't come to this country to complicate my life by falling in love. I never thought of falling in love with someone from a foreign country. I came here with an agenda, not to get involved with love. I debated if I should call her the next day. No, on second thought, maybe I'd better cool it for a week or so.

Chapter 20

GOLD

A thump . . . a curse. Awake now I saw a form in the darkened room.

"That's a stupid place to leave a chair. Rolly . . . Rolly, wake up and get dressed."

"Bulldog! Why are you always waking me in the middle of the night?"

"Why are you always sleeping? It's not the middle of the night. It's morning; four thirty to be exact." Then Leon cussed the chair again.

"Four thirty? You must be drunk. What do you mean 'get dressed'?"

"It'll take two weeks to move that drilling rig to a new location. Which means we've got two weeks to go gold mining."

"Go to hell, you crazy bastard."

"I'm telling you . . . get up. I'm not leaving here until you get your ass out of that bed.

We got to hurry and catch a bus to Rondino by six o'clock."

"Tonight?"

"No, this morning, asshole. Come on. We've barely enough time to get to the bus depot Before our bus leaves."

I managed to roll out of bed and stand dazed in my shorts as Leon shouted, "Here, catch."

And with that he tossed me a backpack. I almost dropped it.

"What's this for?"

"When you prospect for gold, you camp out, get it? Both backpacks have enough food if we need it. There are peanut butter cookies, chorizos, and hard-boiled eggs—all good sources of protein. Also, fresh fruit and candy bars—good sources of energy. I also included mosquito netting and a hammock for each of us."

"Maybe I don't want to go gold mining." I was thinking about Marisol, maybe meet her this afternoon.

"Rolly, you're going gold mining with me. I ordered this stuff from the States when I heard you were coming to Colombia. When we were mapping geology last summer in Nevada, our last class before graduating, we agreed we wanted to do some gold prospecting."

"Yeah, but that was in California, not Colombia."

Leon hot-footed it down dark early-morning streets with me reluctantly tagging behind. Ahead we could see glaring floodlights high above Medellin's bus terminal illuminating bright, colorful buses.

Campesinos—wearing straw hats, *ruanas* or *ponchos* over their shoulders, heavy, dusty baggy pants with balloon pant legs, and sandals or boots shod with thick leather—milled around, reflecting a raw sense of what life close to the soil was like. Some people mounted buses that deft artists artistically painted showing off designs in red, blue, green, and yellow. All buses offered hard benches, nailed to roughly hewn wooden plank floors, that stretched across the width of the chassis in six or seven rows from front to back of the bus. The left side, where people mounted, was open from floor to roof, where as the opposite side was open only to a person's shoulders and it had no doors. The buses were built on flatbed trucks; they were far from being elegant but were at least serviceable.

Leon located a crude kiosk selling steaming coffee and sugared shortbreads, *empanadas,* and *pandebonos.* That was my breakfast. I envied Leon's easy way of blending in with these country people. Would I ever be capable of doing the same? He hustled around asking people for the bus to Rondino. Finally he found one and proceeded to climb up onto its roof, which was loaded with gunnysacks full of goods destined for bucolic homes and other *pueblos.* Everyone was laughing and joking excitedly, as if they were going on a thrilling world tour, not just home after visiting family and shopping in the big city of Medellin.

The first rays of sunlight peeked over the eastern Andes. "Hurry up, Rolly. Get your ass up here or you'll miss the bus."

"You son of a bitch, I'd be smarter if I missed it and went back to bed." After I hoisted myself up, I heard a few snorts. I turned toward those snorts and found my traveling partner: a hog-tied hog stretched out and slumbering fitfully.

After a roar of the engine and a few sharp bucking jolts, we were on our way out of Medellin over an unpaved dusty road full of potholes as big as our traveling companion, Mr. Hog. Riding on the roof was still more comfortable than being squeezed like sardines inside on hard benches.

I asked Leon, "I just had a thought, what are we going to do about food on this wild goose chase?"

"I told you, don't worry. I've got everything in this bag I've been carrying. We will stop along the way and buy some mangoes, bananas, chorizos hot off the grill. Don't worry, you're not going to starve."

We rumbled along for an hour. City scenery slid away as we began to climb higher into the mountains. Midmorning was cool and clear. High mountain peaks and steep V-shaped valleys abounded. The narrow road hugged one side of the mountain, which fell off precipitously hundreds of feet below into an angry, churning river. Cresting waves thumped against rock walls, sending a hissing spray into the air. We could hear the river's roar as it echoed off the mountainsides, drowning out the sound of gravel and rocks crunching and pinging under the bus's well-worn tires.

We rounded a cliff and were driving into a blind curve when suddenly we came face-to-face with a big black monster—a huge truck loaded with cattle. Horns blared; brakes squealed; we were frozen with fear—fear of falling, bouncing off mountain walls, into the maelstrom below. The two beasts stopped inches apart. After a brief standoff, the black one reversed direction, backing into a carved-out cul-de-sac made for such near collisions.

"Did you shit your pants?" was all Leon said. Then he lay back to stare at a cloudless, blue sky, unaffected by that brief encounter. I stretched out, propped up on one elbow, to take in some high mountain scenery. We rattled along on a washboard, teeth-chattering road, with a refreshing cool breeze in our faces.

To our left, the mountainside plunged several hundred feet, almost vertically, and then leveled. I could barely see a rust-red roof of a house under a solid riot of banana leaves protecting coffee bushes from the burning sun. Only a few houses could be seen under such thick foliage. Farther along, the view changed to a wide, gently sloping valley. A *finca* cradled between mountains stretched over many acres, or *hectares,* with the perimeter marked by a stone wall maybe six feet high. Inside the wall were neatly sectioned plots of vegetables and other greenery for food. I focused in on a white-walled hacienda, with window frames painted red, in the middle. Such a well-organized place must belong to a wealthy landowner. I could barely pick out ten people working rows of coffee bushes. On the other side of the wall light green grassland broadened out for grazing cattle fenced in with barbwire.

We slowed as we approached a man riding a horse, neither horse nor man in a hurry to let us pass. A loud blast from our bus's horn did nothing to prod them out of our way. The sun was slowly moving higher in the blue sky. I was getting hungry and glad to see we were approaching a roadside brick shanty with a large weathered sign on its moss-encrusted tile roof boasting *LAS MEJORES EMPANADAS DEL MUNDO.*

"Shall we try the 'best empanadas in the world'?" Leon asked me.

"I'm game," I said as our bus braked in front of the rustic place. Our fellow travelers scrambled off their hard benches. I thought they would be searching for empty dining tables, but, no, they lined up shoulder to shoulder across the street, where they frantically whipped out their short arms to relieve themselves. Leon joined them, so I thought, what the hell, I did also. The women disappeared down a dank hall to a place in back of the building and did what they had to do.

An *al clima* beer tasted so good, even though warm. We had another while eating greasy, spicy *chorizos* on sticks followed by roasted, buttery ears of corn on the cob. It made for a royal lunch. Before we were ready to pull out, we grabbed two more lukewarm beers. As soon as we continued our jarring journey, our beers started to foam up faster than we could drink them.

We rumbled into Rondino in late afternoon. Leon said we had to hurry, although he didn't explain why. I realized he never explained anything about this wild-ass gold mining venture. We located a taxi, probably the only one in town, and piled our gear in the backseat with us. The driver nervously sped out of town in the opposite direction we came. Several kilometers later he stopped in a valley between steep green mountains and began to turn around.

"What's going on, Leon? Why's he turning around?"

"This is where we get off." He paid our driver, who slammed his taxi in gear and spun around like a hot-rodder. "He's afraid of being attacked here after dark."

"So why the hell are we out here?"

"We don't own a car. We have nothing to worry about. They don't bother poor people on foot."

I figured the word *they* must mean bandits or robbers. I had an ominous feeling I would regret this for the rest of my life.

Leon pointed up to a sloping gap in the mountain in front of us and a rough trail winding to it, where, he said, we would find a run-down way station. I was tired and didn't bother asking why we were going there. Leon seemed to grow more energetic as we climbed, venturing into an unknown world.

It grew dark along the trail littered with small- to large-sized rounded stones cemented in mud, making progress slow as we stumbled along. Leon pointed to the top of our climb, where a weak light glowed forlornly in the dark sky.

We reached the gap with little sunlight left for us to view an encampment: horses behind a fenced corral, a small withered house, and a blazing fire pit. Chunks of meat roasted on crude spits. The aroma made my digestive juices flow. A few men milling about made me uneasy. *Were they* banditos? Disheveled types—masked in darkness. All I could make out were faces full of whiskers like fallowed weed patches, wrinkled hats pulled low over their eyes, and their beat-up, muddy boots.

"Leon, we'd better get the hell out of here."

"Bullshit. They're just back mountain people."

They were eating what looked like beans and rice with chunks of meat on tin plates. I hadn't eaten since midday, and my stomach was growling. A gray-haired hag wearing a faded apron brushed a shank of unruly hair out of her eyes before offering us soup spoons and tin plates, which she then filled with beans and chunks of meat. We washed everything down with hot coffee. Men talked occasionally to each other in low grunts.

One grizzled old man asked in a whispered growl, "You boys on your way over the mountain?"

"That's right, to see Bonifacio Abricio." Leon's Spanish was better than mine, so he did the talking.

"That's him, that slim *hombre* with a gray *ruana* draped over his shoulder." He yelled over to the earthy fellow: "Hey, Boni, couple of *gringos* here to see you."

Boni turned and ambled over toward us with his head stretched forward as if to see us better. "*Bueno*, I'm Bonifacio. What do you want?"

Leon told him our names; we extended our hands and shook his limp paw. Leon explained what we wanted. It was a friend of Leon who sold him the map and told him Bonifacio would help with mining or panning for gold. Bonifacio told us we had to be prepared for an all-day trek over an ancient trail to the other side of the mountain. So we spent the night in hammocks inside a barn listening to rats scratching and fighting over scraps on the floor and horses snorting and crapping. We got up early the next morning and breakfasted on cornmeal muffins with *quecito* and hot coffee.

"You need horses?" I couldn't tell if Bonifacio was asking or telling. Leon understood and told him we needed just one horse to pack our gear.

"That'll be fifty *pesos*," Bonifacio said. In the early morning sunlight his steely blue eyes radiated unfriendliness. I was able to see him better now, and he was all bone and gristle, like a man who didn't waste time with idle chatter. Leon hesitated before paying.

"Well, what do you say?" the mountain man demanded.

Leon drew fifty *pesos* out of his pocket. We swung our packs on the back of a big, powerful horse. Boni led us on a heavily traveled trail that dated back to the days of the Spanish Conquistadores. It was worn deep, as much as six feet, into red earth bottoming in rain-filled puddles. Soon the path cut into a forest, where no light penetrated through its dense canopy. Around noon we stopped to dig into our backpacks for hard-boiled eggs and a warm beer. Boni ate something wrapped in banana leaves.

"Mind if I ask you what you're eating?" He didn't answer, just sniffed the air, and said,

"Vamos."

"He probably didn't understand your Spanish, Rolly."

We hoisted our backpacks up on our horse again, while our guide smoked a cigarette before continuing our march.

By late afternoon our trail emerged from forest into a stretch of knee-high grassland that overlooked a tumbling river. Boni's bucolic encampment lay ahead on one side of the trail. It appeared to be a trading post; boxes of fruit, potatoes, yuca and other provisions sat outside his small cabin on a narrow porch made of saplings. Tired, Leon and I dropped our gear as we dropped our butts on old canvas-backed chairs. Boni awarded us river-cooled beer and charged us each twenty *pesos*. He was a man of few words and seemed to prefer being left alone.

Even though we were exhausted, we still had to stow our gear under a shelter made from palm fronds supported by four sturdy tree trunks, designed to protect us from rain or an intense sun. Only an hour of sunlight remained before a dark, moonless night. Boni fed us salty fried yuca (tasting better than french-fried potatoes), something resembling chicken, and warm *arepas* topped with *quecito*, and charged us thirty *pesos* each. In the shelter we strung our hammocks between four posts and hung mosquito nets over us as we slept.

We woke at sunrise, ate some of Leon's trail mix and drank thick, sweet coffee, which cost us ten *pesos*. Boni handed each of us a wooden platter-like bowl—large, round, and shallow—used for panning river gold. We followed him down to a gravel beach along a slow-moving stream. We took off our boots, rolled up our pant legs and stepped into the cold current. Crystal-clear water magnified rounded pebbles and coarse-grain sand. In this serenity, the only sounds were birds flapping wings, insects buzzing, and the stream lip, lip, lapping against our chilled ankles.

Boni took his pan and tersely explained: "Scoop up a pan full of sand and gravel, swirl its contents around and around, allowing large pebbles to escape and lighter slurry to spill out, leaving heavier sand and gravel. Then study the remaining sediments to see if you can find any gold. If you don't see any gold, try again."

Optimistically Leon and I went to work panning. At first we were excited to see an accumulation of glinting gold flakes mixed with black silt. On closer scrutiny, those gold flakes turned out to be mica flakes and cubes of pyrite—the mineral iron sulfide, known as fool's gold. We spent the rest of the day panning in different areas of the river without any luck. My bare feet were cold and sore from walking on rocks.

"You know, we should have brought tennis shoes instead of boots," Leon said.

"You're right. You keep panning and I'll go back and get them."

"Shut up, wise ass, and keep panning."

"I'm ready to give it up and go back to Medellin."

"What do you mean, go back to Medellin? Forget about that little sweetie you're so hot for. We just got started panning. In a few days we'll begin to get results."

Leon was thoroughly pissed at me, so I kept my mouth shut. No need for a big falling-out.

Boni suggested we try a stretch upstream where the river bent and the current slowed down.

"What do you think, Rolly? Shall we give it another shot tomorrow?"

"Yea, why not?" Maybe I'm not cut out for this placer mining stuff; it's too much like fishing.

It was late afternoon, so we trudged out of the river and up to Boni's layout. We each had a beer; it was warm, but that didn't matter to us. Boni prepared an unnamed concoction called dinner for the three of us. It tasted strange, so I didn't eat it, whereas Leon, with his voracious appetite, ate his portion and asked for seconds. I was satisfied with boiled corn-on-the-cob and an *arepa* washed down with a beer. Because we were both tired and a little discouraged, we hit our hammocks soon after nightfall.

I woke at sunup with little enthusiasm panning for gold, but I was determined to make the effort. Leon was still asleep. I had to wake him so we could start panning right after breakfast. He was awake but didn't move. "Leon, are you all right? It's time to get up."

"Yeah, yeah, yeah . . . go to hell." I gave him a few more minutes before he finally dragged himself out of his hammock.

After breakfast Leon and I spread out and waded partly in the stream and partly over sand and gravel beaches. Boni kept an eye on us high on the riverbank. Leon slowly made a sluggish attempt to pan sediments. I was committed to do my best even if my heart wasn't in it. I scooped up some dry sediment, dipped it in water and swirled it and eventually was left with grains of sand and pebbles and silt—same results as yesterday.

After several pans, Leon shouted, "I found a nugget! Rolly, take a look."

I dropped my pan load and ran splashing over to him. He proudly handed me his pan drained of everything except a skim of silt and three flecks of shiny gold-colored cubic crystals.

"Leon, that's pyrite, you asshole."

"Bullshit."

"Ask Boni."

Who agreed it wasn't gold. We waded upstream around a bend, where the current slowed. We panned until late afternoon without stopping for lunch, although Leon managed to chew on something he found in his backpack. He also picked some berries to eat. Boni didn't know about those berries, so I didn't eat any. Boni turned them down also.

"Let's do a couple more pans and then call it quits," I suggested. Leon agreed. He was working downstream in ankle-deep water. I worked upstream in water at the same depth. The sun burned my bare back. A small school of minnows nibbled on my toes. Off to my right, willow branches hung low over the river, obscuring the riverbank. I pushed away leafy branches and noticed a flow of water in a small gurgling creek. Why not give it a shot? I scooped up a pan full of sediment. I swirled its contents. I discarded larger rounded pebbles and continued to swirl. With my hand lens I could see angular pyrite, sparkling quartz crystals, and black, flat, tabular minerals, but no gold. I tried another pan with almost the same results except for one rounded rice-size, shiny grain. In the bright sunlight, its yellow luster made me gasp. I picked it out of my pan with my fingernails and put it in my palm. My heart beat faster. Gold! I shouted to Leon. He heard me and came running, splashing through shallow water, falling down twice to reach me soaking wet. After he saw it and agreed it was gold he shouted, "We made it! We've got gold!"

Frenzied, we both started panning. I didn't know how long we were there, but when sunlight dimmed we had to stop. We had three rice-sized grains and one slightly larger we called a nugget of gold. Where to put them was the question. Back at our campsite Leon mixed them with a small vial of aspirin to hold our riches. Boni asked if we had had any luck panning that day. I just said it looked promising and that we were planning to spend a few more days.

At sunup we quickly got dressed and started down to the river. We wanted to start panning before Boni got up. We both realized that we needed to locate the mother lode to get rich.

"We might find it in a dike or a sill," I said.

"Or a pegmatite."

"Or a pot as in pot of gold."

"Right."

We waded upstream looking for a dry beach to put on our boots. We started climbing the steep slope. Slippery scree made poor footing, so we had to grab hold of bushes to pull ourselves up. Bushes thinned, and larger chunks of scree covered an area below a granitic outcrop.

"Look, over to your left; looks like a narrow path," Leon said.

We followed it and found scattered pieces of rusty broken shovels, rusty dented buckets, and other metal scrap. "We are really stupid, Rolly. We left our geology picks and machetes in Medellin."

"I know. Remember, this whole trip was your harebrain idea."

We started to make a study of the rock. We found weathered granite pockets where we dug out several decayed mineral grooves with our fingers. We found pea-sized, dull red crystals. "Aren't these garnets?" Leon asked.

"I think you're right."

"This gotta be a pegmatite."

"Yes, could be loaded with gold."

"And looking at those rusted-out tools, we're not the only ones who figured that out."

With no mining tools, we sat down on rough rock to figure out what to do. Neither of us had any ideas. We had a view of the mountains around us and the river below. The only sounds were chirping birds, a breeze ruffling tree leaves, and our own muted voices. Then suddenly a sharp CRACK echoed off the mountains around us, and then silence.

"What the hell was that?" we both asked.

Then another sharp CRACK, and small sharp chips of granite fell on us from higher up on the outcrop.

"Rolly, those are goddamn gunshots."

"You're right . . . we've got to get the hell out of here!"

"Let's go." When Leon stood up, another shot rang out; he grabbed his left arm. Blood streamed down his arm and dripped from his fingertips. He fell on the ground. I was so stunned I couldn't understand what had just happened. Leon sprawled out on the ground in front of me, terror on his face. He groaned, "I'm shot, Rolly . . . everything is black . . . Rolly, I can't see . . . do something. We've got to get out of here and fast, or they'll kill us." He looked dead. I slapped him across his cheeks. He opened his eyes. "Help me, Rolly."

I slipped off my belt, wrapped it above his wound in his arm and tightened it up. That stopped the flow of blood. I grabbed his other arm and pulled him. He gained enough strength to get on his knees.

"Ho man, I'm dizzy."

"We'll slide down to the river on our butts; it's faster than hiking down." He couldn't stand up, anyway. We hit the water in seconds. "Better keep your wound in the air. It might get infected if it gets wet." My fright made my voice high-pitched and unrecognizable. *I need to control myself and not panic.* "Just lay back and let the current carry us."

"My arm hurts like hell, Rolly," he growled.

We traveled faster with our backs pointed downstream, but we couldn't see obstacles in the river until after we hit them. I paddled with my arms. Leon had a problem keeping up with me, so he held onto my boot. We stayed together until we neared our camp. I could see a trail of red dissipate in the water behind us. I hoped his arm wouldn't get infected.

Leon stumbled as he tried to walk up the trail, his face white as a sheet. Boni spotted us from his cabin and ran down to help. We both grabbed Leon and dragged him to our camp.

"You heard gunshots. You must have gotten too close to someone's claim," Boni said.

"Do you know who it is?"

"Maybe." Then he saw Leon's arm drenched in blood. "Oh my god. We've got to get you two out of here," he warned.

I needed to get Leon to a doctor right away, and Boni agreed to help. Time was crucial as Leon's condition was growing worse. We were lucky it was downhill to the way-station and to the road to Rondino. Boni brought one of his horses from his corral. We both hoisted Leon onto the horse, and Boni led us down the trail to the road. It was a rough ride; Leon bounced precariously from side to side as he hung on to the horse's neck. I had to make sure he didn't slide off and become an amorphous blob on the wet, muddy ground. At least he didn't pass out and wasn't moaning.

About an hour after we left Boni's place, the horse stumbled on smooth, round stones on the path, and Leon couldn't hold on. He slid from the horse into mud, cursing, "Goddamnit, Rolly, you let me fall." I rushed back to him, afraid he had broken something. "Leon, what happened?"

He didn't speak, just lay there on the muddy, rocky trail. Finally he whispered, "You let me fall. I'm hurt . . . Rolly, I can't get back on that goddamned horse. Maybe I'll try walking the rest of the way." His face was as bloodless as a dead man's.

"Leon, you can't even walk one step and you know it. How about if I tie this rope around you and let the horse drag you?"

Leon broke out laughing. "And you'd do it, too, you heartless son of a bitch." *Glad to hear he hasn't lost his sense of humor.*

Leon was too weak to stand by himself. Boni and I put our shoulders under each of his arms and raised him to his feet and leaned him against the horse. Boni and I put our fingers together to form a sling and Leon stood on our hands. As we straightened up, he grabbed the horse's mane, and we hoisted him up onto the horse again. He swung his other leg over to straddle the horse's back.

We reached the road by afternoon, exhausted. Traffic amounted to an occasional car, truck, and one bus that barreled toward us fast. Boni jumped into the middle of the road in front of the speeding bus. The driver jammed on his brakes and swerved onto a shoulder before he could stop. The bus was full of *campesinos*. Some men tumbled out of their seats to see what had happened. Immediately they wanted to help carry Leon. Boni and I and four men lifted him.

People on one bench crunched together to make room for Leon. One wizened old lady could see he was dehydrated and rummaged through her carpetbag for a jug of water. He eagerly drank what was left in her bottle. Then another lady came forward and poured a cup of some kind of tepid herbal tea that she carried in a special earthen jug. Many passengers lauded her reputation for being their local witch doctor. After Leon drank several cups, he said he felt better, but I doubted it. He drifted between drowsy and unconscious, his face a pale-green mask.

I shook hands with Boni and attempted to give him fifty *pesos* for renting us his horse. He held his palms up and uttered. "No." I then realized Boni wasn't so money hungry after all. I told him we would come back after Leon regained his health. He smiled and mounted his horse and then waved good-bye and rode away.

As we jostled along on the bus over a rough road toward Rondino, the riders chattered good-naturedly, asking me questions I either didn't understand or didn't know the answer. I kept my eye on Leon to make sure he didn't fall off the bench seat. He rested his semiconscious head on a *señora's* lap when she scrunched up next to him. She patted his head to console him in a low voice, which was drowned out by the bus's tumultuous threat of falling apart. Twenty minutes later we slowly clattered into Rondino. Ahead was a white stucco building with a large sign that said HOSPITAL. We pulled up in front, and several men helped me unload and carry Leon into the building. A white-clad giant single-handedly lifted Leon to put him in a wheelchair and wheeled him through a private door. I thanked the men from the bus and offered to give them money, but they all refused it.

I waited in the reception room while Dr. Gonsalvo examined Leon. At six o'clock in the evening, Leon was wheeled out on a hospital gurney, his face sickly pale, his voice a whisper. "I want to go home" was all he uttered.

"We'll get a taxi and go to Medellin," I told him.

Leon countered with "No, I said home. I want to go home. I want to get away from here."

"He should stay here for a few days," said the young doctor who followed Leon out of the examining room. "He has a dangerously high fever." He spoke perfect English.

"Did his wound get infected?" I asked.

"Yes, but I'll know better after a complete examination. The bullet went through his arm without doing much damage but lodged somewhere in his gut. That could be where he is infected." I didn't want to leave Leon alone in the hospital, but I explained to him the company might be trying to contact us. I told him I would come back as soon as possible and take him to Medellin.

Chapter 21

AGUAS NEGRAS

I answered after the third ring. "*Bueno.*"

"What's this '*bueno*' shit, Farrington? You trying to sound Colombian?" John Turner's voice was loud and irritating.

"That's how everybody here answers the phone, John."

"I tried calling you for the past two days. Where the hell have you been? Your maid didn't know shit."

Do I tell him about panning for gold and Leon in the hospital? Think, man. Think of something and fast.

"Geez, John, I never can understand her either. She talks so fast I can't get one word she's saying, so I ignore her."

"Forget all that bullshit and just listen to me. I'm glad I got you first before I talk to anyone else. I know you want to make as much money as you can in the shortest time possible, so I've got a great offer for you. How'd you like to earn double what you're making now?"

Baffled, I had to give it the once-over twice before answering. "John, what the hell are you talking about? Sure, I want to make as much money as I can. What's the hitch?"

"No hitch— it's a one-man opportunity. You work this well alone, have sample catchers bag your drilled-up rock cuttings so you can study them during daylight on your regular eight-hour tour. It's a lot of responsibility, but I know you're just the man to handle it."

He waited impatiently for my answer. I let him wait. Why did he think I was the right man? These other Brocton geologists have more experience than I do. Is he trying to screw me because I showed him up in that Chanara well?

Before I could reply, he continued, "I offer you the chance because those other guys would jump at this opportunity. I convinced Vickers you're right for the job. You're always on the ball and don't make mistakes."

"When do I go to work?"

"Right away."

"How about if I have breakfast first?"

"No, hell no! There's a flight out in about an hour from Medellin to Aguas Negras. You can eat one of their stale sandwiches on the airplane. Remember, double pay. Oh, and also remember to buy yourself a round-trip ticket, and don't take too much cash. I don't want you blowing those extra bucks on a bunch of easy women. I hear there are a lot of good-looking ones hanging around Aguas Negras." He hung up before I could ask him any questions.

All single seats on the DC-3 were taken, so I settled for a double and left the aisle seat vacant, hoping I was the last to board so I wouldn't have to struggle making worthless conversation in my poor Spanish with someone I'll never see again.

I was mistaken. A loud voice thundered even before anyone showed up in the doorway. A heavyset guy with a round, jovial, white-washed face, eyes bulging behind thick, steel-rimmed glasses, stopped to chat in loud Spanish with the stewardess. There were a couple of empty seats left, so I thought I wouldn't be bothered with him sitting next to me. I was mistaken again.

"*Hola, yo soy* Howard Jenkins," he said with a noticeable *gringo* accent. He continued in English as he squeezed in the seat next to me. "Almost missed this plane. Been talking business with a couple of big shots from Bogotá. They're amateurs when it comes to business. I had them eating right out of my hand. Sold them a machine we've been trying to unload for years at a price three times what it was worth."

He talked fast and then took a deep breath before continuing. "I'm a businessman with an expertise in international relations dealing with coffee, gold mining, oil, you name it. I travel all over this goddamn world representing most companies you've heard of and a lot I bet you've never heard of. I can smell a deal, that is, a good deal—(he punched up *good*)—when I see one."

He didn't seem to notice the mixed logic in his deals. He went on and on until we were almost ready to land at Porto Brano before continuing on to Aguas Negras.

"You haven't said much."

"Haven't had a chance to, *How-weird*." He didn't seem to catch how I pronounced his name.

"Maybe you don't understand Spanish."

"I understand a lot of Spanish."

"Oh well, as I said, I'm Howard Jenkins."

"Yea, I got that. I'm Bert Bankowski, with the International Fair Trade Association. From what you've been boasting, I think you'll be hearing from us real soon after I turn in my report about sales personnel cheating companies right here in Colombia and the rest of South America."

Howard's face changed to a scared mask. "Well now, look." His eyes bulged; his face reddened. "I might have been exaggerating. That machine I referred to is really top-notch as far as I'm concerned, and if folks here don't like it, we'll take it right back and refund their money. I've heard of your association, and you're doing a great job." He wasn't going to admit he didn't know what the hell I was talking about and neither did I . . . But it didn't matter. He was getting off at Porto Brano. But as he buffeted toward the open door, I called out, "Look forward to seeing you real soon, How-weird."

The rest of the flight seemed to be noisier because window frames started rattling and the overhead racks began to creak. I tried a conversation with our sweet, young stewardess, who spoke only Spanish. She knew about this place with the unpleasant name *Aguas Negras*—Black Water. "I've never liked to spend time on the ground there. Just be careful there," she warned.

I didn't expect to hear that. She didn't specify what to be careful about. I spent the rest of the flight preoccupied with what kind of a hellhole awaited me. I tried to watch the land below, but thick clouds made it impossible. Suddenly we made a 360-degree turn and dropped altitude. My stomach jumped to my chest. Still in thick clouds. Another 360-degree turn and down again. Now at a lower altitude I could see beyond scattered lacy clouds, a brown river snaking through solid green vegetation and ahead a gray straight gash that I assumed to be a landing strip cut in dense jungle. On my right were a few scrubby thatch or terracotta roofed huts, weathered black from age or neglect. This must be Aguas Negras—not a welcoming sight.

Landing on a muddy runway was, as I expected, rough. Stepping down from the plane, I sank in soft, ankle-deep muck that sucked at my boots with each step. Pesky insects buzzed around my ears. In the burning sun I sloshed over to a little concrete building that must have something to do with the airport but no one was inside. Behind the building I found a parked tired looking, dusty, dented jeep. It was after ten o'clock. The driver, a young man with straight black hair streaming over his brow and covering his eyes, dozed in the cab.

"*Muchacho! Despiértese. Tiene que llevarme al pozo de petróleo, por favor.*" I ordered him to wake up and take me to the oil well. But then I thought what if he wasn't from the well? What if he didn't know what I was talking about?

"*Hay, señor, perdón lo siento mucho.*" The fearful youth jumped out of his seat, grabbed my suitcase from my hand and stowed it in back of the jeep. What was he so nervous about? I wasn't going to get him fired or anything. I introduced myself and asked his name—Paco.

Once we were out of the airport and on a rough, unpaved road, I asked, "*¿Estámos cerca del poso?*" If we were near the well site?

"*Sí,*" he muttered. I had expected a longer answer.

I thought we were heading toward town and an easy ride to the well, but instead we turned into a forest. The canopies of tall trees spread dark shadows over the rutted road and gave no escape from the heat. My shirt stuck to my sweating back. Rainwater that filled deep gouges in the road splashed up onto the windshield, blurring visibility but not causing us to slow down. After a tortuous rough ride, we approached a small group of adobe buildings in the middle of an imprisoning riotous jungle. A charcoal brazier searing juicy meats, *empanadas*, and sausages, gave off an aroma too good to resist. After all, I hadn't had breakfast that morning.

"Paco, stop here! I need to eat something." Breakfast was greasy meat skewered on long sticks served on top of a banana leaf. I didn't forget Paco. He was shy but ate ravenously. Maybe this was his only meal so far this day. After guzzling a warm beer, we hit the road again. I chatted with my young driver, and he seemed to lose his shyness. I even screwed up enough Spanish to make him laugh.

The road steepened. Soon a vertical wall of rock soared straight up on our left. On our right a sheer cliff that plunged down a swift river below. Our jeep began to struggle as it climbed higher. Paco shifted down to his lowest gear, but the engine couldn't climb anymore. It died.

"What do we do now?" My anxiety made my voice gain an octave.

"*Esperamos.*" Which I knew meant we wait. "As soon as the motor cools, we'll continue." As we waited, I peered to my right over a sea of green jungle stretching like an endless Garden of Eden with no sign of civilization. After the engine cooled, we attacked the steep trail again. The long mountain drive was taking too long. What if it gets dark? Paco could drive us right off this road. Then what?

"Are we almost there, Paco?" I couldn't hide the panic in my voice. Was this insufferable heat and humidity cooking my brain?

"No," he mumbled.

After another hour or so, we had to stop again. Silence prevailed except for the ticking from the overheated engine as it cooled and an occasional argument coming from a squadron of flapping parrots.

Ahead, a new sound, a barely detectable distant purr. It wasn't a far-off airplane, more like *barrrroom* from diesel motors, then at a distance a sudden *whoosh*, like airbrakes on a drilling rig. Our engine cooled, and we continued. Noises grew louder on our approach to a level stretch of road. Then we veered off onto a long, graveled side road. Dust almost hid what could have passed for a sight mimicking a skeletal neck stretching skyward—an unearthed dinosaur—bony neck of steel girders and crisscrossing braces. It sat on top of a drilling platform with faded letters ANTON OIL WELL DRILLING COMPANY in the middle of 100 square yards of bulldozed level brown earth. A crew of sweating roughnecks lowered joints of steel casing into the well. They usually drill down about 500 feet, run casing, and then cement it in place. Their last step would be to hook up blowout preventers before drilling ahead. My work would begin after that.

Roughnecks waved and yelled at us, pointing to a trailer with Brocton Geological Services painted on its side. Paco dropped into low gear again, challenging slippery ruts around stacks of drilling machinery, and passed long racks of drill pipe to my trailer. I jumped out, unlocked the trailer door, and swung it open. I found a thick layer of fine tan dust covering everything. I had to hurry and locate my crew of Colombians to help me clean up my equipment so I'd be ready to start work.

A hundred yards away, I spotted a large clapboard structure like the one in Chimera with screened windows to keep out mosquitoes and every other bloodsucking bug. It must be the kitchen and eating area. On the other side of that structure a cabin perched on 18-inch-high blocks hooked up with wires along with a water pipe. It looked like someone had comfort. Next there were several pup tents on the ground. Inside one pup tent a man slick with sweat was stretched out on a cot in his underwear snoring. I knew better than to wake him. I assumed one of those tents would be mine. Back at the large tent, I met a short, smiling Colombian wearing a white apron stretched around his ample girth.

"My name is Eduardo; can I help you, *señor*? How about some late lunch?" he offered in lyrical Spanish. His grin was a welcoming sight.

"Thank you. My name is Rolly Farrington. I'd like some iced tea, and I'll take you up on your late lunch."

"*Sí, señor, con mucho gusto.*" He turned to a tiny, barefoot *mestiza niña* in a gray faded dress and said, "Tulia, *un vaso de té con hielo para el señor.*" The sallow-cheeked child with sad eyes was so nervous my tea almost splashed out of the glass.

"*Muchas gracias, señorita.*" I gulped down the sweet, icy drink and requested another. Sensing an injustice, I asked, "How old is she? Isn't she too young to be working here? Shouldn't she be in school?"

"She is twelve or thirteen and has to work because her father is dead and her mother makes very little selling *arepas,*" he answered with an avuncular arm around Tulia's thin shoulders.

"What about other children in the family? Can't they work to help out?"

"No, they are all too young to work."

I was concerned for her welfare, so I asked, "How much does she earn here?"

"The camp manager pays her five *pesos* a day. She comes to work on the bus with the daylight crew at eight in the morning and goes home at four when that crew's tour is over."

"Five measly *pesos*? Isn't that against all child labor laws?"

"There are no laws here, *señor* Rolly. I give her five more *pesos* from my own pocket. She's a good little worker. She helps with washing laundry, and when she's finished she helps me."

"You know, Eduardo, if poor people didn't have kids or, at least, not so many, their lives could be a lot better. The young die from curable diseases as it is."

Judging from Eduardo's deadpan expression, he didn't agree with me, or maybe he thought I was nuts. It didn't matter. I handed poor little Tulia a 10-*peso* bill, and as I did so, the drop that landed on my hand didn't come from a rain cloud. She raised her sparkling eyes, wiped them dry, and said, *"Mi Dios le bendiga, señor." My God blesses you.*

I was not sentimental, but that little girl could have made a liar out of me. That's why I avoided emotional situations like this. I just walked away. After our first meeting, I entrusted Eduardo with money to give to her every day but only after I had left the table.

I shuffled down the road to the rig. Three laborers squatted next to my trailer; their silvery hardhats glistened in the burning sun. They must be the sample catchers that were promised me. *Oh God, now I have to teach them what their job entails: setting up my equipment on the rig, a line for water, connecting up electricity, running sensor cables, a drain hose, and anything else I can think of. Then I have to teach them how to collect and preserve sample cuttings for me to study. With my limited Spanish, it's going to be difficult.*

One man, their leader, introduced everyone. *"Yo soy Julio, los otros son Miguel, y Jaime."* We all uttered *"mucho gusto"* and shook hands. *"Señor, es usted el geólogo de* Brocton?"

"Sí, señor, I'm the geologist. I'm going to teach you your job, that is, if you can understand my Spanish."

"Sí, señor, we are your sample catchers," he announced proudly.

133

I prepared to teach them how to collect samples for me. But first we had to make all the connections. I opened the trailer door to enter, but Miguel beat me inside. He grabbed a rolled-up hose and pulled it out; next Juan dragged out a coiled-up electrical wire, and Julio wrestled out a narrow-gauge hose for methane gas detection. All three went to work hooking up lines to the rig. Afterwards they connected the drain from the sink to the wastewater sump pit. From my grin they must have understood I was surprised and happy with their work. Next I picked up a spatula and pan for scraping drilled-up rock cuttings from the shale shaker. Juan took them from me and beckoned me to follow them to the shale shaker to demonstrate how they collect cuttings. I couldn't believe it. They had already been trained.

"How'd you men learn all these hookups?" I asked.

"From Mister Connors," they said proudly, all at once.

"Connors? I've never heard of him. Who's he work for?"

"Brocton."

"Brocton?" *How come Turner didn't tell me about him?* "Where is he now?" I asked.

"Dead."

Dead? That stunned me. "What happened? Was he sick . . . or did he have an accident?"

"He was killed," Juan said.

"Who killed him?"

"Bandidos."

"Bandits? Where?"

"*Aquí, cerca.*" Julio said it was near here. I envisioned bloodied, machete-wielding madmen chopping heads randomly throughout the camp. I remembered John Turner told me about *corte franela*—cutthroat.

I wanted to know more about Connor but was interrupted by a grizzled old-timer with a red wrinkled face who had just driven up.

"You in charge here?" he asked me. His voice sounded like a crowing chicken. He was short and thin. I watched his Adam's apple bob up and down like a yo-yo as he spoke or swallowed.

"Yes, my name is Rolly Farrington, and I'm the geologist for Brocton Geological Services."

The stranger gave out a hoot. "Well, I'll be. That there's quite a title—Rolly Fare-thee-well. But I'm not so fancy; I'm just Roy Tyler, drilling pusher for Anton Oil Drilling Company. How's that for an easy name to remember?"

"I'm impressed," I answered, not knowing if he's a funny "good old boy" or a sarcastic son of a bitch.

He broke out in a big grin and added, "You're impressed . . . that's a good one. I can see we're going to get along just fine. You all set up now?"

"Yes, we're ready to drill ahead."

"Good. Will your partners arrive today or tomorrow?"

"No, I'm working this well alone, that is, along with my three sample catchers over there by the rig."

Roy pondered for a moment and then said, "That's mighty unusual." He took a deep breath like he wanted to ask more questions. "Well, by ginger, you'd better get a good night's sleep 'cause after we finish running casing and cementing it in place, we'll hook up our two blowout preventers, test them, and then we'll drill ahead. It's going to drill fast. Could be down a thousand feet or more by tomorrow evening."

I could handle fast drilling. I still felt maybe John Turner screwed me by giving me this one geologist job nobody else would take. And why was John Turner giving out jobs instead of Brad Vickers, the boss here in South America, whom I never met or talked to?

I entered my trailer-lab and with my back still to the open door, a voice behind me boomed, "Who the hell are you!"

I wheeled around puzzled. "I'm Rolly Farrington—"

"What the hell are you doing in this goddamn trailer?"

"I'm the geologist from Brocton."

"The hell you are. Where's that weasel Turner?" His face was red with rage. "He's supposed to take Connor's place." He was about six feet tall and middle aged, had thick shoulders, black hair trimmed with gray around his ears, and a serious mean squint.

"He's the man who sent me here to work this well. If you don't like it, take it up with him," I answered, ready to have it out with him.

He let it drop. "I'm Randall Marsh, chief engineer for Mueller Oil Company. Get set up—they'll be drilling ahead real soon. You'd better be ready." It sounded like a threat.

"It's all taken care of. I'm ready to go work as soon as they've hook up their blowout preventers."

"You worked wells alone before? By that I mean with no other geologists?"

"No, this will be my first."

"It works out with one geologist and three sample catchers. Connor was able to keep up with the drilling and did a good job."

"What's this I've hear about Connor getting killed?"

"Before he got killed, I'm saying. . . . Well, mighty fine. I got to go to Aguas Negras. We don't have any communication here. We need a goddamn shortwave radio." He climbed back into his jeep, but before he left, he called out: "Do I need to tell you that this is a no-dope-hole? Nobody allowed information or in your trailer except Mueller engineers." He didn't wait to answer my question but sped out without a comment about Connor.

This is going to be one well I'll never forget.

Early next morning I felt someone shaking my shoulder to wake me. The night before, I had fallen asleep on a padded bench inside my trailer. The rig's double diesels revved, making the rig shiver and clang as they raised a section of drill pipe up into the derrick. From my window I could see men up on the rig floor ready to drill. I darted outside to see if one of my sample catchers was ready to collect rock cuttings while they drilled. Julio was at the shale shaker ready to scrape up my first sample.

They started to drill. The first cuttings sample was cement from cementing casing. After that, cuttings were gray-white fine-grained sandstone. I had forgotten about breakfast while I worked steadily testing and studying rock samples until Miguel interrupted me. He had a plate full of scrambled eggs, bacon, toast, and a cup of strong black coffee. I gulped down breakfast and got back to work.

I was studying a sandstone fragment in my microscope, naming the different minerals, along with size and angularity, when I felt the trailer rock back and forth like a rowboat in rough seas. I looked up and saw a solid man as tall as I was but too thick to fit easily through the narrow doorway. His hard hat was pushed back on his head, exposing a round, jovial face that lit up with a smile. His dusty denims, faded-blue cotton work shirt with its long sleeves rolled up, and steel-toed boots marked him as one of the American tool pushers. Then I remembered that no one is allowed in the trailer. What should I do? Screw it. Randall Marsh's jeep was nowhere to be found; he must still be in is in Aguas Negras.

"Didn't mean to disturb you," the big man said with a voice like a foghorn. "My name's Tiny Warner, daylight tour pusher. Hope I'm not interrupting your work."

"No, not at all. I'm Rolly Farrington." We shook hands.

"So you're working this well alone just like that other geologist, Connors?"

"That's right."

"Anybody going to spell you so you'll have some time off?"

"Nope. I'm on my own."

"Didja know you could be out here for two or three months or more?"

"Well, no. Nobody told me anything except I'd be working alone."

Work was steady until late afternoon, interrupted only by a quick lunch brought to me by one of my sample catchers. I had just finished studying a sample when another man stuck his head through my open door.

"You got a minute?" he asked, dressed like Tiny so I figured another tool pusher.

"Sure, come on in. I'm Rolly Farrington."

"My name's Matt Clarkson." We shook hands. "I'm the rig mechanic. Got mechanical problems, let me know, I'll fix 'em for you." He looked to be in his fifties, medium height, and well-built but with a beer drinker's gut hanging over his belt.

"Pleased to meet you, Matt. I'll let you know if I need help."

"I suppose I'll see you later at dinner, if your work is done by then. I'll save you a place."

"Is it crowded at dinnertime?"

"Naw, just an expression is all."

Dust rose from the road. Randall Marsh came speeding over the bumps and parked in front of his cabin and entered. I went back to work studying cuttings. Soon a dusty sedan pulled up to Marsh's place. A girl got out—high heels and a body-hugging slinky green dress—followed by Jesse Logan. *Jesse Logan*? What was Jesse Logan doing here with a girl dressed like a *puta*? My guess: Logan's a pimp. The cabin door opened again, and Logan scurried out, jumped in his car, and fled away, leaving the charmer with Marsh. I wouldn't have guessed Randall Marsh was the type to go after young stuff. He must be human after all.

The sun was painting a red smear above the western Andes when the drilling slowed. I reminded my sample catchers to save cuttings in liter jars with depths labeled for me to work the next morning. I washed up in the outside bamboo and palm frond makeshift bathroom facility and then made my way through knee high green brush and hoped not to encounter any snakes on my way over to our dining room.

"Evening, boys," I said to a small group seated at the dining table.

They made room for me. I nodded to Tiny Warner and Matt Clarkson. There were two men I hadn't met, so Tiny did the introductions. "This here's Terrance Kirby, afternoon pusher, but before that a Marine who fought in Korea." He looked to be solidly built, age about thirty, round face with an easy smile and short, brown, thinning hair. "And this other fella's Wilbur Freshner, evening pusher." He looked to be an older, serious type, probably in his forties.

"Why did you ever agree to work this well solo?" Wilbur asked me.

"Could be that I'm just stupid."

They chuckled and agreed that's probably true.

Before I could take my first bite of steak, the screen door burst open and Roy Tyler stomped in. His face was a scowling mask of rage, and he smelled of alcohol.

"Fare-thee-well, your goddamned sample catchers are making a muddy fucking swamp out by my shale shaker." He squinted squarely in my face and continued. "You'd better get your ass out there and get it cleaned up, you hear?"

Startled by his seething anger, I couldn't reckon what had happened to his "good-ole-boy" spirit. Tired as I was, I held my temper. I was in no condition to argue with this skinny old man anyway. I got up, eased past Roy, and trudged down to the rig, hoping not to find a big cleanup job waiting for me. Rig lights illuminated everything around the shale shaker. My three sample boys shoveled dry dirt over what was left of that "muddy fucking swamp." I thoroughly inspected the area and was satisfied there was no crisis.

"A roughneck from the rig watered down everything on the rig floor and soaked this area," Miguel explained. "It was his fault. There wasn't anything to get so mad about."

Back at the dining table, I sat down across from Tyler. "There's no swamp, and if there was, it was your roughneck's fault." He didn't say another word to me or anybody else. Now I knew what to expect from Roy Tyler.

After dinner, before anyone left, Tiny Warner asked me, "How do you feel about having a friendly little game of poker with us boys?"

I couldn't think of why not, so I nodded yes. "Sounds good to me. Haven't played poker for a while, but I'm willing to join you."

"Don't worry, it's really just sort of penny ante—just a few *pesos* is all," Terrance added.

Our game started after the dishes were taken away. Five of us sat around the dining table. I noticed they all drew out a few *peso* notes and some small change. I pulled out my wallet and shuffled through my large bills looking for smaller denominations.

"Holy shit! Look at this man's bankroll. We said a friendly little game. Why are you bringing heavy cash with you to Aguas Negras? Don't you know this is *bandido* country?"

I had forgotten about bandits. "Well, I heard about that today from my sample catchers; nobody in Medellin told me about bandits," I answered.

No one said a word, just stared with blank expressions.

I wanted to know about Randall Marsh, so I asked, "I'm wondering how to deal with the chief engineer, Marsh. Is he rough with everybody or just me?"

"Not you personally, just geologists in general." That comment from Tiny was followed by chuckles.

"I thought that might be it. Now I'll know what to expect from him." We played until midnight. Nobody won or lost much. I broke even. These guys weren't out to scalp the new geologist in camp.

Sunlight pierced through an open flap in my sleeping tent and through the mosquito netting around my cot. I rolled away from those burning rays, not anxious to go to work. but I knew I'd better get up before Randall Marsh came around. I pushed my sheet away, swung my feet over the side and onto rough wooden flooring. It was already too hot to sleep anyway. After I pulled on my wrinkled suntans, shirt, and dusty boots, I staggered half asleep to an open-air wash basin next to an open-air shower. I splashed sun-heated water over my unshaven cheeks—I'll shave later. A row of two-by-twelve planks led to a palm-frond-covered shithouse, open-air like the sink and shower. On my hike over to the mess tent, ominous dark clouds threatening rain rolled in like a murky tide.

Conversation was light at breakfast. Only an occasional, muffled voices—from jaws grinding away on sausages, potatoes, eggs, and beans—broke the silence when someone asked for salt or butter or ketchup. No cheerful talk, no smiles, no good-natured laughter. What's wrong? What happened to that friendly chatter? I attributed their malaise to an impending storm brewing.

I hiked down the slope to my trailer-lab grousing to myself about not being warned about the threat of bandidos. Dust rose on the road ahead. I could barely make out that Logan was driving. He passed by me and gave me the high sign as he spattered me with a face full of dust and grit. He stopped at Randall Marsh's cabin and picked up Marsh's *puta,* girlfriend. No surprise. Back in my trailer, I picked up last night's samples and started working them and soon forgot about Logan.

Thunder exploded echoing in every direction followed by heavy rain pounding my roof. Tiny Warner opened my door and stuck his head in and asked, "Do you mind if we come in out of this goddamn gulley washer?"

"Come on in before you drown." He sat on the side bench while I finished working cuttings samples. I welcomed his easy conversation. He started working the oilfield at sixteen—big enough to pass for eighteen—as a roughneck in Oklahoma, Texas, and Rocky Mountains. He worked so many states he never settled down long enough to feel he belonged anywhere. I asked him how he liked Colombia, and he said about as much as any place.

After the rain let up Tiny said, "After dinner I'm heading to a little village up the road and have a few beers with one of them bargirls. If you're interested, you're welcome to join me. What do you say?"

That sounded good to me. I could use a change of scenery. Tiny drove the company's pickup truck with me hanging on. "I think I hit every pothole in this poor excuse for a road."

"Well, almost every. I think you missed one back there a ways."

"Don't worry; I'll get it on our way back."

After twenty minutes, we drove into a poorly lit shantytown with a handful of cantinas belting out raucous music. Memories of Chanara. We pulled up to a tall wrought-iron gate with a low-powered light bulb dangling from a nearby tree. A dark figure dashed from the shadows over to our truck. "*Señor* Tiny, *tanto gusto, been venido.*"

"You been here before?"

"Once or twice maybe," Tiny grinned.

Tiny led the way. It was a never painted dark wood construction that fit the description of a barn more than *cantina*. Multicolored Christmas lights brightened the atmosphere. A group of gaudily dressed and painted bargirls rushed Tiny, throwing their arms around him and pawing his shoulders and chest.

"Only two times, huh?"

"Well, I never count how many times I've been here."

Everyone finally settled down. One girl took my arm and led me to a table to share with Tiny and his charmers. Tiny ordered a round of rum and cokes for everyone at our table. It didn't take long for me to realize that these were the same brazen type I had met up with at other drilling locations. We danced to a few tunes from a scratchy phonograph record. I wasn't willing to do anything except dance here. Colors from the Christmas lights glistened on our sweating brows. After I had enough of what passed for dancing, we went back to our table. I ordered two more rum and cokes, which probably meant mostly coke for my girl. Conversation was limited to my limited Spanish. My girl—I had forgotten her name—massaged my drinking arm, so I switched my glass to my left, making it awkward but manageable. When Tiny returned from his girl's bedroom, he was ready to leave. I thanked my girl and told her I would be back soon, maybe in a coon's age. She looked sad and wanted to know why I wasn't going to her room with her. I didn't want to say I wasn't interested in her, so I paid what they normally charged for bedding a girl. She looked at me with contempt in her eyes and hissed, "*Gracias, marico. ¿You prefer little boys?*"

"You insulted her because you made her feel she wasn't good enough for you, so she called you a queer."

We were back at the well before midnight. I thanked Tiny for the outing and appreciated getting away from camp for a few hours.

Several days later the mechanic Matt Clarkson stopped by my trailer and asked, "You got any plans for this evening, Rolly?"

"No, not really." How could I have plans out here in no man's land? "Maybe a little game of poker if others are going to play. Why, what's on your mind, Matt?"

"I seen you and Tiny leave a few days ago to go up to that little town to visit the ladies. I haven't been away from here since we started drilling, and I'd kind of like to get away and have a little change of scenery. What do you say about us taking a drive up the road tonight?"

"Well, sure, Matt. That sounds like a good idea. I'll be ready to go after I shower and have dinner."

Matt drove the pickup truck to the same settlement but to a different *cantina*. Same loud honking music; same tables filled with horny men and avarice women. We took a table and waited for our drinks. From a dark table across the dance floor, voices grew louder. Someone was pissed off; I didn't know why. Our drinks came, and our lady friends immediately became affectionate. On the other side of the room, I glimpsed a man stand up and make a motion I couldn't see very well. The next thing I heard was a whoosh and glass shattering against the wall right over my head. He shouted something about *gringos*. Before we could hear another word, Matt and I dropped a handful of *pesos* on our table and darted out to our pickup and headed home.

Randall Marsh had a habit of stopping by my trailer every day to hector me about why or how I did my job a certain way. He wanted to see what kind of rock we had drilled up and if there were signs of oil or gas. He always left disappointed.

On the fifty-sixth day of drilling I strolled down to my trailer ready to study cuttings drilled the night before. Suddenly I heard a blaring alarm coming from my trailer, shrieking like a disaster warning. I broke out in a dead run, swung open the door, and saw the depth gauge registering a sharp increase in depth. I darted outside and up a rig ladder.

"Pull your bit off bottom a few feet but keep your mud pump on," I shouted to the Colombian driller. When I was back down the ladder, taking two steps at a time, I scrambled to my trailer and recorded a drilling rate increase from 30 feet per hour to 120 feet. I calculated it would take thirty-seven minutes for the drilling break cuttings to reach the surface. I turned off the alarm and sat back and waited.

Randall Marsh burst through the door. "What's going on?"

"We just had a drilling break."

"Well, what the fuck are you doing sitting on your ass? Why aren't you evaluating what's in that drilling break?"

"I've got about thirty minutes before the contents come to surface. It's only partway up now. Don't worry, I'll handle it."

He gave me that threatening stare I saw often when he didn't believe me.

Minutes ticked by, with him hulking in the doorway. Finally I watched the gas analyzer needle rise from 0 to 10 to 20 and then jump to 100 units. I sprang out of my seat, bumping the surprised chief engineer, grabbed my sample pan and spatula, and ran to the shale shaker to scrape up cuttings. Back in the trailer again I put a scoop of sample into a Petri dish and slid it under my UV lamp. While I kneaded the mushy sample, dark golden-brown flecks spread out on the surface in an irregular pattern, much like what you would see in a mud puddle along a road. Only a few pops surfaced and spread out in a green and blue rainbow of live oil, but those golden, irregular flecks meant dead oil.

Immediately, Marsh peered over my shoulder. "What've we got?"

"Take a look," I said, thinking he would see so much dead oil that he would realize that we didn't have an oil well.

"That's a goddamn pretty sight. You did all right. I'm going to town and call for a tester."

"Hold on, Randall. That's dead oil you're looking at. You test that and all you're going to get is a puff of methane."

"Bullshit! You don't know what the fuck you're talking about, you lame-ass rock hound."

He barreled out of the trailer in a flash on his way to town. I was stunned. What if I had goofed? Undoubtedly he had seen more oil than I had.

Along came Roy Tyler, eyes popping out of his head. "Well, boy, what do you think? We got an oil well or what?" he asked, his Adam's apple bouncing up and down like a ping-pong ball.

"Well, Roy, it's like this: You roll the dice and wait to see what comes up," I said, much to his dissatisfaction. "I've got more work to attend to, Roy. Thanks for stopping by."

Three days later a flatbed truck pulled up to the well with the tester strapped on back. It took all day and into the night to pull miles of pipe out of the well before hooking up the tester and then running it back to bottom before starting to test. The chief engineer wanted to test during daylight the next day. The sting of uncertainty plagued me. I wanted to hurry up and test. I wanted to see if I had made the right call. Did we drill into dead oil, or was it live oil? Get it over with.

Randall gave the driller the okay to start the test. He waited impatiently for oil to surge to the surface. The part of the pipe sticking out at the top of the well began to vibrate. We could hear a low rumble. The pipe began to form ice crystals as compressed humid air was allowed to escape, absorbing heat from the surrounding pipe. Then it grew quiet. Rumbling stopped, dead silence. Everyone stood around with questioning faces.

"What happened?" the chief engineer blurted out.

"Nothing . . . no oil, no gas," I said under my breath.

"Pull that tester out of there. I want to see if it's got oil in it."

When the tester was out of the hole, we found just a few cups of oil in it—dead oil. I wanted to shout, "I told you so!" but sucked in my emotions and kept my mouth shut.

"Okay, get that test equipment out of here and put on a new bit. We're drilling ahead," Randall Marsh shouted as he jumped in his car and hightailed it toward Aguas Negras.

One morning about three weeks later I arrived at my trailer ready to go to work. I checked the drill rate chart for the past twelve hours. Drilling had been fast up until an hour ago, when it showed no penetration at all. That, I figured, couldn't be right. Was my equipment broken? Suddenly the rig began to shake, screeching and pounding, drill pipe bouncing and torquing up.

"Oh my God! They've lost a cone off their bit," I said aloud to no one. I darted out the door and up a ladder to the rig floor. The noise from the bouncing and grinding was so loud the Colombian driller couldn't hear me. I yelled louder and motioned for him to pull up on his pipe, get the bit off bottom but keep the pump going. From the back of the rig, Tiny came running up and asked what was going on. I told him I wasn't sure, but I believed a cone broke off the bit; we'd know after I checking my sample now. If pieces of the bit broke off, that would be our problem. We might have to fish pieces of the bit out of the hole or grind them up with a mill.

I had my sample catcher bring me cuttings that were coming up. Under the microscope I could see gray-white shards of rock. Tiny was right next to me. "Whadda ya got?" I let him peer into the microscope. "That sandstone looks mighty sharp. What the hell you smiling about, Rolly?"

"I'm smiling, Tiny, because that isn't sandstone, although you might call it suitcase-sand, because we're done drilling here."

"What do you mean?"

"Those are granite chips."

"Granite? Can we drill through it?"

"Not in a million years. That's solid granite. We'd never find the bottom of it. Here is something else you can see."

"What's that?" Tiny's face was a confused mask.

"Slivers of steel from your bit." I could hardly contain my joy, but I managed a weak, "I think we have just finished our drilling on this location. We are in granite, and there's no drilling through granite; there's no oil in granite."

After Tiny understood what I was talking about, he ordered his driller to keep circulating mud to make sure the hole was in good shape and then to wait for orders from chief engineer Marsh."

At dinner Eduardo quietly placed plates of fried steak, onions, potatoes, and corn in front of the five of us at the dining table. Those present were Matt the mechanic; Tiny Warner, daylight tour pusher; Terrance Kirby, afternoon pusher; and Wilbur Freshner, the evening pusher. Roy Tyler the bull pusher was the last to sit down. We ate fast as usual. Conversation centered around drilling into granite.

Roy Tyler said he had never heard of such a thing. He cleared his scrawny throat and spoke: "How about a friendly game of poker this evening, boys?"

Everyone agreed to play right after dessert. A single light bulb cast a dull glow over our well-worn cards. We anted up, the cards were dealt, and then bidding started. No excitement when anyone won a hand; the pots never amounted to more than ten or twenty *pesos*. This went on until around eleven o'clock. No one seemed to be ahead or behind much. The last hand was quiet, all of us studying our cards and planning how to win that last pot, the biggest of the night.

"Hey, did you guys hear horses?" I asked.

"I didn't hear nothing," Roy answered. "Are you going to call or fold, Fare-thee-well?"

From nowhere a loud deep voice broke our concentration. "¡*Manos arriba!*"

"What? Who said that? What's it mean?" Roy squealed.

"'Hands up' was the command, Roy!" Tiny roared with uncontrolled fury.

"Tiny, a bandit raid is no time to get pissed off and get ourselves killed," Matt warned.

A group of ragged men kicked open the screen door and crowded in; their hats were pulled low and thick mustaches obscured their faces. Tiny, his back to the door, twisted around to look at our intruders. He then turned back for us to see a grin light up his face.

"There's Grumpy and them other dwarfs, so can Snow White be far behind?" he howled.

"Take another look, Tiny. These five ain't no dwarfs," Wilbur cautioned.

"Looks like they could cause some serious pain. Let's not fuck with 'em, Tiny. Raise your goddamn hands," Terrance added.

We stood and put our hands up except Tiny. Roy looked ready to piss his pants when he uttered, "Tiny, you'd better stand and raise your hands or get us all shot."

When I first met Tiny, he was such a good-natured guy, but now he was a bomb with a lit fuse. Guns were pointed at us and machetes held ready for a swift chop. I was certain they were capable of using them—killing Connors pictured in my mind.

Tiny finally stood with his hands up but continued with his levity. "I think they want to take up a collection to buy bullets for them guns." Only Tiny chuckled. In a low voice he added, "If you've got any knives, try to drop them in the mud without them seeing you. If you can, that is. They'll want to search our pockets."

"*Afuera, gringos.*" They motioned us outside. As we shuffled our way out, I sidled up to Tiny to warn him: "Don't do anything stupid and get us all killed. It's not worth it."

All he replied was "No shit."

A dull light bulb mounted on a pole outside made everyone's face a waxy gray. They lined us up single file with our backs to the wall. Suddenly a blue-white flash pierced the night sky, followed by an ear-splitting rumble of thunder. Rain began to beat down on us. The ground became a swamp. Tiny was last to follow orders. His bearing let those ragtag thugs know they didn't scare him. Our brave leader, Roy Tyler, seemed unaware that his pants exposed a dark stain emanating below his belt and down both pant legs. We stood quietly while our pockets were searched.

"Go ahead, you assholes, take our money and then get the fuck out of here," Tiny growled. Even if they didn't understand English, they got Tiny's message because the grizzled leader stepped forward, looked up into Tiny's eyes, and growled, "*¡Hijo'e puta!*"—*son of a whore*. That was too much for Tiny. He took one long step forward knocking the bandit chief back into the arms of his comrades as he raised his rifle and pulled the trigger. The explosion momentarily deadened our hearing and froze everyone, including the bandits. Horses snorted and screamed. Tiny gripped his chest, his eyes wide with surprise, as if he couldn't believe he was actually shot. As he slumped, he groaned, "Ah shit." At that moment, muddy chaos erupted. Matt charged two bandits holding the leader and knocked them down in the mud. I grabbed the rifle barrel and twisted it out of the surprised shooter's hands. I pulled the trigger. Nothing happened. No more bullets. High on adrenaline I rushed toward another man, who raised his gun, and I kicked him in the groin. He dropped into the mud, his hands gripping his pain. Terrance struggled with a guy wielding a machete, who missed his target, allowing Terrance to land two good punches. The assailant dropped his machete and fell face first in the mud. He got up, put his hand to his bloody nose, and scuttled away in the downpour.

At that point Roy began to scream insanely. One of the bandits stepped forward and smashed Roy's face with the butt of his rifle, crunching bone and making Roy's face a gory mask. Roy fell unconscious in a splash next to Tiny.

The bandit leader bound forward, shrieking at his men: "*¡Matenlos, maten todos!*"—*Kill them, kill all of them*! Another man, his finger on the trigger, raised to fire his rifle, as I leaped forward, knocking the barrel to one side just as the he pulled the trigger. The bullet went wide, striking the leader. He fell into a muddy pool. The other bandits rushed up, not to fight but to carry the wounded chief back through the quagmire to their horses. His voice rang out: "We'll be back to kill every one of you *malditos gringos!*" They fled as the rain stopped, aiding their escape.

It became strangely quiet as I continued I bent over, my hands gripping my knees trying to catch my breath. I tried to talk; my voice came out a weak whisper. I had to wait for my adrenaline to wear off. Finally I could stand. My hands were still shaking, my mind was blank. Everything happened so fast I must have reacted instinctively. I couldn't remember until Terrance—sitting hunched over on a piece of drilling equiptment, also visibly shaken—asked me, "Where'd you learn to kick like that, Rolly?"

My mind cleared; I answered, "My uncle taught me that. He said I might need it in a street fight sometime."

"I'd say he was right."

I heard someone gagging and saw Matt's ghostly white face. He stumbled a few steps and then threw up on the ground but mostly on his boots. That didn't help my queasy stomach. "You okay, Matt?" I asked.

"Yea, I'll be okay. Where's Wilbur?"

"I'm over here stretched out on the pickup seat." He sat up and said, "Now, how do we handle our biggest problem?" The morning clouds lifted making way for another hot and humid day.

Chapter 22

ADIÓS AGUAS NEGRAS

We slopped through mud over to where Tiny and Roy sprawled in pools of muddy water. Tiny's voice was weak but his mind clear. His voice a congested wheeze, "Bring me a bottle of whisky. I got a terrible thirst."

"There's no whisky, Tiny. What we got to do is hurry you and Roy to a hospital, and fast," Wilbur said. Matt trudged through mud over to Roy and searched for a pulse in his neck and wrists. "Roy hasn't moved since he fell on the ground."

"Those bastards killed Roy."

Sprawled on his back, Tiny oozed blood from a wound somewhere in his chest or gut. He tried to speak again, but no words came out.

"He's in shock," Matt said; the others agreed.

Terrance splashed his way through the mud over to Roy's tent, hauled his mattress outside, and placed it in the back of the pickup truck. Then we lifted Roy and placed his body on the mattress. That was no problem. He was easy to lift. We knew we would have a problem with Tiny. We placed Tiny's mattress alongside Roy, and then we tried to lift him. There was nothing to grip. He kept slipping out of our hands. We took his mattress out of the pickup, placed it in the mud, and then rolled him onto it. Now we were able to grab a handful of mattress and lifted his moaning body onto the pickup truck next to Roy. We agreed Roy was dead. There was nothing we could about that but with Tiny; it was hard to say if he was alive or dead.

"We've got to get to a doctor quick," I panted, my voice unsteady and nausea in my throat. I tried to calm down and not show I was still in shock from the shootings and the exertion of lifting Tiny's body.

"What about the well? What should we do about that?" Terrance asked. "All those Colombian rig hands fled like scared jackrabbits." We agreed that Terrance, Wilbur, and Matt would stay and take care of the rig while I drove the pickup to Aguas Negras to find a hospital.

I started down the narrow, winding road to Aguas Negras miles away. I was sure that bouncing over the ruts was not helping Tiny survive. He was unconscious but still breathing, although weakly. I wanted to slow down, but knew I had to get Tiny to a doctor as soon as possible.

After hours of my not being sure we would ever get to Aguas Negras, a pale glow reddened a faded cloud bank in the eastern Andes, illuminating a dusky village that, to me, **resembled a war zone. We finally rumbled into town, where I found adobe and cement block hovels, some with walls but no roofs. It appeared that people living there had virtually given up battling against an infestation of weeds. Other hovels had slumped roofs resembling tired shoulders. No light shone from any building. It took only minutes to patrol a few streets to find no hospital or doctor's office. Bars and whorehouses were usually near large rivers, so I headed that way hoping a bar or whorehouse was still in business. No luck. I randomly stopped at one hovel and banged on the door. No answer. I banged harder and longer. A sleepy-eyed girl grasping a dim flashlight opened her door and focused the beam on my face. I apologized for waking her.**

She was pissed and fired a question at me. "What do you want? Can't you see we're closed?"

"Sorry, but I need to find a doctor right away, a matter of life or death. My friend's been shot and needs a doctor now." I could see on her shadowed face in the dim light that she had trouble understanding my Spanish and probably didn't trust me.

"Please, for the love of God, is there a doctor here in town?" I was growing impatient and bothered by a headache that began to throb.

She pointed up the gravel road I had just come down. She tried to tell me where a doctor lived—I imagined he was the doctor who checked all the whores for VD. She must have sensed that I didn't understand, so she climbed into my pickup next to me. Her thin

nightgown didn't hide much. With this heat and humidity, she wasn't overly dressed or uncomfortable.

Aguas Negras was beginning to show signs of life. The sun peeked and then gained intensity to promise a torrid, sweaty day. The girl's name was Faviola, and she told me to stop at the building with a high white wall and a door painted green. She climbed out and tugged on a bell cord by the door. We could hear faint jingling. As we waited for the door to open, I got a better look at Faviola. Her hair was brown and wavy, skin smooth and bronzed, eyes and eyebrows black. She had natural beauty; she didn't need makeup. She probably had never gone to a beauty parlor. Her fiery charm must have attracted men to her like a bear to honey. Without lingering my gaze on her, I noticed her nightgown was so sheer it was clear she wore nothing underneath. Well, in such tropical weather I wasn't surprised. Her small firm breasts pointed straight at me, and I began to forget my headache. I realized I had become more interested in sex than in Tiny's life.

No one came to the door. She yanked insistently several times until it finally opened partway. A short, thin boy nervously peered through the opening. "Eucebio, we must see Dr. Morosco right away. A man is dying."

Dr. Morosco was young and probably serving his required tenure as the only doctor in this Godforsaken shanty town. He must have dressed hurriedly because he was barefoot and his shirt was only half buttoned. He rushed out to the pickup bed to check Tiny's vital signs. He shook his head and then confessed, "I don't know if I can save him. He has bled a lot, too much. I have only limited facilities for treating bullet wounds."

With help from his wife, three servants, Faviola, and me, Dr. Morosco carried Tiny, still on his mattress, into the house and into a white-walled examining room. Then we carried Roy inside. Dr. Morosco confirmed he was dead. He checked Tiny's pulse and blood pressure. He took a blood sample from each of us except Faviola. None matched Tiny's blood type. I explained what had happened during the bandit raid. He stared into my face and said, "*Señor* Rolly, are you all right? You don't look so good."

"I'm okay, only a headache and an angry stomach."

"I would like to give you something for your headache and stomach, but my medicine supply is very limited. I shall have Eucebio take you to our local *farmacia*. Be sure to swallow any medication with bottled water; I do not recommend drinking our local water."

Faviola stood solemnly by the front door, looking anxious to go home. She accepted my offer to drive her there. She didn't say a word except to give me directions. When we pulled up to her front door, I thanked her for helping and said, "I don't know what I would have done without your assistance." She said nothing, then opened the pickup door and got out. "Wait, please," I said and handed her twenty *pesos*. She took the money in one swift motion. "I would like to see you again," I added.

She smiled broadly, almost leering, looking me in the eyes, and then vanished behind her front door. *Before I leave this pueblo, I'm going to pay her a visit.*

I drove back to Dr. Morosco's clinic, where I told his wife that I needed to call two companies in Barranquilla. "Could I use your telephone? My company will pay for the calls."

"That wouldn't be necessary, but our telephone has been down for over a week now, but you can find the *farmacia* on *Carrera diez con la Calle cuatro.*

Hey lady, I'm new here, I wanted to say but said instead, "I'm sorry, *Señora*, could you direct me? I don't know *carreras* from *calles*."

"Oh, *señor, perdoneme.* Eucebio can take you there and then to the telephone company office. They're easy to find on foot."

We walked several partially paved streets to a *farmacia*. Its outside walls were coated with broken and chipped tapia—cow shit and mud—exposing supporting bone-like bamboo stalks. Although primitive, the drugstore was well stocked with medicines labeled "Made in USA." They had pills for my headache and stomachache, and I remembered Dr. Morosco had told me to take them with bottled water. Across from the *farmacia*, I spotted an open-air *cantina* called Bar Nuevo, a tattered brick structure that had been painted white at one time. I sat outside at a rickety table under a ragged beach umbrella. Neither the wobbly table I leaned on nor the fragile chair that threatened to break were significant problems compared to the pain I felt in my stomach and head. The rolling and twisting in my stomach was like some scaly serpent eating my gut.

A somnolent bar girl, painted up and ready to party, announced, "*A la orden, señor.*" Then she yawned. I ordered a bottle of soda water— room temperature, because I figured ice was made from dirty river water. Many *gringos,* foolishly, swear that rum mixed with water kills all the bacteria in the water. I ignored the smudges on the glass that accompanied my bottled water. Better to drink straight from the bottle and hope the top is clean. I swallowed two pills from the *farmacia* and chugalugged my carbonated water.

As I waited for relief, I stared at some ancient outside wiring tacked on to buildings. Strands of wire—either bare or covered with black flaking insulation—ran under the eaves and occasionally fastened to chipped ceramic insulators or on a nail or wooden peg.

From Bar Nuevo we plodded along to a white stucco building that featured a modest sign over a wide open doorway labeled "*Compañía de Teléfono y Telegrafía*" in fading black letters. A line of people waited to be attended in the cramped office. Across the street another *cantina* beckoned me to sit and have a drink. I asked Eucebio to please save my place in line. This time I ordered, "*Una cervesa al clima, por favor.*" I doubted they had ice-cold beer, anyway. I waved the filmy glass away. With my sweat-stained shirttail, I wiped the mouth of the bottle. Well, it was my sweat, so it didn't matter. The beer tasted good anyway.

Halfway through my second bottle, Eucebio motioned with his cupped hand from across the road at the telephone company office. Momentarily, I was baffled by his hand signal—he waved like the way we wave good-bye.

"¡*Señor* Rolly, ¡*venga*! ¡*Teléfono Barranquilla*!" Eucebio yelled.

I ran across to the telephone office, a stuffy place with ceiling fans creating a desert wind. It didn't seem like a telephone company office—there were no telephones on the dark, weathered counter behind which a studious young man stood flagpole straight, clip-on bow tie slightly askew, and a pencil behind each ear adding to his business-like aura. His brow glistened with sweat, as did mine. A badge with his name, Enrique Corona, was pinned to his chest.

"One moment, please, while we complete the connection to Barranquilla," Enrique informed me in polite Spanish.

"Okay, but where is the telephone? I don't see it anywhere."

"Oh, one behind door number two in that booth over there." Pointing, he gave me a questioning look, like he was either struggling with my accented Spanish or he'd guessed perhaps I wasn't used to using a telephone, a public telephone. "Good, we've made the connection. You may go into booth number two now."

"*Gracias, muy amable,*" I triumphantly uttered, proud of my improving vocabulary.

"*A la orden*" was his reply with a slight questioning frown.

In the booth I heard a series of distant buzzes until finally a voice came on: "Brocton Geological Services." A warm and soothing voice, very sexy.

"Hmm, who am I speaking to?" I asked.

"To whom am I speaking?" Firm, but low. A purr like a kitten. "I'm telling you the correct English."

"Who taught you English, honey . . . Shakespeare?"

"Mister"—rrrs rolled along like a smooth running motor—"Sandwich."

"Don't you mean Mr. Sanderhitch?"

"It sounded like Sandwich to me. What do you want?"

She's getting testy; must want me to stop playing games.

"I need to talk to Brett Vickers."

"He's not here."

"How can I reach him?"

"I don't know. He didn't say."

"How about John—"

"I don't know where he is either."

"What kind of an outfit is this?" I didn't wait to let her answer. "Tell Brett Vickers we finished our well. We drilled into granite."

"Oh, is that good or bad?"

"Depends on your point of view. Bad for the oil company but good for me. Now I can get the hell out of here."

My next call: "Mueller Oil Company, Winslow here." A voice loud and forceful hit me like an explosion.

"Hello, Mr. Winslow. My name is Rolly Farrington, the geologist from Brocton . . . I have bad—"

"I know who you are . . . what do you want?"

"Bandits raided us this morning. Tiny's been shot in the chest and might not make it, and Roy's dead." I waited for Winslow to say something. He must have been stunned by the news.

"Goddamn, son-of-a-bitch! We'll fly right out there. Tell the boys at the rig to pull the bit up into the casing and wait for further orders."

"Oh, I almost forgot: We drilled into granite."

"Any oil? How deep into it did you drill?"

"No oil; drilling rigs can't penetrate granite. You just wear out good bits for nothing."

"Okay, what I want you to do is make one copy of your finished log, put it in my safe—it's unlocked now—then spin the dial so no one can open it. Understand?"

"Don't worry, I understand."

"After that, you are released. Just tell the crew I'll be there tomorrow to E-log the hole and then cement her up. *Adiós.*"

I needed to get a ticket out of there for the first flight either to Barranquilla or Medellin. Fortunately Enrique doubled as a ticket agent.

"There is only one flight tomorrow, and it's to Medellin," he told me. Who knew how many other jobs he had?

"Morning or afternoon?" I asked.

"Sunrise tomorrow morning."

Too early, but what choice did I have? I had to go back to the well, tear out my equipment and get my gear, finish my geological report— my log— and make a copy for me and put one in Winslow's safe. Then get back to Aguas Negras before dawn to catch that flight.

When I arrived back at the doctor's place to check on Tiny, two khaki-uniformed police officers were waiting for me. Good, now I can explain our fight with the bandits. Maybe the police know who those thugs were and can catch them.

Their eyes hid behind dark glasses, and wide-brimmed police hats shielded their faces. Both featured thick wiry mustaches. "We don't understand. We have no bandits here in Aguas Negras. People here are very peace-loving. Did you and that wounded man have a disagreement, a fight or something? What were you two doing here, anyway?"

"We are employed by Mueller Oil Company. The bandits came into our camp about midnight and after stealing our money, started a brawl, which resulted in shooting Tiny and killing Roy."

"I just told you, we don't have bandits here in Aguas Negras."

"Not here in town, but up in the mountain, *la selba.*"

"Tell me the truth." He squinted, put one hand on his pistol, and said, "Did you shoot these two men?"

"No, Officer." I almost started to shout but quickly controlled my temper. "Possibly my Spanish is hard for you to understand. I will simply say that Tiny was shot by unknown men and might die and this other man was smashed in the head and died."

They pulled away to discuss something privately. Then one spoke up. "Do not leave Aguas Negras until our chief returns. He will have questions for you to answer."

"When will he be back?"

"In a day or so." They climbed back into their jeep and sped away. Like hell I'll wait for their goddamn chief to return. I'll be out of here tomorrow morning, so screw 'em. They are probably in league with the bandits.

I followed Dr. Morosco to his hot and stuffy examining room to see Tiny. He lay stretched out on a cot sweating under a white bloodstained sheet. His closed eyes and sallow complexion gave all indications that he was dead. If it hadn't been for the occasional rise and fall of the sheet, I wouldn't have known he was breathing. No fans or air conditioning to allay the heat. When he heard my voice, he gazed over at me, smiled, and said, "Thanks for that rough fucking ride from the rig. Don't think you missed even one chuckhole."

I must have looked uneasy because he quickly added: "Only kidding, Rolly." He paused to catch his breath. "This old boy, Doc Morosco, said you saved my life."

"Bullshit. Purely a selfish act— if I hadn't driven you here, I would have had you on my conscience the rest of my life, and I couldn't handle that."

"No, *señor* Farrington, you got him here just in time. He almost bled to death."

"That's an exaggeration. He's too tough and ornery to let a little bullet stop him. The *jefe grande* from Barranquilla will be here tomorrow and take you to their hospital."

The doctor stepped forward and said, "Glad to see you put a smile on Tiny's face. Could I have a word with you in the other room, Mr. Farrington, for a moment?"

Dr. Morosco seemed uneasy when he said, "I'm not sure how long I can keep Tiny alive. He has lost so much blood. I've put in an order for more blood from the hospital down the river, but they didn't have any to spare. The bullet is still located somewhere in his body, and I need more blood before I can find it and take it out. At the moment I am more concerned with infection. If the bullet pierced his intestines, gangrene could set in. It would kill him." He searched my face before saying, "Are you all right, *Señor* Farrington? You don't look well."

"Oh, I'll be all right. It's been a rough night. Haven't had any sleep since yesterday morning."

I drove over to Faviola's house, knocked on her door, and waited, and almost gave up. Finally she opened and invited me in. Maybe she thought I wanted her now. That would have been nice, but I had to get back to the rig. "Faviola, I'm leaving Aguas Negras early tomorrow morning, and I would like to sleep here with you, if that's no problem."

She looked at me with her big dark eyes, a wisp of a smile on her full lips. "Of course it's no problem. Come any hour. I'll be waiting for you."

Back at the well, Wilbur, Terrance, and Matt had just finished pulling the bit up into the casing. I gave them Winslow's orders and then went up to the mess tent to eat. An aroma drifting from Eduardo's primitive kitchen made my mouth water.

"*Hola*, Eduardo. I smell something delicious. Can I have some? I'm starving. I know it's almost dinnertime."

"Claro que sí, señor Rolly." He answered. He placed a large bowl of beef stew in front of me. Tulia sauntered toward us from the laundry shed, her eyes downcast. She was tired after helping with the washing. "Tulia, come here. I want to say good-bye to you." She came into the dining area shy as ever. She stared up at me with eyes as big and trusting as a lamb's.

"I won't see you again, so I want to give you this before I leave." I handed her fifty *pesos.* Her eyes lit up and tears streamed down her cheeks. Gently, her thin arms reached up and hugged me. That was too much. Before I choked up, I stood and walked away, determined not to look back into those haunting eyes. That's the kind of a weak coward I am.

I found Matt Clarkson in the equipment shed and told him I needed someone to drive me back to Aguas Negras that night.

"No problem, Rolly. Go find Paco working over yonder on that tanker truck. He can drive you to town."

Paco didn't mind giving me a ride in the old tanker truck; he would enjoy my company. He told me he was going to *Aguas* Negras to pick up a load of diesel fuel. I was warned it would be a rough ride. That didn't bother me; I had ridden in worse heaps. But before leaving I had to pack up all my equipment in my trailer lab. I found Julio, Miguel, and Juan perched on scattered drilling equipment next to the trailer. We shook hands. Without being told they knew the drilling was over. Then we got busy tearing out my equipment from the rig and cramming it into the trailer. Before we said our good-byes I gave them each an extra twenty *pesos.* I wanted to give them more, but I was low on cash. Colombians are emotional, sentimental people; they each gave me a manly hug—*un fuerte abrazo.*

Riding back to Aguas Negras in a tanker truck at night was a rough ride and more dangerous around sudden curves and perilous cliffs. One front headlight jarred loose from our hitting countless ruts and bowling-ball-sized rocks along the way. As we rounded one curve, I swore a boulder the size of our truck jumped out at us. But it was only an illusion made by that loose headlight. After a few more bumps, the light gave up and dangled by its thin wires. Paco stopped, got out, and tried to put it back in place. Success, but only for a few more kidney-jarring miles. He finally gave up. We continued traveling way too fast with only one headlight and moonlight as our guide. At times I thought Paco had lost control and I was set to grab the wheel.

It was late when we arrived in dirt-poor sections of Aguas Negras. Paco had trouble locating Faviola's house. No problem; it was fresh in my memory. The light above Faviola's door barely lit the doorknob. *Do I knock first, or do I open and walk in?* Before I did either, the door swung open and a short thin boy welcomed me: *"Bien venido, señor."*

I picked up my small suitcase from the truck. "Don't take that bag in there with you," Paco warned.

"Afraid someone will steal it?"

"Sí, leave it with me and I'll pick you up in the morning and take you to the airport."

I thought it over. "Good idea. How much do I owe you?"

"Nada, hombre," he answered, grinning. "I was going to Aguas Negras anyway. I'll pick you up tomorrow early."

"Can you get here real early so I can check on Tiny's condition before I leave?"

"Sí, ¿cómo no?" he said as he pulled away, calling out, *"Buena suerte, amigo."*

The room was large enough for six tables, two for seating four people and four for seating two people. Two men sat huddled over their drinks and talked with two dolled-up prostitutes. The men's faces were obscured by darkness and thick beards. Could they be the *bandidos* from last night? When they looked up and saw me, they stopped romancing their girls to size me up.

I took a table for two and said, "I would like to see Faviola if she's not busy?"

"Con mucho gusto, señor. What would you like to drink?" I ordered a rum and coke and prepared to wait. I figured he would make Faviola wait so I would order a couple more rums to kill time.

It wasn't Faviola who swept in wearing a slinky dress that showed off her curves. This short, well-stacked seductress approached and leaned into my face. I could barely make out her face in the shadows. Her name, she said, was Antonia. She murmured the usual phrases, like she had waited all evening for someone like me. Well, as I got used to the darkness, she wasn't bad looking. Maybe the lack of bright lights favored her. I asked about Faviola. She acted like she didn't understand me and changed the subject—which seemed to be me. My rum and coke came as well as hers, which I hadn't ordered. I wasn't about to argue the point. The house had already figured that. I finished half my rum in one long gulp. The clinking of ice bothered me, but what the hell? Rum kills everything anyway. But I could see her face now—perhaps because of the rum—a lot of mascara and a lot of lipstick. Her sharp eyes searched into mine, causing my pulse rate to increase.

She snapped her fingers. "Vergilio, bring *el Señor* another rum and put some dance music on."

She took a few sips of her drink—I wondered if it contained any rum at all—and took my hand. We rose; she put her arm around me. We danced to a slow *bolero*. She was good. She knew exactly how to make dancing interesting. I was sure she was aware of the effect she aroused in me. Conversation was limited. We were not interested in anyone's history, but she did ask, "How long will you be in Aguas Negras?"

"I'm leaving tomorrow."

"You are leaving Aguas Negras tomorrow?"

"Yes, on the first flight."

"What a pity. Tonight, I'll just have to make you want to return."

With that we parted from the dance floor, left our unfinished drinks at the table, and swept into her bedroom. Well, it wasn't as romantic as I had hoped. I'm afraid I acted like an old married man: After one moment of bliss, I rolled over and fell asleep.

I woke before sunup with Tiny's condition on my mind. I wanted to see him before I left town or else I might never know if he survived. Antonia was sleeping soundly, breathing softly. I could use a cup of hot coffee, but no one was up, so I forgot about it. I'd get something at the airport. Then I remembered that the airport was just a brick square box too small to even be called an office. Forget the coffee. I laid fifty *pesos* on Antonia's night stand (five times more than her usual fee).

I waited outside for Paco, afraid he was going to pick me up late and I would either miss seeing Tiny or miss my plane. But he surprised me. I could hear that old tanker truck a mile away. When we arrived at the doctor's, I jerked the bell cord twice. Dr. Morosco answered. His face told the story. He explained that Tiny was exhausted and was having difficulty breathing, and then his heart stopped. He tried everything to start it again but failed. I was stunned, unable to comprehend. Did I misunderstand his Spanish? It couldn't be true. Tiny was too tough to let a bullet kill him.

He asked me if I wanted to see his body. I was undecided, didn't know what I should do. Would the sight of Tiny haunt me? "No, Dr. Morosco, better to remember Tiny like he was in life."

It was the sight of the empty airport, vacant of any life, that gave me a hopeless dawning. Something else to make me feel lousy. Paco must have sensed my dejection when he said, "*No se preocupe,* an airplane will come soon."

With my suitcase in hand, I asked, "When?"

"*No sé,* maybe soon, maybe *mañana.*"

"That's fucking great! Well, I'll just have to wait. No other choice. You don't need to hang around. I appreciate your help . . . how much do I owe you?"

"Nada."

"Bullshit!" I grabbed him and shook his hand and then stuffed fifty *pesos* into his shirt pocket. The thought came to mind that for a guy who wanted to go cheap and accumulate a fortune, I had spent a bundle in this town. I waited hours before I heard a welcome drone in the sky and saw the sun's glint off silvery wings.

I fell asleep on my flight to Medellin. Violent air currents over Medellin jostled me awake as we prepared to land. What a beautiful sight—Medellin. I felt like I was going home.

Chapter 23

AVALANCHE

From the airport I jumped in a cab and told the driver to get me downtown Medellin and hurry. He did until we hit downtown traffic. Cars were backed up for three blocks. I stepped out, viewed the problems and heard multi-keyed honking from vehicles going nowhere. I grabbed my suitcase, flipped the driver ten pesos, for a ride that should cost five, and struck out for home on foot. Being gone for so many weeks, I missed the hustle and bustle of humanity—Medellin, spectacular women and parties. I had to make up for lost time.

Florencia met me at the front door. Her broad smile stretched from ear to ear and her drooping spirals of graying tendrils bobbed up and down excitedly when she saw me. "*Señor* Rolly! Is that really you? They told us you were dead."

"They exaggerate, Florencia." Stretching my arms out and taking a deep breath, I exclaimed, "Oh, but it's good to be back. You don't know how much I missed your happy smile."

She laughed then picked up my suitcase. Thurston Thornton, grinning like a toothy clown, approached through the living room from the patio, "Welcome back from the grave."

"Who told you I was dead?"

"Jesse Logan. He said *bandidos* chopped off your head." He said laughing as if it made a good joke.

"And you believed him." I peered over his shoulder toward the patio. "Who's out there on the patio?"

"Don't you recognize your best friend?"

I couldn't see his face clearly just his back. "Are we going to play guessing games?"

The person turned towards us. His face lit up with a smile.

"Leon!" I shouted. "I can't believe it's you. You're so skinny, what happened?"

He grabbed me and gave me a big *abraso*. "Rolly, I was a dead man … almost. That hospital in Bogotá pulled me through. I have to give those doctors a lot of credit. They didn't give up on me."

"You're so skinny, are you even able to go back to work now."

"Rolly, I'm on my way home, back to California and never coming here again. I don't know how to tell you but I found out I really miss home; I miss California."

I couldn't get over the fact that Leon was leaving. "You used to tell me you wanted to live here the rest of your life. You loved it here, the women, the city, the climate; membership in good clubs, even the work and money was great."

He changed the subject. "Have you gotten over your fantasy with that gal Marisol?"

I didn't answer his question. I just said, "Oh, I haven't seen her for several months. You know I've been away working wells." *Marisol was on my mind. I wanted to call her and see if she still remembers me. Maybe she has stopped thinking about me and found someone else.* "I was planning to call her now that I'm back."

Thurston broke his silence, "You're wasting your time. She's not home." Then he chuckled, saying "tough luck, buddy." That's typical Thornton—obnoxious.

"Where is she? When will she be home?"

"Don't know. Left town yesterday."

"Come on Thornton, what gives? Where'd she go and for how long?"

"I told you, I don't know. Dora says she went to see her sister." He took a beer and returned outside in the sun.

I called her house to find out when she'd be back. The phone rang five times before a timid hushed voice answered. "This is the Durán residence. *La Señora* Durán is not available to come to the phone right now. I'm sorry."

Before the maid could hang up, I rushed, "One moment please! Has Marisol returned … May I speak with her?" I hoped she understood my confused Spanish.

"Sorry. I cannot say." And then she hung up,—as instructed, no doubt.

"Son of a bitch," I shouted into the dead connection. I didn't like what was happening.

"What's the matter?" Leon asked.

"I'm being stonewalled. Is the *Señora* Durán trying to shut me out; won't let me talk to Marisol?"

"Maybe my girlfriend knows what's going on over there." Thurston yelled as he stretched out on a *chez-lounge* sunning himself while reading a book. "All I know is she left yesterday to go up in the mountains to see her cousin and help while she has another baby or something."

"Why the hell didn't you tell me that when I first asked you? Well, how long will she be gone?"

"Don't know how long. All I know is she left." He put his book down. "It's high up in those blasted Andes somewhere."

"No crap? That's no place for a girl to be traveling," Leon put in.

"Oh, she left with Bruno. She'll be all right."

"Bruno?" I exploded. "That son of a bitch. He's a cock-hound who tries to screw every girl he can get his hands on … it is common knowledge. He's got lots of money and thinks he's God's gift to girls." I calmed a bit, "Why the hell does he have Marisol's cousin living so far away and in such a bad ass area?"

"That I couldn't tell you. I know he's got cattle and some mines up there and has to keep an eye on the miners or they'll steal him blind."

"Listen Rolly, that girl's got you obsessed. What happened to not getting tangled in a love affair? If you don't look out you're going to screw up your whole life," Leon warned.

I didn't sleep that night thinking about what I'd heard about Bruno. Next morning, I came down for breakfast. Thurston was just finishing. "Hey, Thurston, do me a favor and call your girl friend Dora and ask if she knows when Marisol's coming back to Medellin."

"I just got off the phone with her. She heard over the radio a storm caused landslides in the mountains where they were headed; forced a lot of vehicles over the cliff. A few dead and several injured."

"No shit?" That was a jolt. "What kind of vehicle does Bruno drive?" I asked.

"Dora told me they went by bus."

"By bus? … That's crazy! Bad roads, bad weather, bad people, Jesus Christ, anything can happen— washouts, breakdowns, anything." Wild thoughts spun in my mind. "Thurston, I'm going to find out if Marisol is okay or if something has happened to her."

Leon, on his way down stairs shouted, "Bullshit, man. Don't get so involved. It's a family matter, not yours. Let them handle it." But I had made up my mind.

Next morning before daybreak, Thurston was up. He had a poncho, a small backpack, some energy bars, a jackknife, and a flashlight.

"What's all this stuff, Thurston?"

"You can't tell what problems you're going to run into. That crap is for just in case."

He amazed me. Maybe he can be a nice guy after all.

The sun wasn't up when he dropped me at the Medellin bus terminal. I recognized those weak flood lights that cast a ghostly flush over a motley crowd ready to mount busses. Wildly painted buses about to burst with a crush of country folk filling rows of hard wooden benches lined across splinter floors. I checked out my bus—caged chickens clucking and crowing, a pig snorting, and rope tied cardboard boxes piled on top of the bus. Riding on the roof again, looked better than being squeezed together below.

I sprawled on top of stuffed boxes and gunny sacks for another long journey into the Andes. We jostled along, towing a cloud of brown dust rising from unpaved, washboard roads. Our driver geared down prepared to climb higher into steeper terrain. Although a beautiful panorama scrolled out around me, I couldn't take my mind off Marisol. I wanted to hurry, get to our destination to find her safe and unharmed. But we stopped every several kilometers to drop off people. They quickly disappeared into thick foliage along narrow trails. We rumbled up to rugged, palm frond roofed shanties. The smell of meat sizzling always made me hungry. I dug into juicy meat, chicken or pork. I finished with roasted corn on the cob dripping with butter and salt. I looked over slices of papaya, mangos, and other ripe tropical fruits attracting flies. I didn't know how bug-free they were, so didn't eat any. Bananas were safe so I bought three. I passed up bottled drinks stored in a stream because I wanted to hurry onward to arrive at our destination before dark.

We got to in Barrocete before sunset. This was the town closest to the landslide. I set out to show people Marisol's picture, hoping someone would recognize her. Maybe they would have information how I could locate her. That's all I had to go by. I realized I was wasting time searching for her in darkness. I needed a place for the night and continue my search in the morning. An uncooperative policeman in a khaki uniform hefting a machinegun stood on a street corner. He didn't know of any hotels in town and had never seen Marisol in my photo. I slung my back pack over my shoulder and made my way through a stream of milling *compesinos*.

A sign over a weathered door simply announced HOTEL JARAMIO. When the door closed behind me I mounted a dark, steep stairway. Each riser squeaked as I made my way upward. On the first floor, the main floor, a stout middle aged matron—with graying hair coiled in a bun and wearing a white apron over a black dress like so many widows— greeted me with a big smile. The rustic room had drab wood walls that new paint hadn't touched since the day it first opened centuries ago.

"*Buenas tardes*. May I help you?" she smiled cheerfully, perhaps hungry for tenants.

"Yes, do you have any vacancies?"

"Yes, we do and we are serving dinner in about an hour. You may use our one bathroom, which is down the hall and then have a nice hot meal: *arroz con pollo, sancocho, platano maduro*. Oh, if you have any laundry to wash, we can take care of that for you. We charge two *pesos*."

I lathered then let cool water pour over my head and slumping body to flush away the funk hanging over me. I donned clean clothes and put my dirty ones in my backpack. Down a dark hall I discovered the dining room. Six people sat at three different tables; their faces painted amber in the murky glow from one naked ceiling lamp. Two other tables were empty. Everyone looked to be old married couples. I went to each table, introduced myself, and showed them my picture of Marisol. None of them recognized her. When I sat down at my table, an older gentleman came over to me. "Might I have a moment to talk with you, sir?" By his clear Spanish I figured he was well educated.

"Certainly, please have a seat."

"Thank you; I'll only be a moment. Judging from your accent, you are not Colombian."

"That's right; I'm American.

"Your Spanish is very good." He paused, "Young man, I want to warn you about some very dangerous men in these parts. Outlaws look for innocent people to rob, often killing them first. They descended on victims involved in that horrible avalanche. It's been reported that searchers went through pulling out people dead and alive and stealing everything they could get their hands on. They killed anyone who put up a fight. I pray that your young friend was not one of those poor unfortunate victims. If you continue to search for her you must be careful. They might try to silence you if they have had anything to do with her."

"I'm aware of the danger. I've lived here for a long time now and I've faced tough situations including a bandit raid on an oil well."

"Well, I'm glad you're familiar with the lawlessness we have to put up with.

He stood but before he left my table he muttered, "And I wouldn't count on the police for help. They are as corrupt as any criminal around here. However, you might find it useful to contact *señor* Viscarra. He owns the typewriter and business machine store next to this hotel. He was here and witnessed the barbarism that took place when the avalanche occurred."

Another sleepless night and no appetite the next morning. I drank coffee and ate an *arepa* with *quecito* and left the hotel looking for *señor* Viscarra. He was a small thin man, clean shaven, and about fifty-years old. His hair could pass for raven's feathers, so black and shiny. He couldn't identify Marisol in the picture I showed him. His piercing eyes made me sense he might be a fountain of information. He told me during the storm a bus in the rockslide was pushed over the cliff. It happened just outside town. "At night the scene was chaos. Few people survived. I don't know how many. I saw six dead."

"Were any survivors women or girls?"

"Yes, the next morning I saw one among the dead men. They were still looking for more bodies." I couldn't hide my dread after hearing this.

"Where were the bodies taken?"

"Over to the clinic."

I hated asking but I knew I had to do it. "Can I go there and view them?"

"No, *señor.*"

"No? Why not?" That answer set a fire in my gut. *You can't stop me,* I almost blurted out. I had to stay calm or I'd screw up my chance of getting help or answers.

"That whole area was mass confusion and, I might add, looting was rampant. Some bodies were identified at the scene and were taken by family members; others were buried in unmarked graves in the cemetery."

Unmarked graves? *What if Marisol was one of them?* I had to know the truth. "But why bury them so soon?"

"The law. Dead bodies have to be disposed of right away before they start to stink."

"Was that one girl identified?"

"Not that I know of."

"Goddamit, maybe I could have identified her if they waited to bury them later.

Señor Viscarra reacted to my anger by trying to get rid of me, when he said, "Our priest has photographs of all the dead people. He can show them to you." I thanked him and asked how I could locate the priest? He took me outside and pointed to a tall steeple two streets away. I made my way to the church and went inside. A priest was conversing on the telephone. When he saw me he hung up and came over to me. "You were inquiring about those unfortunate people in the accident. Don't look so surprised, son. *Señor* Viscarra just called me and told me that you would be coming to see these photographs."

First, I showed him my picture of Marisol. That drew a blank. His pictures were black and white. I had hoped for colored prints. Diffused sunlight filtering through stained glass windows made it impossible to recognize facial details. He took me through another door to a brightly lit room with a large window. I gasped when I saw the first picture. "Do you recognize that person?" The face was grisly bruised but I was sure it was Bruno. The next photograph all I could see was a grotesque misshapen face with black dried blood or dirt and one half opened eye. It was impossible to identify any of the photos: men or women.

"*Padre*, I don't know what to do." I felt only anger and frustration. He suggested there was nothing I could do. I should take an afternoon bus and go home.

"I heard there is a clinic nearby. Could you tell me how to find it?"

"Yes, of course. This is a small town. You'll find it two blocks then around the corner."

Even though the smell of food cooking wafted in the air as I walked down the street, I had no desire to eat. The clinic, a sterile looking white concrete building, crowded with people, some injured needing medical attention others waiting to visit injured friends or family. I spoke to a young receptionist dressed in a pale-green nurses' uniform. Her short hair was covered by an unflattering little nurse's cap and her eyes were shyly downcast. I could picture her in a nun's habit.

I introduced myself and explained why I was there. I showed her Marisol's picture. "I'm hoping you might have seen her since that accident."

Her small hands shook slightly as she reached over and took Marisol's picture. She studied it for several moments, making me believe she recognized Marisol and then handed it back to me. "No, I'm sorry, I haven't seen her. … but I hope you find her safe."

She stared blankly at some papers on her desk. I wanted her to take another look. When she looked up, she must have seen grief in my eyes. "You could ask people here if anyone has seen her or if there's anything they can do to help you find your friend."

"Yes, of course," I said with little conviction. "That's very helpful, Rosalinda. I guess that's your name. It's written on your name tag. I've already talked to many people."

I was tired and out of ideas. I found myself in front of a little sidewalk *café* next to my hotel. I hadn't eaten yet and had no appetite. I requested coffee with an *arepa con quecito* while I tried to figure out what my next move should be. A little rag-a-muffin with a soulful face pointed at my feet. I couldn't say no to those bright eyes. As he cleaned and shined my boots, a bare foot girl in a faded torn dress circled tables around me showing people seated something in her hand. People shook their heads no. She approached my table. Her eyes down cast as she shyly held up a broach and asked me if I would buy

it. I was stunned. I opened my mouth but no words came out. I tried to grab it to get a better look, but she quickly jerked it away. "I just want to get a better look," I said. "Where did you get that?"

She wouldn't say, just rolled it around in her palm and started to walk away.

Chapter 24

KIDNAPPED

"*Sí, sí,* I'll buy it." I couldn't believe that it might be the broach I gave Marisol. "Just tell me where you got it."

She didn't speak just lowered her eyes and shook her head.

"I'll pay you whatever the price."

"A man gave it to me to sell it for him. He said he would pay me fifty *centavos* if I sold it for fifty *pesos*."

My hands began to shake as I dug into my pockets for money. Still shaking, I paid her the fifty *pesos* and said, "I'll give you ten *pesos* more if you promise not to tell anybody I'm the one who bought it. I watched her cross the street to another café. She gave the money to a swarthy man dressed in a disheveled faded gray- white suit. His back to me, hunched over, as he read a newspaper.

He looked one way then the other, but not at me. Finished eating, he stood up, taller and thicker than those around him. After he dropped a few coins on the table, he began to walk away. I had to follow him. Maybe I'll find where he got Marisol's broach. I shuttered to think what Marisol's fate might have been. Being taller than everybody around me, I knew he would spot me if I followed him closely. My young rag-a-muffin had finished my boots and waited for his *peso*. "What is your name *muchacho*?"

"Asdrubal, *señor*."

"Asdrubal, you can earn another *peso* if you'll do me a favor." He nodded his head eagerly. "I want you to follow that man in the white suit across the street but don't let him see you following him. Is that a deal?"

I lagged behind Asdrubal as he watched the white suit enter a telephone company office. Minutes dragged like hours until he finally moved along again. He left the main part of town as Asdrubal followed him up a rutted dirt road. Again Asdrubal stopped then came running back to me.

"*Señor,* the man turned left up a path and entered a shanty hidden behind trees and bushes. What should I do?"

"Wait for me here in the shadows of these trees. I may need you again."

Foot traffic was light and only one truck passed us. I hesitated before entering a short path that led to the cabin. What will I say if someone sees me and wants to know what I'm doing here? What if this has nothing to do with Marisol? But where did he get her broach?

I couldn't stop now. I was onto something. I could barely see a palm-thatched wooden hovel obscured by dappled sunlight through a mesh of tree limbs and over hanging vines. I hid in dark shadows. I heard someone's labored breathing behind me, it came from the road. I slipped behind a huge kapok tree. A man shuffled a foot passed me and banged on the door before entering.

When I was sure nobody was outside, I angled up to the side and peered through a hole in the wood-plank wall. Inside a shadowed bundle of cloth stirred. I couldn't see clearly what it was. I heard one man's deep voice ask another, "Oscar, did you make the call?"

"*Sí,* señor."

"Did they say they'll pay?"

It was difficult to understand their muffled Spanish, but I did recognize one word: *rescate*—ransom.

"They said they would try to pay."

"We are going to Medellin now. If they don't come through with the money you know what to do with her."

"Sí, señor."

Hearing the words 'know what to do with her' stung my senses. I had to act quickly. My heart pound faster. I had heard three different voices in the cabin. Feet shuffled across the wooden floor. Then two people bounded outside, brushing bushes out of their way as they trotted down to the road. There must be only one man left inside?

I could barely see the man in the white suit, gray now in the darkened room, approach the bundle on the floor. He muttered something. I couldn't understand. Hands sprang up at him, fists clenched battling. He brushed them away and laughed. The bundle emitted a mournful cry, a female voice. It had to be Marisol's. He was going to rape her.

I blindly dashed around to the front and burst through the flimsy door into darkness. A gray hulk spun around, light glinted off of something shiny—a knife. I charged blindly. His knife flew past my ear clanging against a wall; rebounding it swished across the floor somewhere. I stumbled forward. He had the advantage: his eyes could focus in darkness. He charged from across the room. I sprang toward that shapeless mass. I stumbled, the top of my head butted against his chin knocking him back. He was dazed momentarily. I could see him better now. As he rose up I tried kicking him in his groin, but missed my mark and hit him in his stomach. He fell again, the wind knocked out of him. He got to his feet, bent over panting. I quickly searched for that knife with my hands but couldn't find it. He started straightening up, Marisol screamed. I took my eyes off him to look for her. He landed a hard punch against my face, knocking me back. Another punch missed my face and grazed my shoulder. I aimed my punch for his jaw but hit his throat. He let out a gargled cry. I went for his throat with my hands, my fingers squeezed, as cartilage start to give way. I tried virtually to tear his throat out of his head. His fingernails clawed my hands. I wouldn't let go. His hands loosened and dropped. He slumped lifeless on the floor. From nowhere Marisol screamed; her voice hysterical. Exhausted she slumped sobbing. Her voice quivered, "Oh *God oh God what have I done?*"

I had to catch my breath before I could speak. She seemed lost. She needed me or was it God she needed? She began to tremble. I reached for her and held her. "It's over, Marisol, it's over. You're safe now. Be calm, I'm going to get you out of here." She shuddered mumbling incoherently. Her voice had weakened to a whisper. A deep, painful coughed erupted from her lungs. That scared me. With all she had been through, she must have caught cold or worse—pneumonia. "Rolando?" her voice weak. Then she started to weep. "What came over me? I had to kill him. I wanted," there she stopped to find the right word— "revenge!" Then she wept, "In my heart I was as low as any murderer."

"No Marisol, you did nothing thing wrong."

She calmed herself, shaking less, still scared, still dazed. "How did you ever find me?"

"Luck, but you'd call it divine guidance, I think. It's a long story, Marisol, but now we have to get away from this den of murders before the others return."

I helped her with each step. She was woozy; she almost stumbled, but then she said she was alright. Her denims were dusty, ragged. Elbows of her jacket were torn and shredded. I offered to carry her but she said she could manage. Her hiking boots fortunately were in good shape. She clung to me as we made our way. The overcast sky still too bright for her sensitive eyes; she squinted while we shuffled down toward the rutted road. It suddenly occurred to me—*where are we going? What are we going to do when we get to the road? To town but where in town? Marisol was in no condition to go to a hotel and be subjected to a swarm of questions. Could we make it to the clinic?* "Marisol, we have to decide on a safe place to go."

Asdrubal, behind us, quickly suggested, "My house; my mother will help you. She is very kind and gentle. She always helps people; we have plenty of room."

I didn't think much of that idea but Marisol responded anxiously, "Yes, I want to be in a home." Rough sharp rocks and pebbles slowed our progress; she could only take small steps.

We had to hurry before the kidnappers returned to kill us. There was no traffic until a beat-up Ford sedan rattled up behind us. I was startled when it stopped, afraid they might be part of a gang. An old *compesino* leaned over from his driver's seat to observe, "Looks to me like you need a ride before that young lady collapses. Are you heading for town? That's where I'm going."

Asdrubal sat in front with the old man. Marisol curled up next to me in back. She hadn't said a word since saying she wanted a home. Then suddenly she rose up and asked why it was taking so long? I tried to calm her. She coughed again and started to shake. *What did those bastards do to her?* In town, Asdrubal directed us to his home. We jostled along over cobblestones, past a wall of identical homes with identical doors and small shuttered windows; homes of working people. We stopped in front of one that looked different, a freshly painted bright green door and next to it a hanging basket of red flowers. Asdrubal jumped out, darted inside calling his mother.

She came to the door looking confused at two squalid strangers. Asdrubal quickly explained our situation to his mother. She brightened, curious about what she saw. She told us her name was Marta. I guessed she was in her early thirties, intelligent and commanding, tall, slender and stood her ground. We didn't get out of our seats until she sized us up then bade us enter her home. I carried Marisol into the house. Marta wore a simple housedress slightly faded but fresh and ironed. Her strong voice and proper language suggested she was well educated. Inside her home I respected: cleanliness, order, shiny slate floor wept clean, furniture, a bit worn but neat. Walls looked recently painted white with pictures of Jesus everywhere, and everything in its place.

When Marta noticed Marisol's slight wheeze she offered her tea or coffee and traditional buns made of cheese stuffed with preserved fruit. Marisol murmured how delicious they were. She, and Marta got along well: warm and friendly. Marta wanted to help her relax, to feel at home. She offered to let her freshen up, even offering her clothes to wear. Marisol smiled brightly for the first time, hugged Marta and accepted her offer. I could see she was regaining her spirit, a glimpse of her former self; the same Marisol as before.

I told Marta I wouldn't have been able to find Marisol without Asdrubal. I felt indebted to him and to her. I wanted to find a way to thank them.

She said there was no need for that. She and Asdrubal managed just fine. After her husband died two years ago, she was able to find work as an accountant, a field she had been trained for in school. She does well here at home bookkeeping for several businesses in town. But I noticed an ancient typewriter and a simple adding machine. She caught me frowning as I ran my fingers over the keys but said nothing to me.

Marisol was anxious to leave for Medellin so Asdrubal and I hurried to a taxi stand by the plaza. A group of taxi drivers lingered, either resting on their car hoods or on a shady bench; they smoked and chatted. I caught part of their conversation. "Pepe said the *chosa* was a mess after a brawl. The dead guy had been strangled."

"Yeah, I knew him— Marcelo, a thief, cut-throat, kidnapper, you name it."

"Police are looking for the guy who strangled him."

I was surprised they were looking for me so soon, so in a hurry I picked out one young driver, thin, hungry-looking, and wearing rumpled clothes. His name was Basilio. I told him, "I'll pay you 50 pesos to drive us to Medellin."

"100 pesos, *señor.*"

"70 pesos and I'll throw in lunch."

"80 pesos and you'll throw in lunch, dinner and gasoline."

"Deal."

A policeman sauntering toward us seemed to be in no hurry, "You *Americano?*" he asked in a gruff voice.

"What?" I acted startled.

In a louder voice in slurred Spanish, "Are you *Americano?*"

"No, *Aleman.* Why?" I made my Spanish sound German —I thought.

His eyes bore into mine then he turned and strolled off, occasionally looking back at me.

Asdrubal's voice was a whisper. "*Señor* Rolly, we better leave before he comes back with his chief."

Before we could move Asdrubal noticed, "Oh-oh, you'd better say something good in German because here he comes again with another police."

They looked me over, their hands at their sides clutching pistols. "You don't look German." Remembering movie dialogs with actors imitating German accents, I tried to sound like them and hoped it would work. Asdrubal, standing in back of them, rubbed his index finger and thumb together, the sign of producing money. He mouthed the word *veinte*: twenty.

I got it. I dug out two 20 pesos bills which were quickly snatched from my hand. The inquisitors grinned. "That will cost you another 50, my friend,"

I figured better to pay than argue. On our way back to Marta I asked Asdrubal if he knew how much a new typewriter and calculator would cost. He said his mother had been saving to by them. I peeled off 500-pesos and gave it to the boy. His eyes brightened as if he couldn't believe his eyes. "Please, Asdrubal, give the money to your mother after we leave."

Marta packed baked goodies called *buñuelos* in a clean cloth for Marisol. Putting her arms around Marta she tearfully thanked her. I wrote down their address and telephone number so I could contact them later. We waved good-bye and started our long journey to Medellin.

It was a tooth jarring ride, rocks pinging off fenders, rain made bad roads worse, traffic heavy in both directions, and avalanche warnings posted along all mountain roads. Marisol coughed again and shivered with cold in the back seat with me. I pulled her closer and put my arm around her. She snuggled up, her head on my shoulder. "Rolando, I was so scared, more than I had ever imagined possible. I swore I would find a way to kill myself if they attacked me. I prayed to God and then I made a promise to him."

"And what was that?"

She uttered, "That if I live through this horrible nightmare I will devote my life to the church. I would join the sisterhood."

Stunned at first but quickly realized that I shouldn't be surprised. In the short time I had known her I should have expected that answer. But for a brief happy moment I had found her and at the same time lost her. Would she really give herself to the church, to become a nun? I didn't want to accept that.

The out skirts of Medellin lay ahead. Marisol became alert enough to give directions to her home. When we pulled to the curb I helped her out. She rushed up through the shadowy arched entrance to her front door before I was out of the car. The front door swung open; followed by great shouts and cries of joy as she was swept in by her family. I heard the door slam shut. I hesitated for several moments waiting for the door to open welcoming me inside. It never happened. I turned and slowly returned to the cab.

"Where next, *señor?*" my driver asked.

I thought for moment, clearing my mind. I gave him directions to another part of town to an area of bright lights and lively activity. We stopped at a door painted red. I got out and knocked. A girl dressed for a party opened. "*Don Rolando*, about time you came to visit me again."

I paid off my driver, wished him a safe journey back home, and escorted Violeta back inside. I ordered a double whisky. With her attention she helped me distance myself from thoughts bounding in my troubled mind.

I woke early the next morning; slipped twenty *pesos* into Violeta's bra hanging on the doorknob and arrived back at our house in time for breakfast. Thurston sat at the dining room table eating breakfast.

"Brett Vickers called wanted to know where the hell you've been since Aguas Negras."

"Okay, I'll call him after I call Marisol."

"Don't bother; Dora told me Marisol has pneumonia and is in the hospital."

"Which hospital? I want to see her."

"You can't. It's in Bogotá." And then he said, "You better call Vickers now. He's plenty pissed."

Chapter 25

VENEZUELA

"Hello, I'd like to talk to Brett Vickers," I announced firmly but ready to receive a tongue-lashing.

"This *is* Brett Vickers," said a commanding voice. "Are you Rolly Farrington?" He didn't wait for an answer. "You were supposed to leave for Venezuela yesterday. Get your ass in gear. There is a flight from Bogotá leaving this afternoon. You'll meet Chip Malone at the airport in Bogotá."

What did he mean I'm being sent to Venezuela? I never agreed to work outside Colombia. I didn't like surprises. "How will I recognize this Chip?"

"Red hair, you can't miss him. Don't worry, he'll find you." In passing he mentioned, "You'll be making twice the salary you were making here in Colombia."

That sounded good to me. I made twice the salary at the Aguas Negras well and now twice the salary in Venezuela—not bad.

Leaving Colombia was best for me so I could forget about Marisol. I felt God had become a dividing wall between Marisol and me. It had ended. It was better to go away—out of sight, out of mind. I needed to work and earn money and keep busy so I wouldn't think about her. That was my goal when I came down here.

The redhead in Bogota's crowded air terminal couldn't see me, so I raised my arm and waved. Red hair, freckled face, five foot ten or eleven, chunky build and smiling broadly—I knew I would like him. Chip told me Walter was already in Caracas and the three of us would work together. Chip had worked in Venezuela off and on for several years and knew the lay of the land.

After landing in Venezuela, Maiquetia airport, we took a long cab ride on a modern four-lane superhighway into Caracas. This city reminded me of summer in Los Angeles: warm, clear skies; modern buildings; late-model cars on well-paved highways and streets. One difference: Around Los Angeles, the mountains were studded with upscale homes of rich people with beautiful views of the city as well as the Pacific Ocean. Around Caracas, the mountains were encrusted with shanty homes of poor people without electricity, water, or sewage.

Our taxi dropped us off at the entrance to Caracas's Hotel Tamanaco. I thought I must be in Beverly Hills or a sister city. Our hand luggage was eased from our grips by bellhops clad like generals in full-dress uniforms. They led us through automatically opening front doors to a sumptuous lobby, and there we saw Walter breaking his way through the crowd.

"Rolly, you ole-som-bitch. About time you showed up. What happened? Vickers was ready to fire you but couldn't find anyone else to send."

"Long story; I'll tell you all about it later. You know Chip, don't you?"

"Sure, Chip and I worked together before." They shook hands.

"How about this place? This is luxury." I continued to be amazed.

"This whole goddamn part of town is luxury. Come on, you're sharing a suite with me and Chip. After you guys get cleaned up we'll go out and have us a few drinks at a fabulous bar here. Don't have a heart attack when you see how much drinks cost. Just remember welcoming drinks are on our company."

"What about dinner?"

"Later, we don't eat early around here. After that we'll meet a few ladies. They're going to be a big surprise for you."

After dinner we trolled the wide avenues, bidding *"Buenas tardes, Linda"* to passing beauties. We found a bar with blaring Latino music that entertained a small crowd of men. As we took our first steps inside we were captured by beautiful, partially clad women who embraced us like long-lost lovers. I was picked to pay the round. The joke was on me because I had to pay for our drinks, including drinks for all the bar girls. I realized I had been conned by my not-so-talented con-artist friend, Walter. To make up for that trick, Walter and Chip picked up the tab for the rest of the evening.

When Walter asked me about Marisol, I realized I hadn't thought about her since I left Colombia.

Next morning we headed to the Maiquetia airport to fly to a well site in eastern Venezuela. Our flight was almost full. Walter and Chip sat on one side of the plane, and I sat on a single side seat across the aisle from them. The plane's noise made it necessary to shout so we could hear each other. Walter wanted to know about Marisol—was I going to ruin my life by marrying her? I pretended not to hear him.

"You got to forget her, and being in Venezuela is the best way to get her out of your mind. You came to South America to make lots of money, never to be tied down with a wife and family. Now you've got the best life in the world: plenty of money and plenty of women."

"Did you ever screw her?" Chip blurted out.

"No, Chip. That had never been a consideration. She is a *señorita*, and *señoritas* don't fuck until after they're married. Anyway, after getting free of her kidnappers, she promised to dedicate her life to God—become a nun." Chip's question shouldn't have bothered me, but it did. It rubbed me the wrong way for no good reason.

"See, there's your reason to forget about her," Walter chimed in.

After we landed, a Cadero Petroleum Company engineer met us. His name was Dwain Abernathy, which was printed on his tan short-sleeve shirt under a company logo stitched above a pocket full of color-coded pens. A company slide-rule hung from his shiny leather belt.

The temperature was ninety-five degrees and as dry as a sauna, prompting Walter to comment: "It looks like they have their own version of the California Central Valley in summertime." The terrain consisted of a rolling arid landscape, a mosaic of gray tumbleweed and brown brambles catching occasional dust devils.

We piled our luggage into the trunk of Dwain's Cadero Company sedan, then the three of us stretched out inside. Dwain turned on the air conditioning, to our relief, and started driving the fifty miles to our new well site. The roads were rough and partially paved, but there was no traffic.

"If a car breaks down, would there be anybody around to save us from being cooked?" I asked Dwain.

"I don't know. I never thought about that."

"It has happened before. People get stranded here for a couple of days; nobody's around and they end up dying a horrible death," Chip said. He seemed to think that was worth a chuckle.

It took us an hour and a half before we reached our trailer-lab set up alongside a drilling rig. A pickup truck for our use simmered in the afternoon sun. We had a choice of living back at Cadero headquarters or driving thirty miles in the other direction to a town called Anaco. Dwain suggested it would be faster if we chose Anaco. Then he asked if we had any questions, which we did but didn't know where to start. He handed Walter a folder containing our instructions for this well.

"If there are no questions, I'll be heading back to our company." He spun around and was gone.

"I've lived in Anaco before, and it would be our best choice for a place to stay," Chip suggested. We agreed to drive thirty miles to check out living conditions there.

Anaco was a small, dusty town with a few paved roads—courtesy of local oil companies. Chip pointed out an inexpensive air-conditioned motel where he once lived. Walter and I were surprised to see a permanent oil company camp complete with an Olympic-sized swimming pool and free Hollywood movies several times a week. We didn't need to look any further. We rented a room with three beds and then checked out an American-style restaurant located across the parking lot.

"American oilmen's wives used to hang out in the bar boozing and punching coins endlessly into a jukebox that played only one record named Tequila as loud as possible, and that doesn't seem to have changed since I lived here," said Chip.

We settled on each of us working twelve-hour tours. Next we drew straws. Walter drew the short straw, I drew the middle straw, which left Chip to work the last tour. The next day at noon Chip drove Walter out to our well site. Walter worked until I showed up at midnight, and he left me to work the well until noon. He drove back to Anaco, and Chip relieved me at noon the next day. That's how we rotated tours.

Oil wells in eastern Venezuela were drilled deeper than any I had worked before. They drilled through hard layers of sandstone and shale with occasional blips of methane gas or oil that had squeezed through seams between different sedimentary formations. It was encouraging to see evidence of oil. Our only complaint: Hard sandstone formations drill exceptionally slow. Even the best bits often wore out in one day. It took twelve hours or more for crews to change bits and fix any rig problems. We didn't work on days the rig was shut down for repairs. We had a lot of free time to spend swimming in the oil company's pool, going to movies, or reading paperback books that were left around the motel.

During so much free time, I thought about Marisol only once. I didn't have her address, so I couldn't write her. I decided to write a letter to Thurston Thornton to ask him about Marisol—did she become a nun? I waited several weeks for his answer but never got one. That didn't surprise me. He can be a bastard.

Chip still had contacts in Anaco, some business and some social. He offered to show us the red-light district, but when he renewed his friendship with an unattached young French girl named Lucett. She owned an English-French book and magazine store that kept us supplied with a variety of best sellers and magazines. Chip spent most of his free time with her and forgot about showing us anywhere. Walter and I read a lot of books and drank a lot of beer. Finally we were tired of reading and swimming; we wanted to get to know some girls, the ones in the red-light district. Passing time with them would be relaxing and eliminate boredom.

The two of us decided to go out on our own and found the honky-tonk part of town. We pulled up to a tawdry joint that featured an outdoor bar. We mounted barstools in the diminishing light of evening. A young, slinky, almond-skinned girl tended bar. Before Walter finished his first beer he latched on to her and left me alone with my beer. Then a girl came from a backroom. She was tall and slender and wore a black dress so sheer it could have been painted on her bare skin. She sat at the bar one stool away from me. I expected her to be aggressive. She wasn't. I don't know why, but that made her interesting, like she wanted it known she wasn't easy. Finally I asked, "How about a drink?" She taunted me with a faint smile and eyes without emotion. She uttered, "*Sí.*" I was fascinated; for me she was a hooker with a big hook. I made an effort to chat. She wasn't helping.

"¿Cómo se llama?"

"Conception," she said without emotion. "Do you want another beer?" she asked in Spanish.

"No, rum and coke, *por favor.*" It seemed our chat was going nowhere. I was ready to give up. She must have noticed my flagging interest because she murmured in a sexy voice: "Do you want to dance with me?" She played it cool; just cool enough to add temptation. We danced, and when the record ended we went to her room. She was a different person then. I was the fly caught in her web.

Conception became my regular girl after that. Instead of my always seeing her at night, we got together afternoons also. I even dared to take her for a swim at the oil company pool around midnight when nobody was around. Of course she didn't own a bathing suit. That was beautiful. And of course we didn't have anything in common but sex, meaningless sex. That was good enough for me. I wasn't looking for a long-term relationship. I had a great job with no obligations or complications, just making money.

As the months crept by, with the slow drilling and few cutting samples to study, I began to feel this job would never end until Sam North, the tool pusher for the drilling contractor, told me Cadero was planning to call this a dry hole if we didn't get an oil show in the next day or so.

Chip was due to relieve me at noon. I planned to tell Chip what the tool pusher told me about abandoning the well. Chip always came a few minutes early. Twelve noon passed and no Chip. Twenty minutes rolled by and no Chip. What could have happened to him? A half-hour later, the trailer door swung open, and Chip climbed in. I could see he was really pissed.

"You know what happened?" Before I had a chance to answer, he continued: "I was robbed. Some dirty bastard cops stopped me on the road. Everything was fine until I came around a curve, and there right ahead of me a cop tried to flag me down. I told him to go to hell and picked up speed."

"That doesn't sound like the smartest thing to do."

"Shut up for a second, I'm getting to that. When I looked in my rearview mirror, he had raised his rifle. I heard an ear-piercing rifle blast echoing through mountains and valleys. I started swerving all over the road. I even heard a bullet smack into the back of the truck somewhere.

So, I slammed on my brakes before he was able to shoot again. Now get this: Down the road in front of me I saw a second cop roll boulders out onto the road, blocking me from driving forward. Then on my side a third cop came out of nowhere and cussed me out. He was yelling so fast I didn't understand a word.

"Two of them ran up to my open window and shouted, 'Get out of your car!' followed with Spanish so fast not a word made any sense to me.

"I asked innocently, 'What did I do, Officer?' First thing he tells me I was speeding. Second, I disobeyed orders to stop."

"But there is no speed limit here."

"Doesn't matter," he told me. "You are going to pay a fine."

"How much?"

"He had to think for a moment, and then with a smirk came up with 'Three hundred Bolivars.' The other two officers laughed wildly, each getting one hundred Bs to put in their pockets."

"Goddamn crooks," I groaned.

"Rolly, on your way back to Anaco you'd better take the long way. I don't know if we're going to have to deal with those crooks from now on, or if the local police in Anaco are honest and will catch them and put them in jail where they belong."

Chapter 26

WEALTH

The drive out to the well at night was always monotonous. I tended to drive too fast because I didn't want to be late replacing Walter at midnight. It was another hot, dark, moonless night; my headlights didn't pick up sudden changes until I was almost past them. I raced up an inclined road. Just as it leveled off, a piercing white light blinded me. I should have slowed down, but I didn't want be late. The light grew intense as I got closer to it. Then suddenly it went off. My headlights spotted a huge truck straight ahead. I slammed on my brakes, which threw me out of control. I spun around several times over a slippery surface. I briefly collided with one side of the truck. My lights flooded the road strewn with what looked like black strips of thick rope that caused my car to go bump-bump-bump over them. That rope wasn't black anymore. It glistened red—with blood. And the rope wasn't rope. It was countless wriggling snakes. I jerked into low gear and spun up on asphalt again. Everything my lights washed over was smeared with blood. I veered off the road for a moment to get around the truck. My hands were shaking, and sweat was sticking to my body. I floored the gas pedal; my wheels spun. I eased up on the gas and gained traction and didn't look back. Finally I could see far ahead the light of the rig's mast towering above distant trees. When I got to the well and pulled up to our trailer, Breathless, I broke through the door. "Walter, what the hell's happening with all those snakes I ran over?"

Walter pushed himself away from the desk where he was working and grinned widely. "The pusher told me it's just a snake migration. Happens every year or so; something to do with their mating season, I guess. Isn't that the damndest thing you ever did see?"

I couldn't get those twisting snakes out of my mind. Walter laughed and then headed for Anaco.

Chip relieved me in the morning. "You can smell those dead snakes frying in the sun, polluting the air. I held my breath and raced ahead," he said, then added, "I've got some news for you. The boss is coming tomorrow."

"Brett Vickers?" I asked.

"Yeah, he sent a telegram for the three of us to meet with him here at our motel."

"What about the well? Someone's got to be there," I said.

"It'll be shut down all day tomorrow," Walter said.

The next day we watched Dwain Abernathy drive up to our motel and get out just as a man we took to be Brett Vickers got out of the backseat. He was as tall as I was, slender build, sharp features, probably in his fifties, blond hair flecked with gray.

"Hello, boys. I'm Brett Vickers." We shook his hand. "Got someplace we can sit down out of this sun?"

We walked him over to the air conditioned café and sat in a booth and ordered coffee. I could see Brett was a serious type. If he smiled it was quick, then back to serious. "They, Cadero Petroleum, plan to shut down drilling in a couple of days. You boys will pick up open-dated airline tickets at the airport at Maiquetia and fly back to Colombia. I'm on my way to Colombia now to clear up business before we terminate operations; then I'm off to Indonesia to open up our office there. Listen to this: You boys are in on the ground floor of a really big contract coming up that's going to be worth millions, and you'll be part of it." That left the three of speechless.

Chapter 27

BACK TO MEDELLIN

We left Chip at his home in Bogotá. Walter and I landed in Medellin in late afternoon as clouds gathered and threatened rain. We caught a cab as the first raindrops began to fall. We had been gone for over a year. Fortunately, Walter remembered our address. The rain was coming down in buckets by the time we arrived home. I quickly paid our cab's outrageous fare without bothering to argue. Grabbing our luggage, we made a mad dash to get under the front porch's spreading roof. I rang the doorbell several times, but no one opened the door.

"You didn't do it right. Here, let me show you," Walter challenged.

Before he could act, a little window at the top of the door swung open and a voice said, "*A la orden.*" The voice was unfamiliar.

Walter started to explain that we had just gotten back from Venezuela. The window slammed shut.

"You know what, Walter? We don't live here anymore."

"No shit. What was your first clue?"

We now regretted paying off our driver before he sped off through the mighty deluge. We looked without success for another taxi in the splashing flow of traffic. Walter remembered there was a taxi stand at a park down the street.

"One of us stays here with our luggage while the other gets a taxi," he proposed.

"I'll flip you to see who goes," I offered.

"It's a deal," he said and flipped a coin.

I lost. "Two out of three?"

"Bullshit, Rolly. Hit the road."

By the time a cabby reluctantly agreed to take us, I was soaked, so our savior tripled his normal fare because he said I left his backseat drenched. He dropped us off at the Hotel Burgos. We entered the hotel, and our friend Armando Quintero, the owner, stood before an ornate front desk carved with figures glorified by old master carvers. He frowned as he watched us—two dripping derelicts dragging waterlogged bundles called luggage—leave a watery trail on his bright red carpet, turning it into a spongy dark brown bear pelt.

"Mendicants," he growled. "You will find good food in our trash cans in the alley."

"Armando, that's no way to treat your best and only friends," I retorted.

"Tell me we've never met before, please," he begged, wrinkling his forehead but quickly bursting into a smile.

"Bullshit, we'll be your only paying customers in this fleabag," Walter shouted as he grabbed the tall, slender, and startled, hotelman, making his executive blue suit wet and black. What followed were slaps on backs and laughing like hyenas, as good friends are always wont to do. We explained our situation.

"Well, there's nothing I can do. I have no idea where your fellow rock grovelers live."

He assigned a room for each of us and told us to dry out before digging dry clothes out of our trash-bag luggage. He met us later in the dining room. After dinner he promised we would have a rousing good time with some local ladies. We could count on that; after all, he had brought most of the wild women to our *finca* parties. It was great to be back in Medellin. I forgot all about the funk I had been in hours ago in Venezuela.

Next morning Walter put through a call to Brocton Geological Services Barranquilla to find out where the rest of the geologists were living in Medellin. He didn't recognize the woman's voice that told him to call back that afternoon when someone in charge was expected to be in.

"Walter, I've got an idea. I'll go over to where Thurston's girlfriend, Dora, lived with Marisol and her mother. They can tell me where the guys from Brocton live."

"This doesn't have anything to do with Marisol, does it?"

"It might. I'll check back with you after I find out where we live."

"I don't get it, Rolly, Leon raved about how in college girls spent money on you for everything beyond what your uncle paid for. Then you'd drop them and move on to another girl."

"I met girls who wanted to help me. Remember, I came from a very poor family, and my uncle paid for my education and nothing more; Leon exaggerates. I'll see you later back here at the hotel if I'm not able to find where the other guys are living."

"Let me know if Marisol turns out to be a nun, okay?"

"Smartass."

"You'd better take the telephone number of this flop house in case I find out where we are living now so I can leave you the address."

I couldn't remember exactly where the Duráns' house was located, just that it was among a number of big mansions set back along a wide street with beautiful lawns and gardens, near a church named San Luis Somebody. My taxi driver knew the area, and we drove around ten different locations. I knew we were getting closer when a few of the large homes looked familiar. Then I recognized two massive ceiba trees in front of one mansion, guarding it like sentries. The lawn had a curving russet brick walk that divided one lush garden from another—the envy of every neighbor.

"You want me to wait, or can I collect my fare and leave?"

"Ah, I don't know . . . Okay, I'll pay and you can leave."

I climbed granite steps to a massive front porch, pressed the doorbell, and heard muffled chimes. No one answered. I knocked. Still no answer. I was ready to leave when a small port near the top of the door opened.

"Quién es?"

"Rolando Farrington. I'm a friend looking for Marisol Durán."

"Está en el hospital."

Oh my God. That left me speechless for a moment. "What happened to her?"

No answer.

"Which hospital, *por favor?*"

"Metropolitan."

"Oh my God," I repeated several times as I waved down a taxi.

When I reached the hospital I paid the driver and waited for my change. He kept it and drove away. *Next time I will pay with a smaller bill.*

191

I climbed twenty steps two at a time to the hospital lobby and joined a long line waiting to speak to the receptionist. Finally, I was at the counter making eye to eye contact with a sour-faced young punk with a crop of black hair and an obviously bleached blond wisp dangling from it. He squinted as he told me only family members were allowed to visit patients. I told him I was a cousin. He asked for proof. I told him I didn't have any. His only response was "Next."

How will I find Marisol? Don't know if she is the one who's sick, perhaps still sick with pneumonia? It's been over a year. What should I do next? Looking around I spotted a flower shop down the hall. I purchased a large bouquet and wrote a note: "Para la señorita Marisol Durán. I followed the boy carrying the bouquet to the elevator but wasn't allowed on without a pass. Damn! She's not going to know it's from me.

I paced impatiently for two hours for some kind of communication from Marisol or someone else. My imagination rolled every horrible possibility I could think of. I agonized over prospects that Marisol might be terminally ill.

An elevator door slid open at the far end of the hall, and a crowd flowed toward me. From the rear of the elevator stepped a stiff-white-collared nun, her face partially covered by her garment's black cowl. *It must be Marisol; she really did become a nun. I have to think; what am I going to say?* I was as tongue-tied as I was the first time we met at the Barranca airport. But after a closer look I realized my mistake; this nun was an older woman.

Marisol stepped out from another elevator. Her flowing black hair and perfect heart-shaped face were unmistakable. I could feel my cheeks flush and my heart begin to pound. But then I noticed something different. As she walked toward me her eyes were on a tall, swarthy man in a black business suit behind me. As she came closer, I felt her eyes wash over me. Strange, her eyes failed to reflect even a faint sparkle, just a sternness that was unlike her. My eyes must be deceiving me. I must be wrong. I was ready to rush forward to greet her, but she brushed past me, never acknowledging me at all. What had happened to that loving, happy girl? Then I lost her amidst someone's family crowd. I didn't know what to do until I remembered the hotel's number. I called and the receptionist gave me the Brocton boy's address.

Marisol's appearance left me so stunned I didn't realize where I was when the taxi dropped me at the new address.

I hoped someone could explain to me how Marisol could have changed so drastically, so hostile. A day passed and I wasn't finding any answers until Thurston returned from a well. He boisterously greeted me in his usual irritating way until he noticed my tight jaw and unresponsiveness.

"What the hell's wrong with you? You find out you're not the *bon vivant* Don Juan you thought you were?"

"Go to hell, Thirsty. Can you tell me why Marisol changed so much, a completely different girl?"

"Change so much? She hasn't changed. She's the same girl she's always been. You've been gone a long time."

"At the hospital she looked straight at me and didn't recognize me. She made me feel like she was a completely different girl."

"Sure. That's because you saw a completely different girl."

"What the hell does that mean?"

"You're thinking that maybe she had some kind of mental breakdown? No, it means you were looking at a different girl. You were looking at Marisol's sister."

"A twin sister?"

"That's right, identical twins but not identical personalities. Her name is Agata."

"What an odd name."

"You're right; it is an odd family name, but then she is an odd woman."

"How do you mean odd?"

"To begin with, she's a hypochondriac. She's always going to a doctor. Doctors never find anything wrong with her."

"Has she always been like that?"

"That's beyond my purview—a long time, anyway."

"Then where is Marisol?"

"She's probably still at the hospital looking after her ailing mother."

The same squinty-eyed hospital receptionist shot me a threatening glance just as I heard over the lobby confusion someone calling, "Rolando, Rolando." Through a swarm of bodies Marisol emerged, trailed by a young, tall Latino dude. Naturally, that aroused my jealousy. Her somber smile did not mask her beauty. As she came closer I could see her eyes brighten, but they were also tinted pale red from tears. We stood looking at each other for a moment.

"Marisol, don't you recognize me?"

"Of course I do," she said her voice a sad whisper. She stepped forward and gently hugged me. I could feel her tremble. "Rolando, my mother is very sick."

I'm no good handling scenes of grief. I have to say something to her now but be careful not to make it sound stupid or unfeeling. "I'm so sorry, Marisol." Her mother is too haughty to die. I know that's not a nice comment.

We moved to a quieter area. That young turkey kept his distance. I wanted to know who he was without asking. I tried to forget about him and concentrated on Marisol's anguish. I managed to say, "Is there anything I can do to help you?" My voice lacked any ring of sincerity. Well, her mother and I were never on congenial terms.

She wiped away a tear and said, "I'll be all right, don't worry." She took a deep breath and changed the subject. "Why did you leave without coming into my home the night we arrived from Brochette?"

"I wanted to, Marisol, but they swept you in so fast and immediately slammed the door. I waited but it never opened again."

"They were so thankful to see me safe again, everyone talking and asking so many questions and laughing and crying at the same time. They didn't give me a chance to explain that you were outside. I didn't realize so much time had passed; when I told them who you were, you were gone. And the next day Thurston said you had left for Venezuela."

"I didn't have your phone number or your address when I landed in Venezuela. I wrote Thurston asking for your address, but either he didn't get my letter or he ignored my request. The last thing I heard, you were going to become a nun."

Marisol brightened. "Rolando, you saved my life. I will never forget that. I was so scared I prayed and was ready to die." She wiped away a tear. "Since my mother's illness I have made no plans for the future."

"I called you when I got back from Venezuela, but I was told you were in the hospital. You were sick when I found you in that shanty, so naturally I thought you were the one sick in the hospital."

"I had pneumonia and was in the hospital for a month. I'm completely well now. That was over a year ago."

I walked her to the elevator. "Remember, if there is anything I can do to help you, let me know," I said and left. Maybe it was my imagination, but I didn't feel she was as glad to see me as I was to see her. It had been over a year, and people change. Was that joker tailing Marisol her boyfriend?

I couldn't get Marisol out of my mind. So what if she had a boyfriend? I wanted to talk to her just to hear if she sounded glad to see me or not. So I called.

The maid answered the phone. "I'm sorry but *señorita* Marisol is not here. She had errands to run."

That was a downer. Were those errands excuses not to see me? I needed to clear my head to take my mind off of her so I decided to go to the American Consulate to pick up my mail. The Consulate was located in an old four-story office building with a large, open courtyard at its center. Each office had a wide veranda that overlooked the courtyard, a garden with a lawn, bushes, and trees stretching skyward accommodating nests of chirping birds. A young couple conversing quietly and eating fruit from a paper bag occupied one of the ornate wrought-iron benches. Wide wooden stairs led to private offices on the floors above. As I climbed the stairs, my leather-heeled shoes clicked with each step, the sound resonating throughout the quiet building.

On the third floor I opened the Consulate's massive door and bumped into Thurston and his girlfriend, Dora.

Surprised to see me, Thurston said, "What the hell are you doing here?"

"To collect my mail. What are you doing here?"

"We need to sign some of your government's papers before they will give me a visa," Dora answered.

"You're going to the States?"

"We sure are. What'd you think we were doing here?" Thurston was his usual caustic self.

I ignored him. I waited for the office girl to hand me my mail, only one letter sent to me by an unknown name, Dolly O'Neal. The short message said: "I was your Uncle Hank's third wife before I divorced him. He died

June sixth. He didn't bequeath you no money. Just so you know about him being dead so don't send him no more letters. Yours sincerely, Dolly."

I was shocked even though I shouldn't have been. He had lived a wild life and didn't figure to live till old age. I just wondered if it was a natural death or if somebody had killed him.

Dora could tell by looking at me that something was wrong.

"I'm okay, just a little family problem."

She didn't buy that, so to cheer me up she offered: "Marisol is just on the upper floor at her lawyer's office. We're going to lunch later. Maybe you'd like to join us."

"Well, yes. That would be great." I felt slightly awkward—maybe Marisol wouldn't care to see me.

"Sure, we could do that, but you have to pay half the bill." Thurston was dead serious.

We climbed more stairs to reach Marisol's lawyer's office. Thurston opened the door to a spacious office: A rich dark-green carpet covered most of a hardwood floor, and two leather cushioned chairs were positioned on each side of a dark leather sofa; three portraits of stern-faced gentlemen—I took to be former company big shots—stared down at us from one wall.

Three young beauties sat behind desks each proudly displaying the latest hairstyles and makeup. One was typing and looking at us at the same time. Another one filed her fingernails. The third one stood up and asked if she could help us. Dora explained we were there to wait for Marisol. She suggested we sit down and be comfortable and offered us coffee. I accepted.

She looked over at me seated in one of the stuffed chairs. She smiled and asked me where I was from. I stood up so I could explain my exciting life history, part of it, anyway. I don't think she really cared about my past, but she was a good listener and probably good at other things also.

In the middle of my captivating story a door burst open on one side of the room. Was it Marisol or Agata? I immediately recognized that it had to be Agata because she flew past us and stormed out of the office without uttering a single word, followed by a young stud. We were stunned and looked at each other with expressions that asked, "What was that all about?"

The same door opened again and a short, plump man stepped out smiling. He kissed Dora's cheek before shaking our hands and asking who we were. After we explained, he introduced himself, Alfonso Catarion. He impressed me as a smooth-talking successful lawyer with a reputation for charming a lot of *señoritas*. He affected a jolly timbre in his voice. At his side was Marisol, who slowly walked forward, handkerchief in hand and a sad and worried look on her downturned face, an indication that the office visit had not gone well for her but it had infuriated Agata.

"We can leave now," Marisol uttered without looking at us. When she did look up and noticed me, she said, "Rolando? What a surprise."

At lunch she tried to be her normal captivating self but failed. She ate little, teasing her salad with her fork.

Dora put her hand on Marisol's free hand and said, "Marisol, something awful must have happened in that lawyer's office. Is there anything we can do to help you?"

"Agata insists we sell our home and everything so she can pay her debts and be free again."

Dora was surprised and asked, "What do you mean, Marisol? What debts?"

"Gambling. She owes a huge amount of money."

"Your family has owned that mansion for years and other property. You can't sell it just like that. It's Agata's debt; let her find a way of getting the money," Dora reasoned.

"It's *el syndicato*. They threatened to kill her and they'll do it. They will mutilate her body before she is dead. That's what they do. Everybody knows that."

"What can your lawyer do for you?" Dora asked.

"He will try to work out some kind of deal."

"And if his deal fails?"

"Sell the mansion and property."

I sat back and tried to think what to do. I questioned, "Will your lawyer, *el señor* Catarion, have time to come up with a plan?"

"He must or else."

Dora left it at that.

I planned to help Marisol's family out of this problem, but I was too much of an outsider to know what to do. Later I called *señor* Catarion's office and made an appointment to see him. I met with him at four o'clock the next afternoon in his sumptuous office. He had his suit coat hanging over the back of his desk chair, his sleeves rolled up, and smoking a cigar. He looked like a poker player ready to deal and collect money from a neophyte like me.

"Pull up a chair and make yourself comfortable," he said after we shook hands. He spoke perfect English. "We have a lot of work to do," he began. "I know you're not part of the Durán family, but I could tell from your staring at Marisol you'd like to make her part of yours."

"Friends, we are just good friends," I corrected.

He smiled a disbelieving smile and let it go. "How much money are you willing to spend on behalf of this family?"

That caught me off guard. I hadn't thought about money before.

He allowed me a moment to mull over that question and then went on: "I know you make a lot of money in our oil industry. By money I mean dollars so that when I mention one million *pesos* you're thinking one hundred thousand dollars. Am I correct, Mr. Farrington?"

"Well, yes . . . I guess you could think that."

"Don't worry; I'm not thinking about millions. I know I can work a deal with those cut-throats that will mean far less. Better I don't go into details for your sake and mine. But if you're willing to spend a little of your dollars I can save the Durán family's estate."

"I'll have to think that over a while."

"Time is of the essence."

"Well, I'll let you know tomorrow."

"I must have your answer today."

"In that case I must know exactly how much."

"Let's say five hundred thousand."

"*Pesos* or dollars?"

"*Pesos*, of course."

"Okay, I'm in." What the hell am I doing? I'm getting sucked into something I shouldn't.

Señor Catarion stood up, walked over to one of his filing cabinets, and pulled out several forms. Naturally they were in Spanish. He gave me a brief description of what they were. I didn't fully understand, but that was okay; I trusted him. I signed and initialed them, just as it was done in the States.

"Now, Mr. Farrington, I have a lot of work to do if we are to save the Durán property. You are making a very noble gesture, and you should be commended for it."

"*Señor* Catarion, this is just between you and me. You can tell the Duráns whatever you want, but leave my name out of it."

We shook hands and I left, left to think over what I had just done. *I can't really believe what I did.*

The next day I called *señor* Catarion. I was told he was away. That made me feel apprehensive, but I convinced myself it was stupid to feel that way. He must be busy dealing with the *syndicato.*

I didn't want anyone to know what I had done with Catarion, especially Walter. He would have ripped into me for doing such a stupid thing. I'd never hear the end of it.

The latest news was Thurston and Dora had announced their wedding date, which was set for the next week. I asked if there was any news about Marisol and her family.

"I was told her mother was still in critical condition," Walter said.

"No, not about that; I mean is she still seeing that clown?"

"What clown? You mean Gorge Delgado?"

"I don't know his name. Big, tall, sneaky-looking guy with a scrounge mustache?"

"Yeah, that's Delgado." Then he added, "Marisol and Delgado have been going together since they were kids. I think their parents hoped they would marry soon."

That felt like a kick in the stomach; although I shouldn't let that bother me. I don't want to be tied down with a wife and kids.

I finally got a hold of Catarion. He said, "I'm still working on an arrangement for the delivery of the pay off. It has to be someone that is trusted by both sides and that's not easy to find. If anything goes wrong, we don't want anyone getting killed."

"I would appreciate if you could keep me posted."

"I'll do my best but can't promise."

I left his office and went to see Marisol at her home. I rang the bell and waited. After a long delay the door opened slightly. "So sorry, but no one here can see you." And then the door shut

I went back to our place to ask Thurston if his girlfriend had seen Marisol lately. She told me, she hadn't seen any of the Duráns for several days, besides no one will talk on the phone either.

Three days later I got a call from Cataríon's assistant for me to come to Cataríon's office. It was late afternoon. All the secretaries had gone home. Catarion's assistant asked me to wait for a few minutes in the reception area. Finally he opened the door and showed me into Catarion's office. As I entered his office, he stood up from his desk and we shook hands. He got right to the point: "I am telling you all this because it was your money, Mr. Farrington that sealed the deal but unfortunately there is no way of recovering any of it; I thought you had the right to know what happened at pay-off of Agata's gambling debt. My employee was prepared to accompany Agata with the money to the drop location. A member of the *Syndicato* was the driver. The two men waited for Agata. She showed up with her boyfriend. She wanted him to carry the bag of money. That wasn't part of the deal, but they let it pass. From the beginning Agata was surly and uncooperative. She seemed ready to panic. The boyfriend tried to calm her, to no avail. They drove to the outskirts of town to a rundown neighborhood, and then stop in front of decrepit three story building. Two thugs rushed out of a building, yanked open the car door. Agata screamed and cursed and as one thug grabbed the bag of money, she whipped out a dagger and stabbed him in the arm two or three times. The other thug grabbed the money bag and ran into the building. Agata boyfriend saw blood on Agata's legs and body. It wasn't entirely the thug's blood. Agata bled from cuts she had accidentally made on herself. The *syndicato's man* and my man realized the gravity of the situation and drove immediately to a hospital where Agata was treated and put into a private room. Eventually, she was admitted into a sanitarium for the mentally ill.

I didn't see Marisol again until the day of Thurston and Dora's wedding. In the church she came over to Walter and me. She hugged each of us and then, frowning, asked me, "Have you been avoiding me?"

I could feel my cheeks redden. Before I could answer her question the organ began to play loud enough to drown out my voice. Marisol hustled to her bridesmaid's seat. It was a long Mass, and when it was over, everyone was invited to our house for the reception.

A caterer served lots of food and beverages. Everyone ate, drank, and talked. The more people drank, the louder the conversations and heartier the laughter. I wasn't interested in food. Music played on the stereo so couples could dance. I watched Marisol talking with a group. She didn't seem to be contributing much to their conversation. I caught her glance in my direction, so I walked over to her, took her hand and led her to the dance floor.

"I missed you" were my only words.

"I missed you, too. I thought you were gone for good and forgot me." She pulled me closer and laid her head on my shoulder.

"You can't imagine the times I wondered if you were all right or still traumatized by those kidnappers or if you had become a nun."

"I've tried to forget all about that incident."

We danced, neither of us speaking, until she said, smiling, "That's my toe," whispered in my ear. Her voice charmed me with her kind of easing laugh.

"So? What's it doing under my foot?" I fought to control this sudden joy that came over me.

"You *gringos* have a funny idea about dancing." Our faces were close. Her faint scent lingered on her cheek; I greeted it with a soft kiss. She tilted her head slightly and we kissed. That was our first kiss, and that was all it took for me to realize what just happened or what was going to happen.

I did not sleep well that night. I woke after nine in the morning with the effect of what happened last night. Marisol was all I could think about. I wanted to see her . . . I had to see her and to see her right now whether her family approved or not.

I showered and shaved, put on the best of my limited selection of clothes. Before I left the house I noticed one white glove from the wedding that she thought she had lost. Armed with her glove I knocked hard on the Durán's door. The maid answered a crack. I pushed the door wide open but before I could step inside the frightened maid pointed toward the garden. I found Marisol seated at a table under an umbrella. When she saw me she stood up, opened her arms and welcomed me. "I have been waiting for you," she said as we kissed.

"What are you doing, losing your senses?" Walter cajoled. "Make up your mind. Do you want your freedom, or do you want to throw it all away and become shackled to the trap of marriage and the burden of raising a litter of house apes? Ask yourself that, Rolly."

I couldn't find words to answer. I didn't know the answer.

"You are committed to go to work in Indonesia. You're set up to become very rich and still young. If you're in such a quagmire, better beat it over to Berta's place and get laid," Walter added.

"You're right, Walter." But I knew this discussion was a waste of time. We locked eyes. Neither of us blinked until Walter finally said, "You're not going to Indonesia, are you?"

"No, I'm not."

"You'd better call Vickers and tell him."

Epilogue

I was at my desk in my study finishing a report in Spanish when I heard the front door chimes. I heard Asdrubal open the door and say, "*A la orden*," followed by muffled voices from two men. I put down my pen and went to see who were there. The massive door was still open. Intense sun light flooded the hallway and all I could see were dark silhouettes of two men. One man with a loud baritone voice boomed out, "So this is what the inside of a mansion looks like! I could get used to a life like this." I knew that voice from somewhere, something familiar about it left it undefined. I took a look. "It can't be!" was all I managed to shout. "Oh my god, Leon and Walter, what a surprise! Where did you two come from? And why didn't you let me know you were coming?"

"When Walter and I happen to catch the name of a twenty year old PGA golfer from Colombian named Farrington in the sport section of the newspaper, we knew it had to be your relative—or maybe your son."

"Well, you got that right. My son became a champ here at our golf club and qualified for the PGA."

"Where did he learn to play golf?" Lion asked. "I'm sure you didn't teach him. You wouldn't know the difference between a putter and a driver."

"You're right; he learned right here at our champion golf course. His father was the *mayordomo* at our golf course and his mother worked as a maid. They were both killed in an avalanche in the mountains when he was just a tyke. With no family to claim him, Marisol and I adopted him. His name is Arturo. Besides being an outstanding student, he spent his spare time playing golf with me and other club members. He caught on so fast he could have been my golf instructor.

We took a moment to take a better look at each other. I was sure the three of us could see traces of our youth but now Leon had grown heavier but kept the same hearty humor and Walter's forehead extends farther back on his head giving him more scalp to wash but not trim.

"So what have you been doing since your marriage to Marisol?" Walter asked.

"Well, three wonderful children, counting Arturo have kept us busy. Besides playing a lot of golf I teach geology and English at the university. My entire salary goes to support poor students."

"And you were the one never to get married or have children."

"Leon, I was wrong, completely wrong. Marisol and our kids are the best that could have happen to me. But what about you? Did you ever settle down and get married?"

"Rolly, you're not going to believe this . . . I married Marcia, your old girlfriend. We started seeing each other after I got back from Colombia. We got married and I went to work for Marcia's father. He eventually made me president of his company before he died. I'm retired right now, so we spend a lot of time traveling with our grown children. It's a great life."

"That's a surprise. I never would have guessed it." Then I turned to Walter. "What about you, Walter, did you stick it out working in South-East Asia?"

"I'm still there. I fell in love with a wonderful girl from Singapore and we live there with our four kids of varying ages and only come back to the states occasionally."

I could hear Marisol coming down stairs. "What's going on down there?" Marisol cheerfully asked in her Colombian tinted English. When she came into my study and saw who were here she gave a startled, "*Por díos,* I can't believe it . . . Leon and Walter. This is wonderful. Why have you waited so long to see us?"

"It was your son the golfer that gave us the idea."

"Rolando, take Leon and Walter out onto the veranda to be more comfortable. I'll bring out some *empanadas* I've made and Asdrubal can bring out café or wine or aguardiente or whatever you would like."

"Does Marisol really know how to cook, Rolly?"

"She sure does, she learned after the family cook died months ago. She has interviewed several cooks but hasn't found one she likes. She discovered she loves to cook so she is not in a hurry to find one."

Leon made us pause as he took in our living room. "My God this is as large as our whole house in LA, and the stairs and banister are like from the movies. I bet you can get lost in this place."

"Don't exaggerate, Leon. There are plenty of larger mansions around here."

Walter walked over the wide veranda and stare down at the steep slope covered by lush green vegetation and off in the distance at the bustling city of Medellin. "Do you remember such a beautiful panorama like this, Leon?"

"It's all coming back to me after being away for so many years."

Asdrubal brought out coffee, wine and aguardiente. I explained, "Asdrubal and his mother, Marta, sheltered Marisol from the kidnappers and saved her life. The boy is now becoming a doctor supported by Marisol. She is very active helping poor people. She spends much of her time working at her church." Marisol returned with a plate full of *empanadas* and said, "I'm not the only one volunteering around here. Rolando's whole salary goes to help young poor students and their families."

"Rolly you said you have three kids, what about your other two." Leon asked.

"We have two daughters. They are at school right now. As you might guess, they have their mother's beauty."

"What are their ages?"

"They are twelve."

"They're both the same age?"

"Yes, they are identical twins."

I could see hesitation in Walter's face. Walter remembered Marisol's twin sister, Agata, and her insanity. "Twins run in their family, Leon. Marisol and her sister, Agata, were identical twins," I said.

"Where is Agata? Will I meet her?" Leon asked.

I caught Walter looking over at me, like he might be wondering if one our daughter was going to turn out to be another Agata.

"Is that dogs I here barking?" Walter asked.

"Yes, we seem to have several. We're never quite sure how many," I said.

"The girls often come home from school with a new dog or several new dogs," Marisol explained.

"The twins are into rescuing stray, homeless animals. They take care of them, feed them, nurse them, bathe them and then try to find good homes for them."

We heard young people chattering, a door slammed shut as two panting young girls burst on to the veranda each with a shaggy ball of fur locked their arms. "Mom, dad look what we found!" Suddenly they notice we were having guests. The girls quickly became embarrassed for busting in unannounced.

They started to say they were sorry but both Leon and Walter told them not to worry; they were a welcomed interruption for older people to enjoy.

"What do you say to a little round of golf?" I asked.

"How about you and Leon show me how to pan for gold?"

Printed in the United States
By Bookmasters